SUBMITTING TO THE ALPHA

EMILIA ROSE

Editor: Jovana Shirley, Unforeseen Editing, www.unforeseenediting.com

Cover Designer: Covers by Christian

Beta Readers: Amira Lunderville, Deya, Rukaiya Murtaza, Brittany Pugh-Garand, Joanne Procter, Niyah Howard

First printing edition 2020

Emilia Rose

emiliarosewriting@gmail.com

❀ Created with Vellum

CHAPTER 1

ISABELLA

"*I*'m better in bed."

"Well, I have a bigger ass, and he's an a

"Well, have you ever given hea—"

I took a deep breath and closed my eyes. *Som* *please.*

I couldn't deal with another catfight from Bit Bitch Two behind me about who had a better chance Roman. Neither of them really had a chance with hin both annoying as hell, and I doubted he wanted son that in his pack house.

"Quiet down," Dr. Jakkobs said from the front of m class. "I know you're all excited because it's the la senior year, but we need to get through this review m looked at the class through his thick bifocals and the brow, deepening the creases in his forehead. "After gr latest exams, most of you need the extra review."

gazed down at the exam on my desk and sighed. On the top
in red ink, Dr. Jakkobs had scribbled another big, fat one
red percent with a smiley face.

itch One—the nickname my best friend and I had given
ssa, one of the popular girls, after she made fun of us in
le school for obsessing over wanting to become warrior
es in Roman's pack—leaned forward in her seat until she
nearly breathing down my neck. "What are we learning
t today?" she asked, her overwhelming strawberry perfume
ing me choke. "If it's the female reproductive system, I can
nitely volunteer myself as a model."

What the he—

Derek turned his pen between his fingers and rolled his
wn eyes. "Nobody wants to see you naked, Vanessa."

The class broke out in a fit of laughter, and I pressed my lips
ether, trying to stifle a chuckle. Derek leaned back in his seat
flashed me his infamous smirk.

Dr. Jakkobs walked around his desk, arms crossed, staring
ntedly at Derek and Vanessa. "Enough," he said. "I doubt you
really want to end up in the principal's office this time of the
r."

Vanessa huffed and sat back. Thank the Moon Goddess I
uld finally breathe again.

"Now"—with pink marker, Dr. Jakkobs wrote *Anatomy Review*
large letters on the whiteboard—"let's begin."

I sank down in my seat and gazed at my notebook, which
dn't have a single anatomy note in it. Instead, it was filled with
e names of wrestling takedowns and reversals, different boxing
mbinations, and a list of judo throws that Derek and I had
en studying relentlessly.

High school ended this week, which meant that Alpha Roman
as going to assign us positions in his pack based on our acad-
mic and physical performances. And no matter the number of

2

perfect grades I'd received this year, I was determined to become a warrior.

Since I had been four years old, I had been training almost every day with Derek. I had memorized the *Lunar Battle Manual* that all outstanding warriors read, and I'd even had the opportunity to train with the warriors in our pack last year when Roman was out of town.

Well, Roman never officially told me I could. I just snuck into practice and hoped that nobody would say a word to him about me being there. Derek's neighbor and retired warrior, Mr. Beck, urged me to practice with them; he'd told me that when he was training to be a warrior, he would sneak out to fight rogues during the night and that slipping into practice wouldn't hurt me.

Someone knocked on the door, and Principal Hackle popped his head into the room. "I hope I'm not interrupting."

Dr. Jakkobs raised a brow at Derek and Vanessa and then turned to Principal Hackle. "No, not at all."

The door opened wider, and that was when I saw *him*.

Alpha Roman stood right behind Hackle. Tall, tan, and terrifyingly tense. His muscles flexed through his white V-neck shirt, and I sucked in a breath. When he stepped into the room, nobody said a word.

His gaze was fixed on me and only me.

I glanced down at my notes. Trying to look busy. Trying not to think about last night.

"Hi, Alpha!" Vanessa squealed, her nasally voice in my ear again.

I could feel her toying with the ends of my brown hair. She was so ... damn ... desperate. But, hell, so had I been yesterday.

Hackle said a few words and then disappeared back into the hall. Roman walked farther into the room and stopped when he reached my desk.

Was it getting hot in here? My body felt like it was on fire, like everyone knew what had happened.

He cleared his throat.

Please leave. Please leave.

The more I tried to push away my dirty thoughts of Roman, the more my cheeks flushed. He needed to leave now, so I could learn more about the now-very-interesting topic of the female reproductive system. Vanessa could be the demonstration for all I cared. It'd be so much more comfortable than being stared down by—

"Isabella," Alpha Roman said.

Fuck.

I glanced up at him through my lashes and fiddled with my pen. "Yes, Alpha Roman?"

"Outside. Now."

Without another word, he walked to the door and held it open for me.

Damn it. I stuffed my exam inside my textbook and closed it, so Jakkobs wouldn't see that I hadn't been paying attention.

Derek eyed me, brow raised, but I shrugged my shoulders and sent him a look that said, *Last night, when you called me thirteen times and I didn't answer once, I really wasn't doing anything bad, I promise.*

After taking a deep breath, I walked out of the room. The wooden door closed behind me, but I didn't dare turn around. This was not how I'd expected my Monday afternoon to go. Not at all.

Roman stepped closer to me, and I could feel his body heat behind me. Warming me in places that it shouldn't have.

A kid walked down the hall, opposite of us, and then disappeared into a classroom.

As soon as that door closed, he shoved me against the lockers, snatched my chin in his callous hand from behind, and ran his nose up the side of my neck. "What am I going to do with you?" he whispered in my ear. "This whole fucking week, you've been teasing me."

I shook my head. But I had been. I'd touched myself too many times to count, thinking about him pounding me against my headboard, about his cock inside of me, about his lips on every inch of my body.

It was wrong to think these sinful thoughts about my alpha.

"Don't deny it," he growled in my ear, his canines grazing against my soft spot.

He pressed himself against my backside, and I clenched. He had never been this close to me before—at least, not like this.

His fingers trailed up my leg and slipped under my skirt. "I know you keep your curtains open at night for me. You want me to watch as you rub your sensitive little clit."

"No ..." I said breathlessly. "I-I don't."

"Don't lie to your alpha," he said, the scent of mint over-whelmingly powerful. Just like him.

I gulped and shifted from foot to foot. His fingers hovered mere millimeters over my clit, and my whole body was just aching for his touch.

With one of his hands softly wrapped around the front of my neck, he pulled me to him. "Don't lie to me," he said against my ear.

My core clenched; I was just waiting for him to slip his fingers into my panties and feel how wet I was for him. I didn't care that there were only minutes left before the bell rang and everyone flooded into the hallway. I didn't care that he was my alpha and that toying with him was wrong. I needed him so fucking badly.

"I'm not," I said.

Lie.

He chuckled lowly in my ear. "I bet you think about me as you do it, don't you?"

"No."

"No?" He pushed some hair behind my ear and ground his

hips into mine. "You don't think about my face between your legs, eating you until you're trembling?"

No.

"You don't think about my cock in your mouth?" His thumb brushed against my lips.

No.

"You don't think about my hand wrapped around your throat as I thrust into you over and over and over again?"

I closed my eyes and inched my legs closer together. *Oh Goddess. Oh Goddess. Touch me, damn it.* I needed it.

"Please be quiet," I said breathlessly. The walls were thin, and I didn't want anyone hearing us, especially Vanessa. She'd make my life a living hell by telling everyone in our small town that I was the new pack slut. "People will hear."

"This is my pack, Isabella. I don't care who hears you moaning my name." He pulled his fingers away, taking a deep breath, and pushed himself off of me. "Close your blinds next time."

"Or what?" I asked, turning around to face him.

That was my first mistake of the day.

He roughly grabbed my chin and shoved me against the locker again. "Or you won't like the consequences." He gazed at my lips when he spoke, his thumb harshly brushing against it, and my heart warmed.

The way he touched me told me one thing—that he wanted to devour my body. But his eyes, shifting between a soft green and a piercing gold, told me that wasn't all he wanted. He wanted more.

He took a deep breath, his chest rising and falling against mine. Tingles erupted on my lips, and I closed my eyes for the briefest moment. Not sure why him being so close excited me, but it did.

When the bell rang, he shook his head, shoved me away, and walked down the hall and out the double doors. I stood there, inhaling his scent and staring down the hall in complete shock.

I didn't know what kind of threat that was from him ... but he had said that I wouldn't like the consequences if I didn't close the curtains the next time I touched myself for him. So, being the good girl that I was, I knew the one thing I was going to do when I got home.

Open the curtains as far as they could go.

CHAPTER 2

ISABELLA

S tudents filed out of the classrooms, glancing strangely at me, and hurried out the front exit doors. I pushed myself off of the cold blue lockers and took a deep breath. Roman hadn't even done anything to me yet, and I was aching for him. *And ... why were my lips tingling like that again?*

"What was that all about?" Derek asked a few minutes after the bell rang, tossing me my backpack.

I walked with him down the hall. "Nothing," I said, heat crawling up my neck. Absolutely nothing.

He raised a brow. "Alpha Roman doesn't just pull students out of class for *nothing*." A small smirk stretched across his face. "So ... what'd you do?"

The last few students pushed past us, and I pulled Derek to the side.

"I kinda did a thing," I said, lowering my voice. "A really bad thing."

A thing I planned on doing again tonight.

Vanessa sashayed out of the classroom, her black velvet heels clacking against the beige-tiled floor. She was typing on her phone, her short, manicured fingernails hitting her screen about a hundred miles a minute.

I quieted down and waited for her to pass, but she didn't. Instead, she lingered in the hallway a few feet away from us. Her back was turned, and her Coach purse with a small red-pink-and-purple pin hooked on to the strap hung off her forearm.

"Isabella, Goody Two–shoes, did something bad?" Derek asked, giving me a fake, overexaggerated gasp.

Vanessa lifted her gaze from her phone to the empty hallway in front of us. I knew she was listening to every single word we were saying, probably trying to figure out how she could get called out in the middle of class by her hunk of a crush, Roman.

I tugged Derek down the hallway and to his car, away from her curious ears. "Okay, so …" I said, gushing about last night. I told him everything, from the past week to how I'd gathered all of my courage to look him right in the eye when I was touching myself yesterday to the tingles I'd felt a few moments ago.

Roman had been watching me for weeks. Every night, I could smell his minty scent drifting through my open window. Every night, I could see his golden eyes piercing through the forest. Every night, I could only imagine how he would feel inside of me.

"You're such a ho," Derek said when I finished, pulling on one of his sponge twists.

I playfully pushed his shoulder. "I am not … but I need you to bring me home."

Derek chuckled and opened his car door. "So you can strip for your alpha tonight?"

"Stop it! It's not my fault. He's the one watching me; I didn't ask him to do it."

Derek rested one forearm on the hood of his beat-up white '95 Chrysler and leaned over it. "I'm all for it, Izzy, but just be careful with Roman. He *always* keeps his promises."

"Is that a bad thing?" I asked, leaning against the hot car and batting my lashes at him.

He arched a thick brown brow. "We'll see."

"What do you mean?"

"We'll see when you turn eighteen in a couple weeks and find out who your mate is."

~

"See you tomorrow," I said, hopping out of the car.

"Don't forget to bring your workout clothes tomorrow. We've got tryouts for the warriors," Derek shouted from the driver's seat.

"You know that I won't forget, Derek." I waved at him and walked up the cement path to the house. "Don't forget *your* stuff," I said over my shoulder. "Roman won't be assigning you to the hospital or anywhere else with your grades."

He lifted his middle finger at me through the windshield and chuckled.

I smiled back at him and entered the quiet house. Mom and Dad were still at the hospital, working, and would probably be there until later tonight.

So, after tossing my backpack onto my bed, I sat at my desk to study the *Lunar Battle Manual* for the hundredth time. I had memorized every move and practiced each one at least a thousand times; I even dreamed of them now and then.

Nothing would stop me from achieving my dreams of becoming a warrior and protecting each member of this pack, especially those who couldn't protect themselves … like Roman's mother couldn't.

My gaze shifted from my journal to the forest outside. On the windowsill, there were seven pots filled with moonflowers glowing brighter than I had ever seen them. I brushed my fingers against their soft leaves and smiled.

Dad always joked that I had too many in my room, but since I had been a little girl, I'd loved watching them glow brighter and brighter when the full moon approached each month. And besides, Dad had no room to talk. He had a whole garden of them out back. They glowed especially bright near my birthday but never like this. Lately, they'd been glowing with such intensity that they could suffice as the Moon herself.

There was a small moonflower keychain that Luna Raya—Roman's mother—had given me before she died. She had told me to never give up on my dreams, no matter how hard they might become. And I wasn't going to.

After reminiscing on better days when Luna Raya had still been alive and would invite me over to play with eight-year-old Roman, I climbed into bed. Trying to shake the stress of tryouts tomorrow and … maybe wanting to make Roman a bit angry again tonight.

Since he'd pulled me out of class, I couldn't stop thinking about him. His strong arms wrapped around me, his cock pressed against my ass, his fingers so damn close to my pussy, the way he'd made my heart race faster than it ever had.

I pushed a hand between my legs, rubbed my clit, and pictured one of his rough, callous hands wrapped around his cock, stroking it back and forth as he watched me from the forest.

Was it wrong? Yes. I didn't even know if we were mates yet; I would find out when I turned eighteen.

Though sex between two werewolves who weren't mated was frowned upon and werewolves were expected to be virgins prior to mating, alphas tended to stray from that rule. They were notoriously known to sleep with a handful of women before finding their mates.

I didn't know about Roman's sex life. All I knew was that I couldn't keep it together with him. Every time I saw him training, his thick muscles glistening under the sun, I just wanted him to push me against the nearest tree and fuck me until I could barely move.

A wave of pleasure rushed through my body. I continued to rub my clit in small, quick circles, thinking about him. His hand around my neck, pulling me to him with each thrust. Pumping in and out and in and out.

Oh Moon Goddess. I grasped the bedsheets and moaned softly.

His minty scent filled my nostrils, yet I didn't see him in the woods. He smelled like he was closer.

Someone knocked on the front door, and I ignored it, deciding to sink further into my silky gray sheets instead. Mom and Dad always told me never to answer the door for strangers, so for once in my life, I was planning on listening to their advice.

Heat warmed my core, making my whole body tingle. I was so close to coming; I wasn't about to stop.

My door was suddenly slammed open. I pulled my hand away from my panties, sat up, and yanked the blankets over my body, my heart racing. Roman stood in the doorway, golden eyes ravishing me. I gulped and pulled the sheets closer as he walked to the bed.

Sure, having him watch me from deep in the forest was fine. But now, he was here. So close and so fucking angry.

He growled, "What did I fucking tell you?" His jaw twitched. "You don't listen."

Why was he here? It wasn't even dark out yet. He should be at the pack house, doing alpha stuff—training people, yelling through his phone at someone, giving orders to his guards. Not in my bedroom, not stalking closer and closer to me like I was his prey, not staring at my body like he wanted to destroy it.

He yanked the sheets off me, his gaze lingering on my nipples poking through my thin white T-shirt. "Here I was, thinking you were some sweet, innocent girl." He sat on the bed, making it dip, and pulled me over his knee. He rubbed his large, callous hand over my bare ass. "I'm going to show you how I treat people in my pack who don't follow orders."

One of his fingers hooked under my panties, and he pulled them down my thighs. After gently rubbing my ass one more time, he smacked it hard. I bit my lip, trying to hold back a moan. Then, he did it again. And again. And again. Until my pussy was dripping wet. I crossed one leg over the other, so he couldn't see just how much this was turning me on.

"Are you going to be a good girl from now on?" he asked.

His cock was hard against my stomach. I paused, my core clenching.

"Answer me, Isabella," he said, his hand grasping my ass.

"No," I whispered.

"No?" He pulled some hair out of my face and roughly forced it back. "No?"

"No."

He gripped on to my thighs, forcing my legs apart, and pushed two fingers against my folds. "Does disobeying me make you this fucking wet?" he asked, fingers sliding up to my clit. He rubbed small circles around it and inhaled my scent deeply.

"Yes," I moaned.

"Look at me when you're talking."

I gazed up at his golden eyes and furrowed my brows together. "Yes, Alpha."

His fingers moved faster, and I squeezed my eyes shut. This had to be a dream. This had to be a fucking dream. Here I was … lying over my alpha's knee, letting him touch my pussy like he owned it, while my core pulsed with pure pleasure.

The tension built higher inside of me, so high that I could feel myself about to explode. But he slowed down his fingers, and the pressure disappeared slightly. He glanced down at my parted lips and started back up again, fingers moving faster than they had before. My brows knotted, and his lip curled into a smirk.

I didn't know how many times he'd stopped and started again. My pussy was aching for a release, and I wanted to come for him.

"Please, Alpha. Please let me come," I said, digging my nails into one of his muscular thighs.

"Is that what you want? To come?" he asked.

I nodded, and he tilted his head, his smirk widening.

"Only good girls get to come."

I stared up at him, brows creased. "I'll be a good girl, I-I promise."

His fingers sped up one last time, and I clenched. I was ... I was going to ...

He pulled his hand away from my pussy and tossed me onto the bed. "We'll see about that." He grasped my chin in his hand, his lips brushing against mine. "If you can prove to me that you can be good, I'll reward you, my dear Isabella."

My breath caught in my throat, and I vaguely nodded my head, feeling as if I was in a daze. I didn't know how he did it. It *was* wrong. So wrong. Yet it felt so right.

I leaned against the headboard, wanting him to leave so I could finish what he had started, but he stayed in my bedroom with me, lingering for longer than he should have. Staring at my moonflowers. Looking over at the journals and textbooks about fighting. Glancing my way a few times.

He stood up and walked around the room. "So, this is what the self-proclaimed warrior's bedroom looks like." He cracked a smile at the manual. "I didn't expect any less."

"Watch what you're doing," I said, covering my body with the blanket. "I don't need you messing anything up. I have the exact page open to where I need to study after you leave."

"Still the same old Isabella." He flipped through it, doing exactly what I'd told him not to do. "Always training to be the best."

"Still the same old Roman. Always trying to annoy me."

He walked around the bed and sat down, resting his forearms

on his knees and looking back at me. He didn't say anything for a long time, and my pussy continued to pulse. I let my eyes close briefly, just enjoying his scent, and reopened them.

Moonlight flooded into the room from my window, and a chilly summer breeze rolled in. I listened to him rub his palms together and sank further into my bed, staring at the muscles in his back ripple against his shirt. He looked back at me with eyes so soft that I felt those tingles again.

"You remember when we used to stay out all night long?" he asked, smiling softly to himself.

I played with my fingers. "When your mom used to invite me over so we could play-fight until midnight, and then she'd make you walk me home?"

His smile faltered for a fraction of a second, and then his eyes lit up with excitement. "Remember that one time you bit me?"

"I did not bite you."

He inched closer to me, resting his thigh on the bed and letting his knee graze against mine. "Yes, you did, Isabella." He shook his head and touched his finger against one of his abs. "I still have the scar to prove it."

"No, you don't."

"You want proof?"

"You just want to take your shirt off for me, so I can see just how ripped my alpha really is. If you're so inclined to show me this scar, then"—my heart raced—"I guess so."

He raised a sharp brow, pulled up his shirt, revealing his toned abdomen, and brushed a finger against one of his abs, as if he had done it so many times before. "*If you're so inclined* not to believe me, what's this then?"

The small scar glistened under the moonlight, and I rolled my eyes. "That's just ..."

He cracked a smirk and inched closer to me. "A what?"

"Just a ... line."

He shook his head, his eyes dropping to my lips for a quick

moment. I sucked in a breath. That look. That same look he had given me at the lockers earlier. That look that had made my lips tingle, that had made me feel this weird feeling that all she-wolves being pursued by alphas must feel.

After another moment, he pulled down his shirt and stood. "Still up to no good, Isabella."

"Always up to no good, Roman."

CHAPTER 3

ROMAN

Sunlight flooded in through the windows behind my desk, hitting one of the hundred used pages in my journal. My pencil glided across a piece. Each line I drew imitated Isabella's curves almost perfectly. I had sketched her so many times but nothing like this.

Nothing with her naked. Nothing with her fingers in her pussy. Nothing with her eyes closed in utter bliss. Nothing like what I had seen last night.

Her vanilla scent still lingered on my clothes, and I could feel her fingers curled into my chest. I loved the way she had stared at me with those big blue eyes when I walked into her room, but I loved the way she had smiled at me when I teased her about the little childhood love bite she'd left on me more.

I couldn't control myself last night. I needed to have a taste of her, needed to see how she felt in my hands. She had been driving me crazy for months. I put myself through pure torture, watching her touch herself and listening to her moan. I knew that I shouldn't. I knew that it was wrong.

Someone knocked on my door, and I scrambled to close my journal.

My beta, Cayden, peeked his head into the room. "Ryker's here to see you."

I stood up, clenched my jaw, and nodded. Ryker, the asshole leader of the Lycans, was here to talk my ear off for the next hour about rogues and how he needed more people to join his team of warriors to fend them off.

"Listen," I said, locking the maroon leather journal in my desk, "whatever he says, do not bring up Isabella."

Cayden furrowed his eyebrows. "But—"

"Do you understand me, Cayden? No mentioning her name," I said, hardening my stare.

He bowed his head and disappeared into the hallway. A few moments later, Cayden and Ryker appeared at my door.

I plastered a fake smile on my face and shook his hand. "Ryker, what brings you here?"

"Roman," Ryker said, sitting across from me. "It's always a pleasure to see you."

I bet it was.

He leaned back in his seat. "Rogues are more rampant than ever. I'm here to recruit the strongest warriors from every pack in the area to join the Lycans."

"I thought I'd already told you that the group of trainees coming out of high school doesn't have as much potential as my previous years." I gazed into the thin file on my desk that had the name of every senior graduating this year, except Isabella's, and handed it to him. "You can look through it … but I doubt there is anyone who will suit your needs."

Lie.

Ryker took the file, sat back, and opened it. Tattoos of moon-flowers—the official flower of our Moon Goddess—covered his forearms. Each one represented a rogue he'd killed to help keep the werewolf packs safe. Each one was a reason that I didn't want him to know about Isabella's superior abilities.

"All of our wolves are average," I said.

Lie. Lie to protect her from joining a group of Lycans who fought against bloodthirsty, handsy, filthy rogues every day. Lie to protect her from him.

After placing the file back down on my mahogany desk, Ryker kicked one ankle onto his knee and locked his hands together. "Which one is the most skilled fighter?"

I gazed at Cayden and shook my head. "Derek probably."

Another lie.

My sister, Jane, walked into the room. "Derek? Hell no. Isabella kicks his ass every day in gym class."

"Why aren't you at school, Jane?" I asked through clenched teeth.

She was going to ruin everything for me. Everything that I'd worked so hard to hide for the past three years.

Ryker gazed at her, his eyes lingering on her hips. I growled under my breath.

What a fucking pig. It disgusted me the way he looked at any woman, especially after the rumors of what he had done to Michelle—his *supposed* mate.

I stood up from my desk and hurried to her, snatching her by the elbow. "What would Mom and Dad think about you skipping school?" I asked, trying to talk some sense into her.

"Don't use that card on me," she said, ripping her arm out of my grip. "I'm leaving now. Just wanted to give you this … you left it on the kitchen table."

She handed me a sketch that I'd wanted to give to Isabella last night, but I'd been too scared and too horny to remember to bring it. Hell, I had been too drawn in to think about anything when she sat right on that bed of hers and thought she could just disobey me by touching herself.

Jane crossed her arms over her chest. "You know that it looks awfully like Isabell—"

"School. Now."

She stomped down the hall, and I slammed the door. She had to ruin everything for me, like usual.

Ryker cocked a brow at me. "Isabella? You haven't mentioned her."

Of course I hadn't mentioned her. She wasn't even eighteen yet, wasn't legal age to be considered as a Lycan. Ryker didn't need to know about her. Not now. Not ever.

"I've seen her fight," I said. "She's good ..." I hated lying about her. I wanted everyone to know how great she was. "But ... not great. She has a lot to learn."

Ryker nodded his head and stood. "I'll be the judge of that." He placed the file on my desk. "You're hosting tryouts for your warriors this week, aren't you?"

I clenched my jaw. If I didn't have a pack to take care of, I would kill him right here for even putting the idea of recruiting Isabella on the table.

"Yes," I said.

He slapped me hard on the back, squeezing my shoulder like we were friends. "I'll be by to see her sometime this week." And with that, he walked out of the room.

I just stood there, staring at the empty doorway.

No. No, he would not take Isabella away from me. I wouldn't let him.

I had to do something, anything, to keep her safe. Even if it meant hurting her.

CHAPTER 4

ISABELLA

"*A*re you coming?" Derek asked, leaning against his Chrysler.

I groaned and tossed my backpack into his backseat, still frustrated from last night. How could Roman leave me so desperate?

"Hello?" Derek said, waving his hand in front of my face. "Earth to Izzy ..."

I shook my head, pushing my dirty thoughts to the back of my mind, and clasped Luna Raya's keychain on to my bag. I had to focus on one thing and one thing only today—winning over the warriors and securing a spot on the team. Although there were more people trying out compared to last year, I wasn't nervous.

I'd trained thirteen years for this week.

And Roman knew that I was one of the best recruits. After he'd left me last night, he'd messaged me and said that he expected to see me here today.

Vanessa jogged past me and to her car in a small hot-pink sports bra, her boobs nearly bouncing out of it each time she ran, and in a pair of spandex shorts. "You guys are trying out for the warriors?"

"*You* are?" Derek asked, brow raised.

She smiled widely at me, batting her lashes. "I think I have what it takes." She opened the driver's door and waved at us. "See you at Roman's."

I rubbed my temples. This would be a long afternoon if she was going. All I could imagine was that she would flirt with Roman the whole time, getting so close to him, running her fingers up his chest, and smirking at me.

"You're basically naked, Vanessa," Derek said.

She placed a yellow manicured finger on her lip. "Am I?" She looked down at herself and then shrugged. "Oh well. I'm sure Roman won't mind." She winked at me, then jumped in her car, and raced out of the school parking lot.

I clenched my jaw. She didn't even want to be a warrior. All she wanted was to get on my nerves. That had been her goal ever since middle school.

"If she gets a spot just by rubbing her tits all over the warriors, I will lose it," Derek said, his hand clenched into a fist as he turned to me. "But if you do it, I won't mind."

"I don't have to flirt with him to get a spot."

It was arrogant to say, but it was true. Everyone, including Roman, knew that I had the most potential out of the students trying out. Hell, even Mr. Beck—who thought he was the best warrior to ever live—believed in me.

Derek bumped his shoulder into mine, the sun hitting his brown skin and making it glow. "I'm just kidding."

Nearly twenty students from my senior class were waiting on the pack house lawn when we arrived. I bounced up and down on my toes and looked over at Vanessa, who was sitting on the ground with her legs spread, *stretching*.

Dear Moon Goddess.

The warrior wolves walked out of the pack house, sizing up the possible new recruits. Some of the women and men had necklaces with pendants shaped like the moon on their chests—a cultural symbol of being mated to someone that they loved. Along with a bite mark on the neck, it was the tradition in our pack and surrounding packs to give someone a necklace. It showed love between one's wolf side and his or her human side.

I smiled at Kerrie and Henry, two of the best warrior wolves. They were mated to each other, and each had their own personalized necklace. I couldn't wait until I found my mate, who I knew would be a strong fighter like me. I had been waiting for my mate since I was a girl and used to watch Mom's necklace sparkle in the moonlight every night. Just two more weeks, and I'd officially be able to find him.

The wolves walked down the stairs and tossed their training gear near the side of the house, and then they stood in front of us. I stared curiously at them while Vanessa smiled seductively.

I took one look at her, leaned my forehead against Derek's arm, and tried to stifle a laugh at how stupid she looked. It was immature, yes. But I didn't like her, and she didn't like me. It had always been senseless, childish drama with her.

If she didn't try so hard, she could probably get anyone she wanted. She was beautiful—tall, blonde, curvy. I was all for flirting with people and self-empowerment, but this ... this was too much.

"Is something funny?"

My eyes widened, and I sucked in a breath. *Damn it.* Alpha Roman stood in front of me, his gray T-shirt hugging his sculpted frame. He gazed at me with those sinister, golden eyes, those same eyes that had devoured my body last night.

"I asked you a question."

Everyone stared at us, waiting for me to answer him.

"N-no, Alpha," I said, trying not to inhale his minty scent and turn to mush.

"And you are laughing, why?" He crossed his arms over his chest, flexing his biceps.

I glanced around, trying to come up with something that would get me out of this, but he gripped my chin and forced me to look him in the eye.

His pure dominance made me want to test him. I placed my hands by my sides, balling them into fists so I wouldn't do something stupid in front of the whole pack. But then, because I couldn't help myself, I shrugged.

He took a threatening step closer to me. "If you're not going to take this seriously, you can leave." He set his lips in a tight line. "I don't need a pup like you wasting my time."

The corner of Vanessa's lips curled. I could just hear her *hmmph*-ing at me in that snobby way she always did.

Roman grasped my chin harder, his fingers digging into my skin. His golden eyes were smirking at me, like I was right where he wanted, like he had pure control over me. "Do I make myself clear?"

"Yes, Alpha."

He released his grip and turned back to the warrior wolves, whispering something to his beta, Cayden. Cayden nodded and looked curiously at me. I let out a breath, fixed my gaze on the kicked-up grass under my feet, and clenched my fists behind my back.

Damn him.

"Five-mile run. Human form only." Roman stared out at the thick green brush. "When you get back here, we will partner up and start the training."

The warriors led the run through the forest, some peeling away and running faster than the others. I gazed at Derek, itching to sprint past everyone and go at my own pace but not wanting to be disrespectful.

Cayden slowed down until he was running beside us. "Keep up," he said to me, running faster. "If you can!"

I glanced at Derek and ran after Cayden, weaving in and out of the other warriors, jumping over fallen tree trunks, and pushing myself harder than I ever had. Cayden ran past Roman, and I followed.

My breathing was heavy, my lungs were full, my mind felt so free. I felt like the forest and I were one. Running had always been a way to connect with my wolf. When we had been small, Roman and I would love getting lost in the woods, running for hours, just to get nowhere.

Cayden slowed down when we reached the clearing near the pack house. He peeled off his shirt, his abdomen glistening with sweat, and pointed to me. "You ready?"

I doubled over, placing my hands on my knees and gasping for air. "Don't we have to wait for—"

He lunged at me, catching me off guard, and slammed me against the dirt. "No. Warriors don't wait for anyone. They fight when they need to fight."

Without waiting another second, I hopped back up and crouched in my fighting stance. Well ... I guessed we weren't waiting for them. I circled around Cayden, trying to find an opening to attack. But each time I went in to take him down, he stopped me and threw me to the ground.

As the others walked into the backyard, I watched Cayden's ear continuously fly back, as if he was listening to them and not paying as close attention to me as he should have. I socked him hard in the stomach with my fist, stepped in toward him, and threw him over my shoulder.

It was the only takedown I had gotten in ten minutes.

Almost immediately, he hopped back up and smirked, turning his attention back to me. We continued to fight for the next fifteen minutes, and he didn't let up once, pushing me harder than anyone had.

But it seemed like everyone else was getting special treatment. Derek. Melissa from Geometry. Even Vanessa, who was trying hard to fight Roman. He let her work her moves—whether those moves were rubbing herself on him or actually doing some type of takedown.

When I was too preoccupied with her, Cayden threw me down. I lay against the ground for a moment, taking a deep breath and envying how easily everyone else had it.

Roman jumped up from Vanessa's takedown, helped her up, and looked over at me. My heart raced with anger, jealousy, and a need to prove my worthiness as a warrior to him. I shoved my palms onto the ground and jumped up.

"Come on, Isabella. You're stronger and *smarter* than that," Cayden said to me.

I growled under my breath and stormed at him. After finding an opening, I came at him with everything I had, lifted him off of the ground, and drove him into the dirt. Hard.

When his body collided with the ground, he grunted, "Damn." He took a deep breath, as if he'd had the wind knocked out of him. "I didn't know you had *that* in you."

After practice, I growled and hurled my sweaty T-shirt at my gym bag. *Stupid. Stupid. Stupid.*

Nobody went easy on me—not that I'd wanted them to. I just didn't want to look like I didn't know what I was doing. Because I did know. I had studied and trained for longer than anyone. Yet they had gone harder on me—purposefully.

"Growling will get you nowhere," Roman said, standing a few feet to my left.

Most of the warriors and recruits had disappeared into the forest to return home for the night.

I pressed my lips together, wanting to do nothing more than to sink into my sheets and release all the tension from today. I tossed my bag over my shoulder and clenched my fist around the strap, turning to him.

Covered in a layer of sweat that made his whole body glisten, arms crossed over his chest, biceps swelling from the sheer amount of pressure put on them from training today, he stared at me with his head tilted to the side and a smirk on those damn plump lips.

"You seemed to be struggling today. Maybe being a warrior isn't for you." His golden eyes shimmered under the setting sun.

My nostrils flared. All that talk about being a good girl because good girls got rewarded. I growled lowly. Fuck being a good girl for him. I wanted to be bad.

Vanessa, the only other pack member still here, walked to her car. "Bye, Roman! Bye, Izzy!" She rubbed a towel across her breasts, wiping off sweat, and I scrunched my nose. "See you tomorrow."

Roman nodded, offering her a smile and a small wave. I narrowed my eyes at him.

Who did this man think he was? Why the hell was he going easy on *her*?

When she pulled out of the driveway, I brushed past him.

He snatched my wrist and pulled me back. "I didn't dismiss you."

"I don't need you to dismiss m—"

He snaked a hand around my throat, squeezing tightly, and shoved me against the side of the house. "What did I tell you about disrespecting me?"

I grasped his hand, my fingers tingling. "I don't need any reward from you," I said between clenched teeth.

He pushed me forcefully against the siding, thrusting his hardness against my thigh. Warmth pooled between my legs, and I cursed myself for reacting like this. He moved his hardness further up my leg until it pressed into the front of my leggings. I swallowed hard and closed my eyes, my core pulsing.

His lips grazed against my ear. "You don't seem too sure about that." He rubbed two fingers into the front of my pants, massaging my clit.

I parted my lips, my head falling back slightly. *Don't give in to him so easily, Isabella.*

"You're not even … fucking … good at this." I pushed his hand away.

He stared at me, eyes darker than ever, canines emerging under his lips. He gripped my chin and shoved it to the side. His fingers slipped into my panties and thrust into my wet pussy. "Not good at this, huh?"

"Cayden could probably please me better than you could."

His fingers roughly pounded into my pussy, sending me further and further against the side of the house with each thrust.

"His hand around my throat," I said.

Roman tightened his grip on my neck.

"His fingers—those long, rough fingers—destroying my tight little pussy."

Roman entered a third finger into me, and I clenched. His hand traveled down my neck, and he roughly grasped my breast.

Holy …

I squeezed my eyes shut and gripped his wrist. "His fingers … Moon Goddess, his fingers tugging on my nipples."

Roman pinched my nipple between two fingers and tugged on it. I rested my forehead against his shoulder, whimpering as my whole body trembled. And when Roman's canines scraped against the sensitive part of my neck, I couldn't stop myself from moaning. Wave after wave of ecstasy rolled through me. I had never felt so good.

After a few moments, he shoved me back harshly and stepped away from me, trying to gather himself. Though he was furious, his eyes were tinted the lightest shade of gold, just like the early morning sunrays.

I smoothed out my leggings and took a deep breath, hiking

my gym bag higher onto my shoulder. Roman was ... he made me feel ...

We stood there, staring at each other for the longest moment. No, I had never felt this way before, but nobody had ever made me feel the way Roman did. Being with him was dangerous and oh-so exciting.

He didn't leave me in the yard alone, like he had at the school. Instead, he glanced down, clenching his hands into fists. "What's this?" Roman asked, noticing and grasping the keychain on my bag. In an instant of realization, he widened his eyes. "My mom's keychain? You still have it?" His face contorted into one of strain.

I gave him a shy smile and looked down at it, a feeling of warmth washing over me. "Yes."

It seemed like it was yesterday when she'd thrust it into my palm, wrapped my small fingers around it, and told me not to tell anyone because this keychain was our little secret.

He curled his lips into a small—a very small—smile and stayed quiet for a long time. "You know that she always loved you." He looked as if he wanted to say something more about it, but then he shook his head. "Even more than me sometimes." He chuckled to himself and looked down at his feet. "Always told me to take care of you."

"Of me?" I asked, brow raised. "Only me?"

"Of everyone, Isabella."

"But especially *me*?" I teased.

He gazed at me, eyes lighting up. "Especially you."

After another second of silence and a torn expression crossing his face, he grabbed my hand. "Come on. I want to bring you somewhere."

CHAPTER 5

ISABELLA

*R*oman held his hands over my eyes and led me through the woods, making sure that I didn't bump into any twigs or trees.

"Where are we going?" I asked, trying to peek around his fingers.

"Patience, Isabella," he said.

We walked for five more minutes with me in complete darkness. And then he suddenly stopped.

When he peeled back his hands, I gasped. "You brought me back to the cave?" I asked, walking around it.

We hadn't been here since we were pups, when Luna Raya would invite me on playdates with Roman and we'd get lost in the woods.

It had been so long. So fucking long.

Moonflowers hung from the top of it, growing through rocks and dirt and twinkling softly. I grinned at them, bringing one to my nose and inhaling its scent.

30

"Roman," I said breathlessly.

He stared at me, trying to suppress a grin, and crossed his arms over his chest. "Do you remember this place?"

"Of course I do!"

His grin widened, and he walked to one side of the cave, drawing his fingers across the stone and over the stupid little drawings that we used to create in here. "My favorite part about coming here was drawing these things."

I walked over to him, gazing over his shoulder, and sighed softly. "Is that a turtle?" I asked, trying to make out the disfigured animal carved into the rock.

"You tell me," he said. "That was your drawing."

"Was not!"

"Was too!" He walked a few feet forward to the last drawing that we'd ever made here. Though they were all ruined just a little, this one was clearer than the others. "This one is mine."

It was a beautifully detailed carving of a full circle, representing the moon, and a silhouette of a woman in front of it.

I stared at it for a long time and smiled. "The Moon Goddess."

He tensed—as if it wasn't of the Moon Goddess but he didn't want to admit to who he had drawn—and stared down at me, parting his lips to peak but no words came out. Instead, he leaned down, picked up a small rock, and handed it to me.

"You want to draw another one?" I asked.

"For old times' sake," he said, cracking a smile.

He sat down on the dusty ground, taking a stone in his hand, too, and I sat next to him.

"What're you going to draw?" I asked, leaning over his shoulder and inhaling his minty scent.

He pushed the rock into the wall and carved. I watched him with excitement, blurting out guesses now and then. He chuckled each time, asking me if his drawing was *that* bad when I guessed he was drawing a stick figure, and continued.

I stared between Roman and the drawing, my heart racing.

31

The way his eyes shifted effortlessly around the rock, the way he moved his hand so smoothly, the spark in his eye … it made me feel young again.

He glanced over at me, and I knew he felt it too. It was like those tingles he had given me but something more, something deeper.

His eyes drifted to my smile and then to the rock in my hand. "Let me help you," he said, scooting closer to me.

He rested one leg beside my thigh and one behind me, so I sat directly between his legs.

When he grasped my hand, we both tensed. But then he leaned closer to me and placed my hand against the stone wall, moving my wrist in all different directions to create a carving of a werewolf.

His breath was on my neck, his heart was beating against my back, his scent was enveloping me. We were close and not close, like we had been earlier.

I shifted slightly, letting him rest his chin on my shoulder and enjoying when he took a big breath of me.

After we finished the drawing, he reluctantly released my hand and put down the stone. We didn't move for a long time, just stayed close, stayed so close that we could feel each other breathing.

And I never wanted the night to end.

CHAPTER 6

ISABELLA

*T*he next day, I slumped onto the ground, back against the pack house, legs stretched out in front of me. Everything hurt. My back, my legs, my arms, my abs, even my neck. But of course, Vanessa and everyone else didn't have this problem. They had all been treated like normal werewolves with normal abilities. I had been pushed. Hard.

Two tan and muscular legs came into my line of vision. "Sore?" Cayden asked, his black Adidas gym bag hanging from his shoulder. He tossed it down and sat in front of me.

"What gave it away?" I asked, tracing the bruises on my quads.

At least they didn't hurt as bad as they had last night. After my night with Roman, Mom had made me sit in a warm bath with moonflowers floating around the top to help with the pain. It worked a bit but ... not as much as I had hoped.

Cayden rummaged through his bag and smirked. "That look of misery on your face."

I raised a brow at him and pointed to my face. "Oh, no. This look of misery is not because I'm sore. I just don't want to go through another day of hell while everyone else takes a fucking walk in the park."

After he peeled off his shirt, he scooted closer to me. "Alpha Roman likes obedience."

Roman likes obedience.

I stifled a laugh. I would disagree. Disobedience seemed to turn him on. I'd tested that many times, and each had resulted in the same way—him pushing his hard cock against me any way that he could.

"I think you handled it well yesterday," he said.

The scent of mint drifted into my nostrils, so I inched closer to Cayden—knowing that this would surely be an act of disobedience in Roman's eyes—and smiled. "Well, I do take punishments very well."

Roman growled, and my heart raced. But I didn't turn around. Instead, I sat, smiling at Cayden, suggesting something more sinister than mere punishment.

Something about getting on his nerves, about getting close to Roman however I could, always excited me.

"I'm serious, Isabella," Cayden said, completely oblivious to my flirting. "You're strong as hell. Training with us will give you that extra *oomph*. You'll be kicking my ass in no time. You're close to it."

Roman walked over to us. Cayden's eyes lingered on me for a second, and then they snapped to Roman.

"Cayden," he said, jaw clenched. "Lead the run."

Cayden stood and held out a hand. "Come on. You can make it."

I grabbed his hand, raising my brow at Roman to test him. Oh boy, did I love testing him.

Roman eyed us, his hands clenched into tight fists. When Cayden released my hand and started walking to the crowd, I followed.

But before I could lead the run with him like I had yesterday, Roman caught my arm. "You're not going."

Cayden gazed at Roman, nodded his head, and disappeared through the woods. The rest of the warriors and trainees—except Vanessa—followed, their feet pounding against the dirt like a thunderous echo.

"Alpha, you're not coming?" Vanessa asked. Her tits were falling out of her white sports bra again. She leaned on one foot, sticking out her hip.

My wolf growled inside of me, wanting me to bare my teeth at her. She was too close to him, too damn close. I didn't like it.

Roman gazed down at me with hard eyes, and then he looked at Vanessa, lips curling into a smirk. "Let's run together. The three of us."

I clenched my jaw, turning toward the foggy forest. "No."

Roman grabbed my hand, his skin on mine making me feel some sort of way. Not taking no for an answer, he dragged me to the running path. I yanked my hand away and rubbed it softly. I didn't have time to be distracted by him. I needed to focus.

Vanessa stood on the other side of him, dragging her yellow nails across his bare shoulder. I took off through the woods, Roman hot on my heels and Vanessa actually keeping up.

I wouldn't be surprised if she *accidentally* tripped over a vine and *accidentally* sprained her ankle, just to get more of his attention.

She started yakking about how she planned to work really, really hard this week because she had been dreaming of being the strongest warrior wolf in this pack. Like she hadn't bullied me in middle school for wanting the same thing. She wouldn't be able to last a single practice if they amped up the intensity for her like they had done with me.

Roman gave her his full attention, smiling and staring and even flirting with her. I growled under my breath, leaping over a vine and ducking under a tree branch.

I pushed myself harder, faster, farther away from them. Not wanting to even hear a sentence more of their conversation. Her voice was so shrill, so utterly shrill.

Everyone was already stretching when we reached the practice area.

I pressed my lips together, breathing heavily out of my nose, and walked straight to Derek. "If I hear another word out of her mouth, I swear I will cut my ears off."

Derek eyed Vanessa and Roman as they finally made their way to the practice area. She gazed at me, fingers brushing against his forearm.

What was her problem?

"Is someone jealous?" Derek asked, pulling his knee to his chest to stretch.

I crossed my arms. "Jealous of her?" I asked, watching her talk to some other warrior wolves. At least she wasn't hanging off of Roman's arm anymore. "No, she's just annoying."

He rested his forearm on my shoulder and tugged on a strand of my hair. "Mmhmm, that's what they all say."

"You know, sometimes, I hate you," I said.

Derek gave me a cheeky grin, and I couldn't help but smile back.

Roman cleared his throat. "Get into partners. One warrior wolf with one trainee."

He gazed at me for a quick moment, and I thought he would walk over and partner with me. But then he turned toward Vanessa.

I stifled a growl, not wanting to seem jealous. Because I wasn't. No, I wasn't jealous over the most annoying try-hard here.

She grabbed his waist, her hands clasping behind his back, trying to take him down. Her breasts pressed into his chest, rubbing on him like she was his.

I hated her.

My wolf was jumping around inside of me, begging me to let her free so she could do whatever she wanted to Vanessa. I controlled my innate urges, gazing at Cayden from across the field.

I walked over to him, determined not to let Vanessa or Roman get in the way of what I had studied last night in the bath. No letting Cayden push me around like he had yesterday. I would put up a fight.

He barreled toward me, arms curling around my knees to try to take me down. I looped my arms under his, turned him onto his back, and slammed him onto the ground, his head nearly bouncing off of the dirt. He rolled onto his stomach and dug his fingernails into the dirt, struggling to push my body weight off of him.

"Damn," he said. "I expected you to go easy on me like you did yesterday." He winked and rolled me over onto my back.

I held a strong wrestling base with all of my strength and escaped his hold. Before he could throw me onto the ground again, I stood all the way up and shook my head. "I'm prepared today."

He headed in for another attack, this time a punch-jab-hook combo. I ducked under each one, avoiding contact. He grabbed my wrist, trying to break my stance, but I continued to resist him.

Sure, I hated getting ragged on while everyone got it easy. But if someone was going to go hard on me, then I wanted it to be Cayden. After Roman, he was the second-strongest warrior in this pack. If I could fight him, I could fight anyone else here.

We wrestled for the next half hour, not even stopping when everyone else rested. Maybe it was the way his lips were so close to my neck or the way his body was grinding against mine with each move, but I caught Roman glaring at us during practice. Each time he looked over, he was angrier.

When Roman announced that we would end in two minutes,

I faked Cayden out, pretending to go in for another takedown but throwing him over my hip instead.

He landed on the ground with a thud and smiled up at me. "There's that warrior that Roman always talks about."

I arched a brow and helped him up. Roman had talked about me, about my warrior abilities? Since when? What had he said?

"I expect you to throw me around even more tomorrow." We walked over to our bags, and Cayden grabbed a shirt. "You're the most skilled trainee here."

"Well, *Caydee...*" I said, gazing over my shoulder at Cayden. Roman stood a few feet away, staring at me with those golden eyes. "I'll be ready for you to go *extra* hard on me tomorrow then." I tossed my gym bag over my shoulder and winked, walking right out of the training area, toward Derek's car, and away from an angry alpha that I knew I would see later tonight.

CHAPTER 7

ISABELLA

I brushed my fingers against the moonflowers on my windowsill, smiling and inhaling their natural, fresh scent. Downstairs, Mom and Dad were home early, talking about the hospital. The world outside was quiet, the forest darker and eerier than it had been. But I knew that he was out there, watching me.

This one is for you, Alpha.

After inhaling once more, letting his minty scent calm my wolf, I crawled onto the bed and rested my back against the headboard. The perfect view for him.

Disobedience. Disobedience. Disobedience.

I slipped my fingers into my underwear and massaged my clit in small, fast circles. My nipples pressed against my white tank top. I moaned softly and arched my back.

He must be so angry, so annoyed, so hard because of me, because of the way I continued to defy him, because of my budding interest in his beta.

EMILIA ROSE

From all the way in my bedroom, I could feel his intense stare on me, could see the moon reflecting off of his eyes in the woods. Two frightening, calamitous eyes that turned me on even more.

I threw my head back, knowing that if I was going to get punished—and punished hard—by him, then I might as well do something worth being punished for. So, I rolled my nipple between my fingers and moaned, "Cayden."

One moment passed. Then two. Then, the door to my room swung open, and Roman stood in the doorway. His eyes were dark, hooded, and a suffocating gold. He didn't say a word, just stood there with a clenched jaw.

My eyes widened. "Roman," I said quietly.

Oh Moon Goddess, he was furious. I'd expected him to be angry, punish me for moaning his beta's name and not his, but I hadn't expected him to actually show up in my room with my parents downstairs.

I wanted him to simmer, wanted him to feel some type of way, like he made me feel.

Jealous.

He stepped into my room and gently shut the door behind him, but I knew he would be anything but gentle with me.

"Get up now."

I swallowed hard and pressed my knees together.

You did a bad thing, Isabella. A bad, bad thing. Now, you're going to pay for it.

My wolf jumped up and down inside of me, running around, tail wagging, tongue out like a fucking dog, like she was ready to take this punishment from our alpha.

When I didn't move, Roman snatched my arm and pulled me up. "I said, now," he said.

I stumbled to my feet and straightened my back, keeping my gaze on him.

"I told you what would happen if you didn't stop this."

"What did I do?" my inner brat asked.

I gazed up at him through my lashes. A part of me knew if I kept up this brat shit, he would flip out on me, but I couldn't stop myself. He was too easy to get riled up. And my wolf and I loved riled-up Roman.

He growled and pushed me onto my knees. "You know what you did." His hand snaked around the front of my neck, and he forced me to look up at him. After unbuttoning his jeans, he pulled out his huge cock and pressed it against my lips. "Open your mouth."

I pursed my lips and shook my head. He tightened his grip around my neck at my blatant disrespect, and I clenched. This was going to feel too good; my pussy was already pulsing.

"Now, Isabella," he said in his alpha tone.

It took everything I had to keep my lips sealed.

Wetness pooled between my legs. I was seconds away from him thrusting his cock into my mouth, from him taking me rather than making measly demands. I was about to get it, and I was about to get it hard.

He pushed his cock against me, coating them in his pre-cum. I moved my lips away from him.

When he finally got fed up, he growled, "Is that really how you want to play this fucking game?"

I smiled and batted my lashes, gazing at the moonflowers reflecting off of his golden eyes. His hair was a tousled brown mess. And his pure control was not making disobeying him any easier.

Before I could do anything, he pinched my nose closed, so I couldn't breathe. I pressed my lips together, the urge to open them hitting me every few seconds. My cheeks flushed.

He pressed his cock harder against me. "Isabella," he said. "Now."

I shook my head and furrowed my brows together. My eyes watered. I hadn't expected to be on my knees for him tonight, and I hadn't expected to enjoy it this much.

When I finally gasped, he forced his cock into my mouth and pushed himself all the way down my throat. "There you fucking go. That wasn't too hard for you, was it?"

My lips met the base of his cock, and I gagged. Spit dripped out of my mouth and onto my chin. I placed my hands on his thighs, digging my nails into his skin.

With long, hard, and fast thrusts, he fucked my mouth, making me gag over and over again. "If you wanted me to fuck your pretty little face all along, all you had to do was ask, Isabella. But since you want to make this hard, I will be hard with you."

He grabbed the sides of my head and pulled his cock fully out of my mouth. I stared up at him, my eyes watery and my lips swollen.

"Fuck you," I said.

He pushed his cock back down my throat until my lips pressed against his base. He tugged on my hair, forcing me to gaze up at him. I pressed my hands against his thighs to push him away, but he held me in place.

"Are you going to disrespect me again?" he asked.

Heat pooled between my legs as his eyes grew darker.

"Answer me, Isabella."

I shook my head, desperate to breathe again. "Mm-mm."

"I don't believe you."

I tried to speak, but all I could do was gag.

"What was that?" He smirked and then began thrusting himself in and out of my mouth again, hitting the back of my throat each time.

I gazed at him, pleading with him to let me breathe for just a moment but loving every single second of him like this.

The wild, feral, dominant alpha.

My wild, feral, dominant alpha.

My pussy clenched. All I wanted was for him to plunge his cock into it, for him to brush his canines against my neck, to feel him moments away from sinking them into my flesh and claiming me as his own. My wolf purred at the thought.

He tore off my tank top, the cool night air immediately making my nipples hard, and groped my breast in his hand. With two fingers, he pinched my nipple. A wave of pleasure rolled through me, and I moaned on his cock.

Lacing his other hand into my hair, he thrust his cock all the way down my throat and stilled. "Moan for me again, Isabella."

He pinched my nipple, and I moaned on him. He groaned under his breath, his warm cum filling my mouth.

When he pulled out, I collapsed onto my hands and gasped for breath, my spit and his cum dripping off of my lips.

"Sit up," he said.

I sat back, my chest rising and falling. His gaze raked down my body—from my eyes to my lips to my tits. "Who knew you'd look so sexy with my cum dripping out of your pretty little mouth like that?"

He brushed a finger against my bottom lip, wiping the cum from it, and stuck it into my mouth. I wrapped my lips around him and sucked his cum off of his finger.

His eyes slightly softened for only a moment, becoming an inviting gold. He clenched his jaw, took a deep breath, and shook his head.

Again, he paused and looked strained, as if he was torn between throat-fucking me another time and something else. But I didn't know what that something else was.

Without another word, he zippered his pants and walked to the door. "It's sad, Isabella. If only you could fight as well as you suck my cock."

CHAPTER 8

ROMAN

I walked right out of Isabella's room after trying not to stare at her teary eyes. It only made me feel worse. She was so fucking good at fighting, almost better than me.

But I needed to get her angry, furious, livid for tomorrow. Ryker was going to show up, and I needed her to screw up. I needed her to stumble. I needed her to fail.

I wanted to break her down piece by piece—had been trying to do it all week—so he would think she was just as weak as the next trainee. And so I could keep her to myself.

Her scent still lingered on my body, and I readjusted myself through my pants. I never wanted to hurt her. I wanted to love her. We had fallen out of friendship so many years ago ... and I wanted her back.

But this—*hurting her*—I knew was beyond me. Even the dom in me wanted to take it back. He didn't enjoy degrading her when he knew that she was the most beautiful thing to walk this earth.

My phone buzzed in my pocket as I walked into the pack house.

I'll be at practice tomorrow to see Isabella, Ryker's text message read.

I sighed through my nose, grabbed my journal, and walked to the cave. It was what I did nearly every night that I knew I wouldn't be able to sleep.

Draw her and think about how our life together would unfold.

CHAPTER 9

ISABELLA

I hated Roman so fucking much.

I didn't hate the way he had thrown me to the ground yesterday. I didn't hate the way he'd forced himself down my throat. I didn't hate the way he'd ripped my clothes off and demanded I do anything he wanted.

But this man had the nerve to tell me I sucked at fighting. Everyone knew that he put me through hell during each practice while they didn't even have to try. Nobody—*nobody*—from my class would dare challenge me to a fight.

I threw my gym bag down next to the pack house and angrily fumbled through the contents to find whatever I needed—I couldn't even remember anymore.

He did it to get on my nerves, to break my will. His job was to keep his pack in place, and he knew exactly what to do to make me bend to his command. Challenge my fighting skills.

"What's got Izzy all angry today?" Vanessa asked, gaze lingering on me for a moment longer than it should've.

She placed a hand on her hip and sashayed over to me. I clenched my jaw, trying to hold myself together.

"Is it because you aren't getting any better at fighting?"

I froze and glared over at her. *This bitch.*

She giggled and twirled a finger around a strand of my hair, inhaling deeply and closing her eyes. "You know I can give you a few tips. It seems like you really need—"

"I'm not in the fucking mood, Vanessa."

"All I'm saying is that maybe you should at least try."

I wrapped my hands around her neck. I was done with this shit. I was done with being put down by her and Roman. That sick fuck had probably told her this to get on my goddamn nerves.

Her big green eyes widened. She clawed at my fingers, trying to tear them off.

This is for the past six years of dealing with your shit, Vanessa.

"Isabella!" Derek said from across the field. He ran over to us, wrapped his arms around my torso, and pulled me away from her. "Isabella! Stop it!"

Vanessa doubled over, coughing and making a bigger scene than she needed.

Moon Goddess, what a damn drama queen.

Derek tugged me to the side of the house. "Are you crazy? Doing something like that will get you kicked out!"

I crossed my arms over my chest. "I don't care. I'm done with this."

"Don't say that, Izzy. You've wanted this for years." He placed his hands on my shoulders, brushing his thumb across my cheek.

"I get bullied by him every single day that I come here."

"He's just pushing you to get stronger."

"He's not pushing anyone else as hard as he's pushing me."

Derek tilted his head, lips curling into a smirk. "Well, not all of us can be born under the Second Wolf Moon like you. We can't be innately stronger, asshole," he said sarcastically.

I arched a hard brow at him and sighed through my nose. It was just damn frustrating. Roman wasn't even training me; he was just pushing me to my absolute limits.

"We have one more day to get through ... just please ..." He gazed around the house. Roman, Cayden, and a few other warriors stood around Vanessa, glancing between her and us. "Shit."

Roman stormed toward us. His eyes shifted between a soft green and a blazing gold. "Did you attack Vanessa?" he asked.

I pursed my lips. If I told him the truth, he would kick me out. I knew he would. It seemed like he had been looking for an excuse to kick me out since the first day.

"No," I said.

"Don't lie to me," he said, jaw twitching.

I wanted to scream at him. I wanted to wrap my hands around his throat. I wanted to scold him for talking to me the way he had yesterday. My wolf hadn't let me sleep all night. She'd continued to moan and moan about how our alpha didn't think we were good enough for him.

By the way Roman's lips curled into a smirk, he knew that he had me right where he wanted me. I couldn't make a scene, or I'd risk being kicked out. I had to listen to him, had to respect him.

"Am I lying to him, Derek?" I asked, glaring at Roman.

Derek paused and tensed behind me. "No." His voice was quiet, and I could tell that Roman sensed his lie.

But instead of saying anything, Roman gazed between us, eyes lingering on Derek's hands on shoulders, and then clenched his jaw.

"You can leave now," I said. "Practice doesn't start for another fifteen minutes. Why don't you go see what's wrong with Vanessa?" The annoying-ass bitch who couldn't keep her hands off of him. I turned away from him and tapped my foot on the ground.

Was I jealous? Yes. He was driving me crazy. I didn't know

what was going on between us, what to call it even. Were we fuck buddies? Friends with benefits?

I'd thought so, but then he'd brought me to the cave the other night. That wasn't just any spot. That had been our spot when we were younger, and then there was all that talk about us being kids and his mother liking me and him letting me keep one of his mother's most valuable possessions. It'd made me think—hope—that maybe there was something more because I was feeling all these weird emotions that I hadn't felt. But ... now ... I didn't know what to think.

A tree branch broke in the woods to our right. I gazed over to see a wolf with thick black fur shift into a human. Moonflower tattoos covered his forearms. A large scar ran down the side of his neck. The man had the natural aura of a warrior—strong, stoic, and stony. His eyes were cold, his arms were crossed, and he was staring right at me. I sucked in a breath.

Roman growled lowly, glaring at him, and then turned back to me. "I hope you'll try a little harder today, Isabella. Try not to get on my nerves, try not to embarrass yourself ... just try."

I snapped my head to his. "Get on your nerves? I think you need to reevaluate yourself before you start telling me—"

"You should just leave," he said suddenly. "If you don't want to respect me, if you want to continue this little game that you're playing with Cayden and not take this seriously, you should leave."

Derek threw an arm around my shoulders and *playfully* placed his hand over my mouth to shut me up. "She will try today, Alpha. I'll make sure of it."

Roman looked between us and then back at the naked man walking through the woods. Without another word, he turned and started toward him.

Derek smacked me on the arm. "All right, listen. I don't know what happened between you two, but you can't go talking to him like that." He shook his head. "Just please ... control yourself today. Give it your all without hurting anyone, especially Vanessa."

I pressed my lips together. "No promises."

~

Roman didn't practice with us. Instead, he and his annoying-ass attitude watched from the side with that wolf. They barely looked at each other; Roman would just nod his head now and then.

The man lifted his hand to rub the stubble on his jaw. My eyes widened when I saw the silhouette of a werewolf tattooed on the back of it. It was a symbol of the Lycan Warriors.

The Lycan Warriors were a group of the best warriors from all packs. There was nothing physically different between a werewolf and a Lycan, but Lycans tended to be smarter and better in combat. They dedicated their lives to protecting werewolves from vicious rogues, like the ones who had killed Roman's parents.

Cayden threw me onto the ground and landed on top of me, but I couldn't stop gawking. Lycans were everything that I'd trained to be but more. Since I was young, I'd had dreams of protecting my pack. I would even pray to the Moon Goddess that I could be as strong as a Lycan someday.

I pushed myself off of the ground and turned back to Cayden.

Why was the Lycan warrior here? Lycans rarely visited packs to oversee practices.

Whatever the reason, I wasn't going to let him see Cayden push me around so easily. Even though I didn't know him, I respected him. More than I respected Roman at this point. I was going to show off my abilities to this Lycan, maybe even get him to recruit me.

Cayden lunged at me, but I sprawled back, curled an arm under his shoulder, and turned him onto his back, pinning him to the ground. He struggled underneath me, but I didn't let him up. I continued to drive his shoulders into the ground until Roman growled at me and told me to stop.

Throughout practice, I took down Cayden over and over. Only letting him slam me twice during the whole two-hour period. I fought like my life was on the line and harder than any other students from my class.

When practice was over, Roman and the Lycan disappeared into the pack house, arguing with each other, but not before Roman gazed back at me, clenching his jaw, a conflicted expression on his face.

"Do you two want to join us?" Cayden asked, sitting next to Derek and me while rummaging through his bag for his clothes. "We're all going out to The Night Raider's Café for some drinks. It's a tradition that the warriors and the trainees go out the night before Roman assigns positions."

I gazed across the yard to see Vanessa grinning at a female warrior wolf. My hand tightened into a fist. "Is she going to be there?"

Cayden followed my gaze and sighed. "Unfortunately." He turned back to me, lightly tapping my shoulder. "But, hey ... last day she'll be bothering you."

"Last day?" Derek asked.

Cayden tugged on his shirt and looked around to make sure nobody was listening. "You think she'll make the team? She can barely do a sit-up without complaining. Roman already can't take her shit." He smoothed out his shirt and slung his bag over his shoulder. "So, you coming?"

CHAPTER 10

ISABELLA

"So …" Vanessa said, sipping on her second Brawl Brew of the night at the Night Raider's Café, a large tree-shaded café perched between five different packs that doubled as a club during the wee hours of the morning. She leaned closer to me, her breasts brushing against my forearm. "What's going on with you and Roman?"

I pressed my lips together. "Nothing," I said. Not that it was any of her business.

The waiter came over, setting another drink down in front of her.

"Isabella needs another one too!" she said.

The guy raised a brow at me, and I shook my head. Moon Goddess, I didn't want to end up like Vanessa, who had undone the top two buttons of her shirt and was nodding her head offbeat with the music.

She leaned even closer, and I pressed against Derek's arm,

trying to put as much space between us as possible. I didn't want to snap again and ruin my chances of becoming a warrior just because Vanessa got on my nerves.

After a moment, she dropped her gaze to my lips and frowned. "I know something's going on."

She rested her arm on the table in front of us, sighing to herself. I glanced down at it, noticing the shiny scars on her skin that looked to be from something other than a physical wolf fight. They looked almost too straight, too *planned*.

"Come on," I said quietly, grabbing Derek's hand and pushing him to the edge of the booth, needing to get out of here as soon as possible. "We'll see you tomorrow. Thanks for inviting us."

As soon as Derek stood, I hopped up and tugged him to the door. Vanessa had been flirting with everyone she could tonight, even *me*. It was desperate, and a part of me felt bad for her. Hell, all of me felt bad for her, and I didn't know why. I didn't mind her flirting with people, but it was her flirting with Roman that made me and my wolf anxious.

"Bye, you guys!" Vanessa shouted from across the pub as I hurried to the door with Derek. "Bye, Isabella!"

"I don't know how her parents deal with her," Derek said when we walked toward his car.

The sky was a dark blue, and the moon was blazing so brightly above us. I could just imagine how beautiful my moon-flowers were glowing on my windowsill.

"Me neither," I said.

Derek opened his door and froze, staring behind me. "Alpha."

I clutched the door handle, my knuckles turning white, and looked at him. He just had to ruin the night, didn't he? Coming here, looking like a fucking sex god, probably going to flirt with Vanessa since he hadn't had time to earlier.

Roman walked up the sidewalk, eyes dark as the night. "I'm taking Isabella home," he said, his gaze not leaving mine.

"Derek's taking me home."

He stepped toward me and clenched his jaw. "Derek is going to get in his car and drive home by himself, aren't you, Derek?"

Sensing the tension, Derek gazed between us. Roman asked him again, this time in his alpha tone, and he bowed his head.

Oh, hell no. I was not going home with Roman. No fucking way.

I yanked on the door handle. "Derek, unlock the car."

"Sorry, Izzy."

"Derek, unlock it!"

He sat, shut his door, and started the car. I grumbled to myself, glaring as he sped out of the lot. He would get it later. Oh boy, was he going to—

"Isabella," Roman growled.

I narrowed my eyes at him, watching the moonlight hit his perfect damn skin. "What?" I said through my teeth.

"Come with me," he said.

He held out his hand, wanting me to take it, but I turned on my heel and walked in the opposite direction—right into the woods. This man had some nerve. Yes, I was still angry from before. Yes, I wanted to hurl my fist right into his pretty face. Yes, I wanted him to tie me to his bed and finally give me what he had been denying me for the past week.

I couldn't wait until my birthday. When I found my mate. When I finally got what I deserved. A man who'd lift me up instead of put me down. A man who wasn't so confusing, like Roman was. One moment, he was taking me to our spot and telling me stories of his mother, and the next, he was shoving his dick down my throat and telling me I wasn't shit.

"Isabella, I'm not in the mood for these games you play. Come with me," he said sternly.

I stepped over some branches, fingers gliding against the bark on the trees in the woods. He could stand there all night and try to convince me to go with him for all I cared.

"For fuck's sake," he growled and followed me, snapping branches and breaking through vines to keep up. "Why don't you listen to me?"

He snatched my wrist, his whole hand enveloping it, and stopped me. I tried pulling away, but he just pushed me against the nearest tree and pinned both of my wrists above my head.

"Stop fucking fighting me."

I growled. *Stupid fucking alpha, always thinking he could just tell me what to do and what to think and ... and ...*

He was so close. The scent of mint and wet bark was driving my wolf wild. She was jumping inside of me, running around in circles, so fucking excited. He trailed his nose up the side of my neck and inhaled, his lips grazing against my soft spot.

"Let me go, Roman," I said.

"No," he said breathlessly. "I've been stressed out all fucking day."

I pressed my lips together. Now wasn't the time or place for this.

"What're you going to do?" I asked. "Force me onto my knees again, so I can relieve *my dear alpha* of all his stress?"

He ground his hardness into me, and I inched my knees closer together. Wishing away the wetness forming between my legs.

Stop it, Isabella. Stop him. I was mad at him. So fucking mad. Mad that he hadn't undressed me already and touched me the way I had needed him to for weeks now.

"Is that what you want, Isabella?" he asked against my ear. "For me to force you onto your knees?" When I didn't answer the question, he released one of my wrists and trailed his fingers down my body, slipping them into my pants. "It's good that I don't like giving you what you want, huh?"

He rubbed my clit in small, fast circles. *Damn him.* I squeezed my eyes closed, tried to steady my breathing, and cursed at him for always knowing exactly how to touch me.

"I give you what you need, Isabella. Not what you want."

He grazed his lips against my neck and sucked the skin into his mouth. My core tightened, and I grasped on to his bicep.

"Is this what you need?"

I let out a whimper.

"Use your words." He lightly trailed his fingers across my nipple through my shirt and then tugged on it. "Is *this* what you need?"

A rush of ecstacy washed through me, and I clenched my pussy. *Oh Moon Goddess.* "Yes."

His fingers moved faster. "Yes, what?"

I squeezed my eyes shut. "Yes, Alpha."

He pushed me further into the tree as his fingers entered me. They curled wildly inside of me, over and over and over and—oh Lord. Wave after wave of pleasure was coursing through my body, making my fingers tingle.

"Come for me, Isabella."

He pinched my nipple hard between his fingers, and I bit my lip to stop myself from moaning out loud.

I threw my head back. "Yes, Alpha." I dug my fingernails into his shoulder, body trembling against him.

My breaths came out short and ragged. I rocked back and forth against the tree, feeling like I was walking on clouds. It felt so good; he felt so good. I hated myself for giving in to him and for letting him rile *me* up so easily.

I just couldn't help it.

When I finished, Roman nodded to his truck sitting in The Night Raider's parking lot. "Come on." He grabbed my hand and tugged me toward the lot. "I'm taking you home."

Without complaining to him for once, I sat in his car and inhaled his scent. It was impeccably organized inside—no empty bottles of water or failed math exams sitting on the seats like in Derek's car. The dashboard was sleek, almost sparkling. He had a maroon journal sitting between us with a few sheets of paper sticking out of it. When he noticed me staring at it, he pushed the papers back into the journal.

"You don't make things easy for me," he said, driving me home. His voice was soft despite the death grip he had on the steering wheel.

"What's that supposed to mean?" I asked.

His eyes flickered back and forth between gold and green, and he stared out the windshield. Quiet. He was so damn quiet.

I frowned and sat back. "Okay, don't tell me."

He parked in my driveway, and I opened the door. Wanting nothing more than to sink into my sheets and sleep for once. This week had wiped me out, and I was finally satisfied.

"Wait," he said, tapping his fingers on his journal.

I stared at him for a few moments, my heart racing.

He parted his lips and looked down at his journal. "I ..."

I waited for him to say something, for him to tell me to stay longer, for him to grasp my wrist and tug me into the forest until it was midnight. But he didn't do any of those things.

He sighed through his nose and frowned down at his lap, looking defeated. He hadn't had that expression since his parents died, and even then, I'd never seen it up close. I'd never felt how I was feeling now for him.

"Have a good night, Isabella," he said.

I stayed in the car for another moment, hoping that he would break. Then, when I knew he wouldn't, I shut the door and walked to the house, not looking back despite my wolf begging me to see him one last time.

Inside of me, my stomach turned. We were wrong. This— whatever it was—was wrong. We shouldn't be getting close to each other. I shouldn't be feeling like this. It was supposed to only be physical, purely physical.

An emotional connection would be frowned upon by my mate—whoever he was—because feeling this way about my *alpha*, well, that was beyond wrong.

When I reached my bedroom, I looked out the window to see his car still in the driveway. He glanced up at me and gave me a small, trying smile.

Good night, Roman.

CHAPTER 11

ISABELLA

*T*hank the Moon Goddess it was Friday because I was done with Vanessa bouncing in the seat behind me. Her warm breath was on my neck again, making me shiver.

I ignored it and gazed at my warrior notebook. All the wrestling moves, punching combinations, types of kicks that Derek and I had practiced over and over were in this journal, to be remembered forever after tonight.

After class, when my name rolled off Roman's lips, followed by the word *warrior*, I would clutch this notebook close and be thankful for it all. Even all the nights we'd stayed up under the moon to improve our skills and all the times old man Mr. Beck had stared over Derek's backyard fence while we practiced, telling us about the good ole times when he had been a warrior.

My gaze lifted to Dr. Jakkobs, who sat at his desk, surfing through his phone and not even bothering to teach class. Seeing that it was the last day of school, he was probably just trying to end the year peacefully—without any disturbing comments from Vanessa about wanting to get naked in front of everyone.

Derek mouthed the words, *Three minutes*, to me from his desk, running a hand over his fade, his sponge twists bouncing ever so softly.

Three minutes until school was over forever. Three minutes until we headed over to the pack house and finally joined the warriors. Three minutes until I didn't have to listen to Vanessa's high-pitched, over-the-top, nagging voice every single day.

Roman would probably assign her as a nurse in the hospital, make her take care of Mr. Beck. Or maybe he'd assign her someplace worse. As long as she wasn't with warriors, I'd be fine.

The bell rang, and everyone stood up. Cheering. Laughing. Racing out of the room. I tossed my journal into my backpack, butterflies fluttering around in my stomach, and walked to the door with Derek. I couldn't wait any longer. Thirteen years had been long enough.

"Isabella!" Dr. Jakkobs said, standing. He smiled at me with his perfectly straight teeth and pushed his glasses up higher onto his face. "Can I speak to you for a moment?"

After reassuring Derek that I would meet him at the pack house, I walked over to him. My wolf was itching to get out of here as soon as possible, so we could see Roman and become one of his warriors. "Yes, Dr. Jakkobs?"

"You've done phenomenal this year," he said.

All of my exams were spread across his desk. One hundred percent. One hundred one percent. Ninety-seven percent. Ninety-eight percent.

"Thank you."

"I think you'd be a great fit at the pack hospital."

I gnawed on the inside of my cheek. I should've known that this was what he wanted to tell me. While I'd worked hard for good grades in his class and while working in the hospital ran in my family, that path wasn't for me.

SUBMITTING TO THE ALP

"Thank you for the compliment, Dr. Jakkobs. I really like Anatomy, but I was born to fight."

He smiled and nodded. "Your mother tells me all the time that being a warrior has been your goal since you were a girl, but if you figure that it isn't for you anymore, you're always welcome at the hospital. We could use someone like you there." He patted me on the back, gathered my exams, and said, "Good luck at tryouts today."

When I departed from his class, leaving the high school behind me, I took my time walking through the woods to the pack house. Everything seemed so much better today. Bluebirds chirped in the distance. Sunlight flooded between the trees, creating patterns on the path in front of me. I walked with a hop in my step.

Unlike the past few days, I didn't have that urge to rip off someone's head. Maybe it was because today was the day I had been working toward since I was four. Maybe it was because Roman had finally let me come last night. Maybe it was because of the way Roman had looked at me after he brought me home. Sitting in my driveway, even after I walked into the house and shut the door. His gaze remaining on my window for the briefest moment.

Green eyes soft. Hair resting against his forehead. Fingers clutching his journal, as if he had something inside that he didn't want me to see. It wasn't a look that I had seen before. He'd looked almost vulnerable, not the alpha who had barged into my room and demanded I suck his dick.

Whatever was making me feel this way, I knew that nothing could dampen my mood. Today was the best day of my life.

When I arrived, Derek and the rest of the trainees were waiting in a large room in the pack house. Pictures of our pack's greatest warriors since the beginning of time hung on the wall, their lists of accomplishments in a frame next to them. Many battles won; too many lives lost.

There was no official practice today, so I didn't bother changing. Instead, I grasped the moonflower keychain and waited. Though Luna Raya had never been a warrior, she'd always seen the strength and fight in me.

"What'd Jakkobs want?" Derek asked me.

"He thought I would be a good fit at the hospital, but I declined."

"The hospital?" Vanessa asked, standing in front of me with her hand on her hip.

I scrunched my nose, her strawberry perfume unbearably strong yet again.

"Gross," she said. "I don't know how your mom and dad deal with that place all the time. There's a bunch of smelly-ass old men and blood and ..." She shuddered. "Just gross."

Instead of getting angry with her—just because she was Vanessa—I actually smiled and kept my temper under control. Nothing would ruin my day, not even *her*.

"Sucks that you'll probably end up there," Derek said to her.

She arched a sharp brow. "We'll see about that. I think I secured a position on the team."

I nearly snorted. *Secured a spot on the team?* She could barely jog three miles without becoming out of breath.

The warrior wolves filed into the room, and everyone quieted down. I clutched the keychain tighter. Roman walked in last, and my wolf purred. She couldn't wait for him to touch her the way he had last night. After Roman said our name and everyone left the pack house and it was just me and him ... we couldn't wait.

Maybe when I started spending more time with him, things would change between us. Maybe he'd take me to the cave again, and we could lie on our stomachs and whisper our deepest, darkest secrets to each other like we used to do.

Roman stood in front of the trainee warriors with dark circles under his eyes and a hard expression. "Today is assignment day," he said.

I tried to suppress a smile and spun the keychain around my finger.

For a moment, he gazed at it and clenched his jaw. Then, he turned away from me. "As much as we would like you all to join us, we do not have space on the team for everything to run smoothly. After much consideration, I have assigned you to where I think you'll fit best. I've based many of these decisions on your performance this week."

Vanessa smirked at Roman, her eyes filling with excitement, and Roman ... looked at her and smiled back? I gazed between the two, my eyes narrowing.

What the fuck was that? My wolf growled lowly, glaring at Vanessa.

Derek picked up on the subtle exchange and nudged me. "Did you see that?"

I clenched my jaw but then forced myself to unclench it. *Nothing will dampen my mood today*, I repeated the mantra to myself until I calmed down.

"All right, let's get started." He cleared his throat. "Alberto, warrior. Alice, warrior. Gene, nurse. Derek, warrior."

A grin broke out across my face, and I leaned into Derek, feeling so proud of my best friend. We deserved this more than anyone here.

"Kelly, businesswoman. Niko, doctor." Roman continued to assign trainees positions. He stopped for a moment, clenching and unclenching his jaw. "Vanessa, warrior."

My eyes widened. *Warrior? Vanessa was assigned as a warrior?*

Vanessa squealed and clapped her hands together, a wave of her strawberry perfume hitting me like a wall. Cayden furrowed his brows and gave Roman a puzzled look. Roman didn't say anything about it, just continued to call out names. Some of our classmates began whispering.

Nobody could believe what Roman had just said. Vanessa was not a warrior. There had to be a mistake.

Roman cleared his throat, silencing the room. "Let me continue." He glanced around at a few people, finally settling his gaze upon me. His face was void of all emotion. "Isabella, nurse."

CHAPTER 12

ISABELLA

*D*erek gasped. Cayden stepped forward. Vanessa laughed. And I blinked in surprise, unable to even comprehend what Roman had just said.

Suddenly, the whole room erupted into a buzz of murmurs. People gazed from me to Roman to Vanessa, who was boasting in her victory. I grasped the keychain tighter in my hand.

"You're dismissed. For those of you who are now warriors, please stay behind for an additional meeting. We'll take a five-minute break." Roman walked out of the room, not sparing me a second glance.

Cayden shook his head and swore, following him.

This couldn't be right. No ... no, it couldn't. Roman knew I was one of the best fighters here. There was no way he'd accept Vanessa over me. No fucking way.

"Are you okay?" Derek asked, placing a hand on my shoulder.

I pressed my lips together. "There is a mistake. There has to be."

Determined on finding Roman, I pushed people out of the way and hurried to the door. The warriors, all surprised themselves, created a path for me to walk through.

Roman's scent led me all the way to his office. Instead of knocking politely, I marched right into the room with a hand on my hip. He sat behind his desk, gazing down at some papers, with Cayden next to him.

"Can I help you?" Roman asked, looking at me with the hardest expression.

"You're fucking with me, right?"

He sat up and leaned his forearms onto his desk, pressing his lips together. "Cayden, leave."

"But—" Cayden said.

"Leave."

Cayden walked out of the room, giving me a sympathetic smile, and shut the door behind him.

Roman's gaze remained on me the whole time. "Why're you still here, Isabella?"

I shook my head. "I'm the best warrior that you have, and you know it." My voice rose with every word, pure anger pumping through me. "Why the hell would you assign me as a nurse?"

His eyes were hard. "Your performance this week was disappointing."

"That's bullshit!" I slammed my hand down on his desk.

He was lying. Every word that had come out of his mouth was a lie. It had to be. It couldn't be true.

My wolf hurt.

There was no regret in his eyes, not even the smallest bit of sorrow. This wasn't a mistake. This was his decision. This was what he thought was best.

"I'm the fiercest warrior you have, Roman. Do you think little Vanessa could fight against anyone stronger than a pup? She can't do shit!"

He stood up, looming over me. "So, that's what this is about."

I slammed my palm onto his desk again, stepping closer to him. "No! This isn't what this is about."

Did he really think this was about Vanessa? About the way she always flirted with him when I was around and tried to get under my skin, the way my wolf always reacted so viciously to her? No, this wasn't about her.

"I came to practice every day, giving it everything I had, which far exceeded anything you could've thrown at me. I've been working for this position since I was four, Roman! And you're just going to take it away from me, telling me that my performance was worse than Vanessa's?"

He clenched his jaw. "I'm giving you one chance to stop disrespecting my decisions. The next time you raise your voice—"

I growled, "You'll do what, Roman? You'll punish me?" I shook my head and walked around the room, unable to even look him in the eye anymore.

Though he was typically neat, Roman's office was a complete mess—papers thrown everywhere, the paint on the walls chipped, desk drawers open.

"I'm done with this little game that we've been playing. I don't give a fuck about you or your stupid punishments."

Lie.

I shook my head and stormed out, slamming the door behind me. The sound echoed throughout the house. Everyone had probably heard it. I pushed past Derek, past Cayden, past Vanessa, promising myself that no tears would fall from my eyes.

None. I would shed none for this.

Punishing me in bed ... that was one thing. This punishment was the worst kind, and I would not give him the satisfaction of seeing me how he had last night. Vulnerable, happy, intimate. If he thought I was just another one of the pack whores he could fuck around with and not give a single ounce of respect to, then I didn't want to see him again. I didn't care.

Except I did.

My wolf hurt so fucking bad. *Why didn't he want us as a warrior? Why didn't he want us?* I didn't know which part of me hurt the worst—my pride, my wolf responding to my alpha's rejection, or me, who had kind of thought he might like me and my wolf.

As soon as I stepped out of that pack house, I shredded my clothes and transformed into my wolf, sprinting into the woods. I needed to breathe, to reconnect with my inner self and make sure she was okay.

The wind whipped through my fur, and rain started drizzling through the trees, hitting my face. The water that ran down my cheeks was just rain, not tears. Definitely not tears.

That man didn't even respect me enough to let me train as a goddamn doctor. He wanted me to be a nurse. A nurse.

Thunder rumbled above me, lightning striking the ground a few hundred feet away. I hated him for it.

There was nothing wrong with being a nurse; Dad was a nurse. But I didn't want his job. I wanted more—more hands-on, more blood, more violence. More. Just more.

Wet branches scraped into my fur, cutting into my side. I jumped over branches and under leaves and around trees, pushing myself to my limits. My wolf let out a howl, her nose lifting to the darkening sky. Running was a sweet release for her.

Not for me.

Nothing would ruin my mood, my ass. This day had turned for the worse, and I didn't think I'd get over it for years. I had prepared for this day. Practiced the fighting moves and beaten them into my muscles' memory with Derek every night. Listened to Mr. Beck's stupid stories of the wars from years ago. Thought about Luna Raya's death every night to motivate me to protect.

Did Roman really think I wouldn't fit well on the team? Had he just lied to hurt me? Why would he lie? Why did he want to hurt me?

I didn't understand it, and I didn't know if I wanted to. Was this all just a game to him? Make me catch feelings and then break me to pieces? Because if it was, he'd won. He'd won it all.

After hours of nonstop running, I went home, feeling both ashamed that I hadn't been assigned to the warriors and embarrassed at how childish I'd reacted in the pack house. I shouldn't have let him see me so upset; I was stronger than that.

Derek was sitting outside, head against the side of the house, dozing off to sleep. My keychain was between his fingers. I must've dropped it. He opened his eyes, jumped up, and wiped his sleep away.

"Isabella!" he said, throwing me a pair of spare clothes that he had in his gym bag.

I tugged them on, trying to hide my tears from him, but he saw right through me. He wrapped his arms around me and pulled me to his chest.

"I'm fine," I said, pressing my lips together.

He pulled me even closer and rested his chin on my head. His chest rose and fell softly, and I leaned my head against it.

"That was a dick move, Isabella. You can be angry."

My body heaved back and forth. Stupid wet tears fell down my cheeks. "He-he … I can't … believe it." I gripped on to his shoulders so tightly that I thought I would collapse if I didn't. "He knew it would hurt me. He knew it."

My heart clenched. Why was this even happening?

"Do you want me to be honest with you?" Derek asked, only pulling away once I stopped crying. He frowned at me, thumb brushing against my jaw. "He's the alpha. He doesn't have to care if his decision hurts you."

It'd sure seemed like he cared about me and my opinion of him—coming into my room after I moaned Cayden's name, using me like a damn doll for his pleasure, giving me what I needed last night. That look on his face when I stared at his journal. That smile he gave me before I stepped out of his car. The way he made my wolf feel so … so fucking special.

"I just don't understand why. I was the best one there all week. Everyone knew it."

Derek shrugged. "I don't know. Maybe he thought this was the best for the pack." He nudged me, trying to lighten the mood. "Maybe he thought you guys would have hot, angry sex after."

"There will be no sex after that." I wrapped my arms around his waist, pulling him into a hug one more time and inhaling his familiar scent. "Thank you for waiting up for me, but you should get some sleep."

He rolled his eyes. "I know ... I have to be up bright and early to listen to Vanessa complain all day."

"I'm happy for you," I said, giving him my best smile. How couldn't I be proud of my best friend for achieving everything that he'd ever wanted? I hoped he enjoyed every minute of it and never took it for granted. "I really am."

When Derek disappeared through the woods, I stayed outside for a few more moments, listening to the rain hit the leaves of the trees and smelling the fresh scent of the woods. I rubbed the moonflower keychain in my hand and walked into the quiet house.

Mom and Dad were probably asleep. And I was glad. I didn't want to face them tonight.

Tears streamed down my cheeks when I closed my bedroom door. I could finally cry alone without feeling judged. But before I let it all go, I did the one thing I hadn't done in weeks.

I closed the curtains.

CHAPTER 13

ROMAN

I hadn't left this empty pack house.

After Isabella had run out of my office, I'd walked back to the new recruits, given them a halfhearted speech, and then sat in my bedroom. Staring at the closed door. Wondering if this was the right choice. Hurting worse than she did.

The pain hadn't faded. Not when I led practice the next day. Not when I ran through the woods and saw her curtains closed. Not when I locked myself in my office and couldn't focus on any task for long enough to finish it.

It was nine p.m. on Saturday. The moonlight flooded into my office through the open windows. If I focused hard enough, I could smell her sweet scent lingering on my desk. I tore a sheet of paper from my journal. The fifth drawing of her I had done today.

I tried not to draw her, knowing that I would only hurt worse, but I did it anyway. She was the only thing that calmed me.

Tapping my pen against my desk, I gazed out the window into

the dark forest. I needed to go on a run. Another run. Run. My wolf wanted to run to her house. I wanted to run to her house.

I shook my head. *No. No, I shouldn't go.* I really shouldn't go.

I sat at my desk in the dark, tapping my foot on the hardwood and deciding to read to take my mind off of her.

Read something. Read anything. Read the used Anatomy textbook Dr. Jakkobs had given me, so I could finish my education. Read the section about mating. Realize that the textbook smelled like her. Realize that it was her textbook. Read her name that she had written in the front of the book. Inhale her scent. Pretend that this was the right decision. Our pack needed doctors. She would be one of the best. She was strong, but she was so fucking smart. Think about her. Think about my Isabella.

Moon Goddess, I couldn't stop thinking about her.

I slammed the book closed, throwing it to the side of the room in anger, and opened to another clean page of my journal, letting my hand sketch whatever it wanted. A curve. Hair blowing in the breeze. Her watching the forest last night through my truck window.

I wished that I'd never gotten caught up with her. I wished that Ryker had never come here to try to take her away from me. Then, I wouldn't have had to stay up all night, going through plan after plan to keep her here, only for her to be pissed off at me.

But being pissed off at me was better than her being dead, like Mom and Dad were.

It was also better than her being in the hands of a man-whore who had marked Michelle, an unmated woman, without her consent. I didn't care if the rumors were true or not; I wouldn't put Isabella in harm's way.

I told myself that I'd made the right decision. She would work at the hospital, where I could keep her safe. She was the smartest wolf that I knew. That was the best place for her. Being forced into a leadership position—especially as a Lycan—when she was so young would ruin her life. Becoming an alpha at fifteen had nearly ruined mine.

Isabella would be stronger than me with proper training. She'd be a perfect warrior, but it was my job to protect her, not the other way around. I was the alpha, and she was ... she was mine.

An unfamiliar howl echoed deep into the night, and my mind link suddenly went wild. *"Rogues. Two of them. South border."*

I closed my notebook, hurrying out of the room. South border, near Isabella's house. Two fucking rogues.

After sprinting for less than a minute, I made it to the borders to see two of my men finishing them off. I pressed my lips together. There were two rogues too many. Two rogues too close to Isabella's home.

Rogues hadn't sniffed around these parts for seven years— when they had torn Mom's heart right out of her chest, when they had taken Dad from me, when they had ruined my life. And now, suddenly, they were back.

Light from Isabella's room glowed through her curtains. I growled lowly. Nothing would take her away from me. I'd do anything to keep her safe. Anything.

No more regretting this decision. This was the right one. This would always be the right one. I just had to get her to see that she meant more to me than she thought she did.

CHAPTER 14

ISABELLA

*E*arly Monday morning, Mom peeked into my room with a soft smile on her face. "Morning, sweetie. I'm heading to the hospital. Would you like to come with me today?"

I didn't want to go. I didn't want to see *him* passing by. I didn't want to hear his voice. I didn't even want to think about him, but I couldn't stop. Every single night this weekend, I'd sat by the window, staring at the moonflowers glowing off of the curtains. I just wanted to peel them open to see the moon, to find some comfort in the forest, but I couldn't get myself to do it.

Without the light from the moon, the moonflowers didn't glow as brightly. They were dull, and their leaves felt brittle. I couldn't stop thinking about that sinister look on his face when he'd told me I'd be a nurse for the rest of my life.

I gnawed on the inside of my lip and sank deeper into my gray sheets, fiddling with the keychain. "No."

She sat next to me on the bed, wrapping an arm around my

shoulders and drawing me closer to her. "Maybe this is a blessing in disguise, Izzy," she said.

I shook my head, a stupid tear falling from my eye.

This wasn't a blessing. The Moon Goddess wouldn't even call it a blessing. She'd call it a mistake. To have one of the wolves born under the Second Wolf Moon become a nurse and not a warrior. It was wrong.

Pups who were born under the Second Wolf Moon in May were thought to be the best warriors in a pack. It was prophesied that these wolves had the strength that the original werewolf had been granted and even possessed powers close to that of the Moon Goddess.

"Your father and I work at the hospital ... maybe Alpha Roman thought this was the best for us."

"No," I said through clenched teeth. "He just wanted to watch me suffer."

She furrowed her brows together. "Now, why would he do that? He's dedicated to this pack, and he has been since he was fifteen. He wants to keep everyone happy."

No, he wanted to keep the Roman in his pants happy.

She sighed and rested her head on mine. "Come on, Izzy. Assignments start today."

"I'm not going to the hospital, Mom. I don't belong there. I should be training with the pack right now, not sitting in the hospital, bored out of my mind."

After pulling me into another hug, she stood. "Please think about it, sweetie." She smiled and tossed a pillow at me, her blue eyes as bright and lively as the moon. "Cheer up ... can't have you sad on your birthday! It's just a few days away! Maybe you'll find your mate."

If she said that one more time, I would probably scream. All weekend, she'd reminded me of my special day. But truth was, I didn't care about the fact that my birthday was days away and that I might find my mate.

When the front door shut softly behind Mom, I rolled onto my side. Though today was the first day of assignments, I literally couldn't pull myself out of bed to go. It wasn't just my inner brat making me feel bad. I felt terrible. My insides were turning over and over, shriveling up, squeezing me tightly, making it hard to breathe. I'd dedicated my whole life for one moment, but he didn't think I was good enough for it.

My wolf wouldn't even let me think of his name. She had cried for most of the weekend, made me curl up in my bed and think about everything that I could've done to please him. To make him like me more. Stop being such a brat. Acting like I didn't hate him with all my guts.

Fuck him. I did hate him with all my guts.

My wolf whimpered, the rejection from our alpha hitting hard.

No. We would not sulk any longer. We would run, run through the woods, feel the wind in our fur, inhale the sweet aroma of the forest. Then, we'd go to the hospital.

After changing out of my clothes, I ran out of the house and shifted into my wolf. With the dirt against our paws and the breeze blowing through our fur, we sprinted into the woods, going off any path that our pack had made within the forest.

This was what I needed. For the whole weekend, I'd refused to let my wolf run free; I'd punished her for Roman's stupid decision. But I was done with that.

She had done nothing wrong. I had failed her, not the other way around.

The blazing sun shone through the trees on us. I let out a small howl and jogged to the pack house. From the trees, I watched the warriors finish their last run of the day. I had watched them since I was just a little girl, but this time, it was different. This time, I had no hope of becoming one of them. I was empty.

All the wolves ran toward the clearing right behind the pack house, even Vanessa, who was a hundred feet behind everyone else.

When they all shifted, I frowned, not seeing him. Suddenly, his minty scent drifted into my nostrils. He was close to *me*. I clenched my jaw and sprinted back through the woods. Paws hitting the ground. Branches scraping my legs. Leaves falling around me. I ran fast but not fast enough.

His scent followed me, and I knew he was hot on my tail. I pushed myself faster. He growled viciously, and his voice rang through my head, commanding me to stop. But I didn't.

He clamped down on the back of my neck with his canines, latching right into my flesh. I squirmed in his grip, my skin tearing. Before I pulled myself away, he sank his teeth deeper in my muscle—into the one place that alphas could bite into to get any wolf to shift—until I unwillingly transformed back into my human.

When he shifted, he gazed down at me, green eyes hard. "Why aren't you at the hospital? Your assignment started today."

"Fuck off," I said, grasping the back of my neck to stop the blood.

"Rethink your next words, pup."

"I said, fuck off."

He snatched my throat in his hand and pushed me against a tree. "I order you to go to the hospital. Your assignment started today."

"I don't belong at the hospital." I ripped myself out of his grip. "I belong out here."

After snatching my neck again, he held me still. "You will go to the hospital, and you will not complain to me again. Do you understand? That is an alpha's order."

Blood rolled down my neck, the bite hurting, but his scent and the feel of his fingers soothed my wolf.

They might've soothed her, but they didn't soothe me.

"You should know by now that I don't listen to any orders you give me," I said. "I never have, and I never will, especially after what you did."

The thought of becoming a rogue crossed my mind for the briefest moment. Going solo? Living out in the woods? Killing rogues by myself to keep everyone in Roman's pack safe? It was more than tempting.

"The other night, you followed my orders, didn't you?" He stepped closer to me, pushing me against the tree, his minty scent so damn strong. "And I gave you exactly what you needed." His other hand traveled down my bare body and brushed against the front of my aching clit. "Be a good girl and do it again."

I swore under my breath, trying to keep my mind clear. He knew exactly—*exactly*—what would get on my nerves.

"Stop, Roman," I said. I pressed my knees together, feeling the wetness pool between them. *Damn my fucking wolf for enjoying this torture. Damn her.*

He rubbed me harder, and I almost let out a moan. Almost. His face was buried into the crook of my neck, his canines poking against my soft spot. My core pulsed violently, the pleasure building higher and higher.

Fuck. I squeezed my eyes shut. *I didn't like this. I didn't like this. I didn't like this.*

But I did.

It felt so fucking amazing to feel good after what had happened on Friday. I didn't want him to stop, but I would not give him any kind of satisfaction, would not let him get away with this.

So, I grabbed his wrist and pulled it away from me. "I said, stop."

Roman paused, raised his brows in shock, and parted his lips. His eyes were a mix of gold and green, and his canines lengthened even more as he struggled to stay human.

Sure, I had pushed him away before, but this was different.

I took a deep breath, seeing his large canines. If I wasn't

angry, I'd probably be turned on. "Don't touch me ever again." I seethed. "If you wanted me, you should've kept me around, but you pushed me away, so I'm not dealing with this anymore."

I mustered up all the courage I had left and shifted back into my wolf, running farther into the forest.

Within a few minutes, Roman would have wolves tracking my scent because I had left pack grounds without his permission and had blatantly refused to go to work. But I didn't give a shit.

The sun burned brightly above me, making my fur warm. I didn't know how far I had gone; I just ran until I heard branches snapping behind me.

After sprinting even faster through the woods for another ten minutes, I hoped that I had lost the wolves Roman had ordered to follow me. I stopped at a small stream and stuck my nose into the water to drink.

More tree branches snapped.

A large wolf with rich brown fur stood at the edge of the forest. I lifted my head and stared at him, wondering if he would approach me. There was a large scar that cut through the fur near his throat. He looked vaguely familiar, but I couldn't remember where I had seen his wolf or smelled his scent.

He slowly stalked toward me, his head low, like he would pounce at any moment. I growled, warning him to stay away, but he continued to advance. I lowered into a stance that resembled his, waiting for him to make a move so I could end his life.

Though he was bigger than me, I would kill him if I needed. All he had to do was leap toward me, and I'd sink my canines into his neck and let the blood rain down on both of us.

After baring his teeth, he growled, the sound rumbling throughout the forest. Yet he made no move to attack. It was as if he was trying to frighten me.

Suddenly, he shifted into his human. My eyes widened, noticing the tattoo of a wolf on the back of his hand. The Lycan from practice the other day. What was he doing here? Had Roman sent him to come find me and bring me back?

The man stared down at me, lips pressed into a line, and nodded. "Shift." Voice full of authority and a presence that demanded obedience, he waited for me more patiently than Roman ever had.

I stood to my feet, shifting to my human, and covered my body with my arms.

He looked behind me. "Carrie," he said.

Another wolf walked out from behind a tree with clothing between her teeth. She placed them at his feet and bowed her head. After dismissing her, he grabbed the clothes and handed me a T-shirt and a pair of jean shorts that were oddly my exact size.

"What's going on?" I asked, tugging on the clothes.

"I need to talk to you, Isabella." He walked to the stream and motioned for me to follow.

I furrowed my brows at him, unsure if I should trust him or not. Where had he even come from? And how did he know my name?

"Are you coming?"

I pressed my lips together and followed him, trying to keep my distance. His authority over me far surpassed any wolf I had ever met, yet there was something about him that I couldn't quite place.

"My name is Ryker," he said. "I am the leader of the Lycans."

"Okay ..." I said, slowly nodding my head.

What did this have to do with me? I couldn't be a Lycan now that Roman had assigned me as a lousy nurse.

"You have tremendous skills. I believe that you will be a great addition to the Lycans."

I stopped walking and gaped at him. "Me?"

When he smiled, my breath nearly caught in my throat.

Despite the scar on his neck, his eyes were light and so refreshing.

"Yes, you." He chuckled and placed a hand on my back to guide me forward.

"I-I can't," I said. "I don't meet the requirements." Something else that Roman had taken away from me. "I'm not a warrior wolf."

He tapped his fingers on the middle of my back, and it was soothing. "We are willing to overlook this. Based on your stats, you should've made the cut. You're ranking just under Beta Cayden, and if you had proper training, you'd rank higher than Alpha Roman. I'm not sure why you weren't assigned as a warrior, but we think you'd do perfectly as one of us."

I felt both intense anger and pride. Based on stats, I could rank higher than Cayden—the goddamn beta! I couldn't believe it. It was crazy to think that was possible. On the other hand, I was furious that Roman had assigned me as a nurse. I didn't know why I'd doubted myself this morning; I didn't know why *he* had doubted me.

"Since you are not eighteen yet, we can't extend a formal invitation for you to join us, but we want to invite you to our pack to have a tour and learn more information about this position. And if you find that you enjoy who we are and how we operate, we will have you complete a test mission on your eighteenth birthday. If all goes right, we'll extend you an invitation to commit to us for a year. Does this sound like something that would interest you?"

"Yes! Yes!" I didn't hesitate. This was my chance. "Oh my gosh. I can't believe this." My heart was pounding against my chest.

The Moon Goddess had answered my prayers. Maybe Roman assigning me as a nurse was fate. I was meant for greater things.

"Good." He flashed me a breathtaking smile. "For now, I need you to keep this a secret between me and you. Go to your assignment at the hospital, stay off of your alpha's radar. You are welcome to visit us in two nights from now. I will retrieve you from your pack at approximately twelve a.m. But if Alpha Roman finds out—"

"I know," I said.

He wouldn't let me go. He wouldn't even think about it. I knew exactly how he would react, so I would keep it a secret and lie to my alpha.

I was sure he wouldn't mind. He sure as hell hadn't minded disrespecting me on Friday.

CHAPTER 15

ISABELLA

"*I*sabella." Dr. Jakkobs stood behind the hospital's front desk, lips parted in disbelief. He excused himself from his conversation with a nurse and walked toward me. "I didn't think you'd show up."

The hospital was a bleak white color and had an eerie kind of silence, the kind that reminded me of the moments right before Roman's father had run into the building with Luna Raya dead in his arms, desperate for someone to help him. I drew my fingers across the desk and frowned. I hadn't been back since. Too many heartbreaking memories haunted these halls.

I gave Dr. Jakkobs a soft, trying smile. "Well, I'm here."

If I had the option, I would already be with the Lycans. But unfortunately, I was stuck in this prison that reeked of blood and bleach.

Just a couple days. That was what I had repeated to myself on the way here this morning. *A couple days. A couple fucking days of torture.* Then, I could leave *Alpha* Roman behind.

My wolf whimpered, but I shook her out of my thoughts. She wanted his attention, and so did I. We wanted—*needed*—it, but we couldn't anymore. Maybe there would be someone else in the Lycans who caught our eye. Maybe he wouldn't be such an asshole. Maybe he would actually respect me.

I followed Dr. Jakkobs through the empty hospital halls to his office. Mom and Dad were in a room, examining Mr. Beck, who had fallen over Derek's fence the other day after congratulating him on becoming a warrior.

Jakkobs handed me a white doctor's coat.

"Alpha Roman assigned me as a nurse," I said.

"He did." He helped me put the coat on anyway. "But I'm reassigning you. You'll work under me until you can take the exam to become a doctor. Let's just keep this secret ours though. No need to get Roman on my ass for it."

I grinned and pulled the coat tighter. "Dr. Jakkobs is a rebel." I shook my head. I never would've guessed.

After catching me up on everything going on inside and outside the hospital, the practices, and the emergency procedures, he introduced me to a young woman named Rachel. She smiled at me from across a desk in the back of the room, twirling a black pen around her chocolate-brown hair. She was a warrior turned nurse after realizing that fighting wasn't for her.

When we finished work, she asked me to get coffee at The Night Raider's Café, but I declined. It wasn't useful to start making friends when I was going to leave in a few days. Besides, I had two nights until I visited the Lycans.

I wanted to spend it in some special way and give Alpha Roman a big fuck-you for not respecting me. That would be fun. Really fucking fun.

After tucking my coat into my backpack and promising Rachel that I'd go to coffee with her some other time, I walked back to the house. The dark forest was almost quieter than the hospital; shadows of trees loomed over me.

Hopefully, Roman would run his nightly route through these woods tonight. I hadn't seen him since my run-in with Ryker yesterday, and the *ho* part of me was actually upset. *I* definitely was not upset, and my wolf, she wasn't upset either. Not. At. All.

We didn't care that we couldn't smell his minty scent drifting through our window last night. We didn't care that we hadn't seen those golden eyes in the darkness. We didn't care about him.

Mom and Dad were waiting at the front door to our house for me with huge smiles on their faces.

"How'd you like your first day?" Dad asked.

"It was good."

Mom clapped her hands together. "We heard that you got a promotion," she said, lowering her voice.

I opened my bag to show them the white doctor's coat.

She squealed, "A doctor, just like her mama!"

Dad ruffled my hair like he used to when I was five. "What suddenly changed your mind about the hospital?"

I gulped and played with my fingers. "Nothing. I just thought that ... I should pull my weight in this pack."

Lie. Obvious lie. And I felt terrible for it.

My gaze shifted from him to the dark window, my heart racing for some odd reason. Two golden eyes pierced through the night and stared right at me. I pressed my lips together and looked back at him.

"I'm going to head upstairs," I said, politely declining the wet-dog-smelling meatloaf that Dad had cooked for dinner. "I've had a long day."

I hurried up the stairs toward my bedroom, shut my door, and gazed at the curtains that I had pulled open this morning. The moonflowers glowed brightly on my windowsill, but his eyes glowed even brighter in the forest.

I wasn't doing this because I wanted him to watch me. I was doing this because I wanted to show him I didn't need him. Not to achieve my goals. Not to have a leg-shaking orgasm.

But when I turned toward the bed, my brows furrowed. Unlike this morning, my bed was made, and a piece of paper that had been ripped out of a journal sat on the center of my black blankets. I picked it up and unfolded it, my eyes widening.

It was a sketch of me, standing among the other warriors in this pack. With my hair braided back, I stood at the head of the pack with the moonlight reflecting off of my eyes and a mark on my neck.

The picture was breathtakingly beautiful. I was speechless. I wanted to sit and stare at it all day long, but something inside of me snapped when I noticed that Roman was in the picture, staring at me with so much love.

It was as if someone was making fun of me for not becoming a warrior and for having a thing with Roman. I crumpled the paper in my fist. *Damn him.* I bet it was the bitch Vanessa; she was set on messing with my fucking life.

I tossed the ball of paper onto my desk and peeled off my shirt. Fucking Roman. He'd probably told her to do that. *Hurt Isabella more. Hurt her so badly.* So he could relish in my pain, so I would need him to help me feel better.

My wolf whimpered inside of me, telling me he wouldn't do that, but he had hurt me before this. I didn't doubt that he would hurt me again.

He stood outside my bedroom window, still deep in the woods, with a fucking smile on his stupid face.

This wasn't for him anymore. This was for me. I needed this release. I needed to feel good after all this hurt. I lay back against my headboard, parting my legs and sliding a hand between them.

Last show for you, you fucking asshole alpha.

My eyes fluttered closed as I rubbed harsh, rough circles around my clit. This was what I needed. I moaned. Long day at the hospital, a bitch Vanessa who thought she was funny, and an alpha who wanted to get on my very last nerve.

Roman walked out of the forest and stood in the open, staring at me. The moonlight hit his fur, making it glisten. My toes curled into the bedsheets.

I imagined us in the cave, me curled into his arm, his fingers brushing against my cheek, making my heart tighten in my chest and giving me so many fucking butterflies.

I parted my lips, lightly pinching my nipple. A wave of pleasure rolled through me. His minty scent drifted in through the window, and I inhaled. He smelled good; even my wolf was purring.

I imagined us the other night when he'd pushed me up against the tree, when his fingers had thrust in and out of me, when he had made me come over and over and over again until I could barely stand straight.

So many undesirable facets of that man, and I was attracted to every one of them.

Roman let out a low growl, and I clenched. I wanted him to roughly thrust me against the headboard, push his fingers into my mouth for me to suck, tug on my hair.

My core tightened.

I bet he'd feel amazing inside of me. His hard cock pushing into my tight pussy. My fingers digging into his back.

He growled again, louder this time. I slowed and stared out the window, eyes glazed over with lust. My alpha wanted me to stop. Too bad I didn't care what he wanted.

My pussy suddenly tightened. I threw my head back, sinking into the sheets and slapping a hand over my mouth to stop myself from screaming to the moon. After a few moments of pure pleasure pumping out of me, I took a few deep breaths.

Trying to calm myself. Trying to catch my breath. Trying to gather my racing thoughts.

My whole body tingled. I pressed my lips into a smile, giggling. It felt like I was walking on clouds with the Moon Goddess herself. I drew my knees together and gazed at him.

He stood in front of my window with those sinful golden

eyes. I wrapped a blanket around my body and walked to the window.

"Roman ..." I said.

He growled again but moved closer.

"I hope you enjoyed the show. It's the last one you'll ever get from me. I don't need you to please me anymore."

CHAPTER 16

ISABELLA

*W*hile I walked down the hospital halls, I gazed down at the crumpled sketch in my hands. It was ridiculous that I hadn't thrown it away yet. But at least, it was better than staring at the bland white-tiled floors.

Screw that.

The sketch was beautiful. Fucking beautiful.

A strand of my hair was blowing against my cheek. There was a tiny scar on my collarbone from when Vanessa had pushed me in gym class in fifth grade. My lips were set in a smile. I looked valued and respected, so strong and happy.

Though I had been drawn in the left third of the piece, every wolf that surrounded me was staring at me in amazement. Even Roman. His dark eyes were fixed on me and only me with the utmost respect.

Too bad that he didn't respect me in real life.

All he wanted was sex.

My wolf whimpered.

I wanted that, too, but some part of me wanted more. Sitting in his truck the other night—just admiring the way he'd seemed so relaxed, lips pressed together softly, dark hair resting against his forehead, that smile he had given me—it'd made me wonder if we could be something more.

But not now. Sex was all I needed from him, all I had ever needed from him. He and I couldn't be anything more than what we were.

When I reached Rachel's desk, I folded the sketch and put it into my pocket.

Rachel grinned at me, clicking her pen. "Morning, Isabella."

I smiled and leaned against the table. "How's Mr. Beck doing?"

She wrote something on a clipboard and handed it to me. "Wheelchair-bound." She grimaced and shook her head. "He's been asking about you all morning. Dr. Jakkobs told me to tell you to go see him when you—" She shifted her gaze behind me, bowing her head. "Good morning, Alpha."

Moon Goddess.

I froze. It was only nine in the morning. I couldn't handle his shit right now, especially after he saw me in this white doctor's jacket.

Wasn't he supposed to be running practice for the warriors?

Instead of turning around to greet my *alpha*, I stood completely still. Hoping he would just disappear. Hoping that he wouldn't even say a word to me.

Rachel noticed my uneasiness, looking back at Roman. "I'll be checking on a few other patients." She stood from her seat and disappeared through the door.

What a great fucking friend.

Roman cleared his throat, but I didn't turn around. His minty scent was tempting, but I wouldn't fall for that trick of his again.

I stared down at the clipboard, flicking through the pages. "Sorry, I have work to do."

Before I walked out the door, he grabbed my wrist—a rush of tingles shooting up my arm—and growled. "We need to talk."

"And what do we need to talk about, Roman?" I asked, turning around and clutching the clipboard to my chest.

"The little stunt you pulled last night."

"I don't know what you're talking about." I batted my lashes at him. "Anyway"—I peered at my wrist, looking at my pretend watch—"looks like I have a patient to get to." I pushed through the double doors and walked down the hallway.

He followed me. "Stop, Isabella."

Room 405. Room 406. Room 407.

"Stop."

Patients and doctors gazed into the hallway as I rushed aimlessly down it. *Room 408. Room 409.* Moon Goddess, the hallway stopped in a few rooms. *Where the hell was room 423?*

"Isabella, don't make me say it again."

Shit. Shit. Shit. I stopped at the end of the hallway. Room 421, Mom's office. The door was opened slightly, her lamp emitting a pale yellow light over her abandoned desk.

Roman grasped my wrist. "I said to stop."

I turned on my heel and pressed a finger into his chest. "You should know by now that I don't listen to you."

Nurses and patients gazed over, gasping. Old man Beck laughed in one of the other rooms, taunting me.

Roman growled, and everyone turned back to their work.

He pushed me into Mom's empty office and slammed the door. Within a moment, he had me pressed against the wall. "I can make you listen to me. Remember that, Isabella."

What was the worst he could do that I wouldn't enjoy? Lock me in a silver cage? Tell everyone at the hospital that I wasn't smart enough to work as a doctor either? Force me to submit to him? None of those punishments was worse than the one he had already given me.

I growled, turning around to face him, and kicked him in the shin. "Don't talk to me like that." I flared my nostrils at his stupid perfect face.

The feelings I'd had before he hurt me were all still there. The excitement. The enjoyment. The passion.

"You know, because of the stunt *you* pulled, someone drew a picture of me." After pulling the drawing from my pocket, I thrust it into his face. "They're mocking me, Roman. They're mocking me for not becoming a warrior, and it's your fault."

He stared down at the picture, then at me, and then back. His face shifting through a variety of emotions. "You don't like the picture?"

Of course I liked the damn picture.

"That's not the point." I stepped closer to him. "The point is that people are mocking me because of what you did."

He smoothed out the crinkles with his fingers, deposited the drawing into his jeans pocket, and shook his head. "I assigned you here because you're smart, Isabella. You should be thankful that you're here and not somewhere else. You should be thankful that you get to help people, not hurt them. The life you think you want is just a life of hurt."

"You know nothing about what I want."

"Moon Goddess, Isabella! If I were in your shoes, I would shut the fuck up about all of this. You have an education. Use it." He pressed his lips together, holding back from saying something worse.

"I appreciate my education," I said, knowing that he hadn't gotten to finish his because the pack needed him to become alpha when he was only fifteen. But that wasn't what this was about. I stepped toward him, staring him right in his green eyes, my heart racing. "But I want to be a warrior."

"Well, you're not!" he said, eyes becoming a dark mess of gold. He moved closer to me, glaring down at me with so much fury. "And why are you wearing this jacket?" He grabbed the collar of my jacket, curling it in his fingers. "I didn't assign you to work under Jakkobs, did I?"

I ripped myself out of his grip and turned around, trying to get away from his intoxicating minty scent. I couldn't handle the way it was making my heart race. "Well, Roman, if you don't want to see me in it, then take it off."

He let out a low growl that made me shiver in ... delight ... and pushed me against the door. His stubble rubbing against the nape of my neck. His warm breath on my ear. His fingers gliding around my throat. Fuck whatever I'd said about not needing him last night.

"Fuck, Isabella," he breathed, nose training up the side of my neck. "Don't tempt me because I will bend you over your mother's desk and rip off every single piece of your clothing. I can't handle this anymore."

"You're all talk."

No, whatever it was between us would never be the same ... but having him touch me—even like this—made my wolf happy. She wanted him even though it was wrong, and I wanted my old friend Roman back. If him touching me like this was the only way I could smell his scent or be comfortable in his arms ... then so be it.

He growled and roughly pulled me closer to him with a fistful of my hair. "All talk?" he scoffed.

In one moment, he pulled up the back of my jacket, pushed down my pants, and pressed himself into me from behind, making me feel his cock through his jeans on my ass. "I would take you right here, Isabella. Would make you beg me to stop. Would leave you stumbling out of this fucking room."

He smirked against my neck, and I clenched.

"But you said you didn't need me."

I dug my fingernails into the door, cursing under my breath.

He plunged a finger into my pussy. "You don't need this?" he asked.

EMILIA ROSE

I tightened around his finger, and he added another one.

"Huh?"

"Roman," I said, grasping his wrist in my hand but not stopping him.

He curled his fingers, hitting my G-spot.

"Holy ..." I breathed out, a wave of heat warming my core, and pressed my knees together.

He growled lowly, his sharp teeth rubbing on my neck and definitely leaving a little love bite for me to admire later, and stepped between my feet to push them apart.

"Roman," I moaned. My pussy tightened, the pressure almost becoming unbearable. I squeezed my eyes shut. "Oh my Moon Goddess."

"Tell me what I want to hear, Isabella."

"N-no." I reached behind me to grasp his cock through his pants and stroked it at the same pace that he fingered me. "Fuck, I want you inside me."

He swore under his breath, lips grazing against my jaw. His fingers moved quicker. I clenched, the tension rising in my core.

"I bet you taste so fucking good."

I parted my lips, my legs collapsing. My fingers dug into the door, trying to find anything I could to hold myself up. My core pulsed over and over and over on him until I released all of my juices.

When I finished, he pulled his fingers out of me. Someone wiggled the doorknob, and my eyes widened. I pulled up my pants and watched Roman suck his fingers into his mouth, his eyes rolling back into his head, as if I was the sweetest thing he had ever tasted.

The door was suddenly pulled open, and Mom stood there. Her dark brows were furrowed as she looked between us. Then, she bowed her head toward Roman, smiling tensely. "Alpha, I hope my daughter isn't being a nuisance ..."

I gazed over at him. He was fighting to keep his wolf contained, his golden eyes shining through Roman's green irises.

He clenched his jaw. "Of course not." Then, he walked right out of the room, leaving me standing in front of Mom, trying not to tremble. "I'll see you at the assignment party tonight, Isabella."

CHAPTER 17

ISABELLA

*R*oman held a party for the graduates every year since his parents had died, celebrating not only the assignments, but also graduating from their education. The parties were always bigger and better than the previous year, and today was no different.

Moonflowers were scattered around the backyard of the pack house and throughout the forest leading to the pack lake, where Vanessa was probably half-naked and flirting with some warriors already.

"I'm gonna find Derek," I said to Mom and Dad after we arrived.

When I disappeared into the crowd, I tugged my hair up into a high bun, showing off the pink mark that Roman had left on my neck earlier.

Derek stood by the grill, stacking three hamburgers on top of each other on his plate. I grabbed a plate from one of the tables that housed food that pack members had cooked for this special occasion. Mel's hot dogs. Toni's chicken wrapped in bacon. Bob's casserole. At least Dad hadn't brought his meatloaf.

Roman walked up next to me, looking around the table for food. He glanced in my direction, his scent so sweet.

"What?" I asked, taking a heaping portion of the casserole.

"Nothing," he said, eyeing the pink hickey on my neck. "Did I say anything?"

I sucked in a breath when he grabbed the spoon from my hand, our fingers brushing against each other. It was such a soft, light touch. Nothing like earlier. Nothing like every other night we had been together. I looked down at my plate and gulped.

He didn't need to say anything for me to wish that things were different, for me to remember that drawing. The way he looked at me. The same way he had looked at me the other night in his truck.

If he hadn't assigned me as a nurse, I wouldn't have thought about going to the Lycans. I just wanted to stay here with my friends and my family and him.

His fingers lingered against mine, my knuckles against his. We didn't speak a single word, just stood there, quietly taking in each other's presence. Then, when I couldn't handle it any longer, I pulled away and walked toward the grill. Away from him. Away from the man who made my wolf feel things that she should never feel.

Derek wasn't standing by the grill anymore. I stopped in my tracks, looking around. Rachel walked up to me in a maroon one-piece swimsuit, her dark hair wet from the lake.

"Hey," she said, wrapping a towel around her body. "What happened when I left the room this morning"—she glanced over at Roman, who had his back turned—"with Alpha Roman?"

I arched a brow, a slight smile stretching across my face. So, she wanted tea.

"Nothing," I said.

"Isabella!" Vanessa walked over to us in a tiny white string bikini, her breasts barely covered by the small piece of fabric. Beads of water dripped down her tan skin. "Are you coming in?"

After ignoring Vanessa, I turned back to Rachel.

She lightly pushed me. "Oh, don't give me that. What's going on between you two? I could just feel all that tension between you both."

I pulled some hair over my hickey. "There is nothing going on between us."

"Going on between who?" Vanessa asked, shaking out her wet hair, her breasts bouncing with it. She puckered her red lips and arched a brow. "Does Isabella have a secret boyfriend?"

Oh my fucking God. What was wrong with her?

"Do you? Is it your mate?" she asked, her expression suddenly blank. "What does he look like—"

"Vanessa, I don't want to talk about it right now."

She looked behind me. "Alpha Roman! Derek!" She motioned for them.

Derek smiled at me, waving. He curled his arm around my shoulders after they walked over to us.

Both Roman and Vanessa gazed at his arm around me.

Then, Vanessa turned to Roman, placing her fingers on his wrist. "Isabella met her mate."

Roman gazed down at his arm and pulled himself out of her grip, his eyes a mess of green and gold. "She did?"

"No," I said between clenched teeth.

Vanessa looked at Rachel. "Is he in our pack?"

Rachel froze beside me.

Don't you dare say anything. Don't you dare say it. I pressed my lips together.

Derek and Rachel both knew that I had been kind of seeing Roman, but if Vanessa found out …

"Yes," I said before Rachel could ruin it. My hand curled around Derek's wrist, hoping that she would put two and two together.

Her eyes widened, and she glanced between us. "You guys are mates? I thought you were just friends," she said, frowning.

She parted her lips to speak again and then wrapped her arms around her body, as if she was shielding herself from us. Not a typical Vanessa reaction, but ...

Derek shook his head. "We're not mates."

"Just seeing each other."

"But you can't tell anyone," Derek continued my lie, and I thanked him twenty times over through the mind link.

"We're just trying to keep it down low," I said.

Vanessa pushed out her hip and rested one hand on it. "I don't believe it," she said, eyeing me. "Kiss him if you're together." She stared at me, her eyes flickering to my lips and her jaw clenched ever so softly.

I felt like I was in middle school with her sometimes. Hell, whether we kissed or not, she would probably go blab to everyone that Derek *was* my mate and not just someone that I was *seeing*.

Roman tensed, his golden eyes staring right at me. I glanced at Derek. We had kissed when we were twelve, but there was no way I would kiss Derek now, especially with Roman standing there. I didn't need to prove anything to Vanessa.

Rachel cleared her throat, tugging on Vanessa's arm. "Vanessa, we haven't talked much before. Let's go get a drink and chat!"

Vanessa wouldn't say no to that, and I silently thanked Rachel when they both walked away. I would definitely have to go out on that coffee date with her after that.

Roman's gaze was burning into me, and I suddenly felt hot. Extremely hot.

I grabbed Derek's hand. "Well, lover boy, let's go get some desert." Because I needed some space to cool off.

Before I could drag Derek anywhere, Roman curled his hand around my arm and gave me a stern look that eventually faded into something softer. He didn't say anything, but he didn't have to. My arm was tingling again, and I bet his was too.

There was something unspoken between us, and we both accepted it without question. Neither one of us wanted to bring it up to each other, but neither one of us wanted to stop—whatever it was.

He released me and walked away.

Two hours later, Derek smooshed a marshmallow between two graham crackers, forgoing any chocolate in his s'mores because he needed to be *lean* for the warriors. I snatched the piece of chocolate that Dad gave him for his s-more, sucked it between my teeth, and sighed in delight.

The moon was glowing high in the sky, and in a few hours, I would have to meet Ryker at our borders. A weird feeling sat heavily in the pit of my stomach. I didn't want to lie to everyone about what was going on, but I needed to.

Vanessa sat across from me, next to Roman's sister, Jane. Vanessa hadn't taken her eyes off of me since she concluded that Derek and I were fucking. She burned her marshmallow in the fire, the light reflecting off of her eyes.

I shifted in my seat, uncomfortable under her stare, and leaned closer to Derek. "I'm going to use the bathroom."

Derek looked over at Roman who was talking to Cayden at the back door. Roman had just taken a dip in the lake, his white V-neck hanging over his shoulder and beads of water rolling down his tan abdomen.

"No, you're not," Derek said.

No, I wasn't. I couldn't handle Roman anymore. Watching him walk around the whole night with a shirt that clung to his body, watching him walk out of the water and flipping his wet dark hair, watching his eyes flicker to gold every time he gazed at me. It was just enough to get my wolf going.

After the whole Vanessa incident, Roman was pissed. I swore he'd growled when Derek and I played together with some pups and when he drew his arms around me. Everything about Roman was driving me insane tonight for some reason, especially his jealousy.

I gave Derek my burned marshmallow stick and walked over to the pack house.

Cayden nodded to me, smiling. "You look happy. You enjoying the hospital?"

"It's doable." I shrugged my shoulders and lingered near the door.

Roman gave me a soft, genuine smile, which made my wolf purr.

"Roman said that you're working under Jakkobs now," Cayden said.

Did he now? He wasn't hiding the fact that I was supposed to be a nurse and not a doctor?

I glanced at him, brow arched, but Roman didn't say anything. Instead, he stood there with his huge arms crossed over his chest, water dripping off his dark hair and eyes such a soft gold.

The epitome of confusion.

He hadn't wanted me to be a doctor. He didn't care that people knew I was.

He hadn't assigned me as a warrior. He'd expected me to practice during tryout week.

He wanted me out of his hair. He couldn't leave me alone.

"I am"—I gently patted Cayden's forearm, fingers brushing over his skin—"which means that I'll be treating you if you end up in the hospital."

Roman growled, his eyes shifting from a soft green to a sharp, scathing gold. He stood taller, fists clenched and canines emerging from under his lips. Well, that was my cue.

"I should be going." I smiled at them both and stepped into the house, glancing briefly at Roman. I walked down the hall, brushing my fingers across the walls to leave my scent for him to follow.

My core clenched when I heard his footsteps behind me, coming closer and closer, his minty scent so fucking strong. I could get high off of it if I wasn't careful. I opened his office door and walked into the room.

When I had been here last time, I had screamed at him. Now, I wanted to scream *for* him.

He softly closed the door behind us, and I hopped up onto his mahogany desk, my skirt riding up the sides of my legs. His gaze traveled down my body and then back up it. He tossed his shirt onto a chair and stalked toward me, each step dreadfully slow.

"Does the alpha want to talk again?" I asked, sucking my bottom lip between my teeth.

Moon Goddess, he was so fucking sexy.

His fingers danced across my knees, sending tingles up my thighs. He parted my legs and stepped between them, pushing his hardness against my thin black bikini bottoms. He roughly grabbed my chin, his thumb brushing against my bottom lip. "I'm about to do more than talk to you."

I raked my fingers up his taut chest. "And what is the *oh-so scary alpha* going to do to me?"

In one swift movement, he pulled me to the edge of the desk. I rested my forearms on the wood, leaning back and watching him yank down my bottoms and throw them to the other side of the room.

He leaned down, tongue immediately finding my clit. I drew my knees together, but he forced them apart and pinned my thighs to the desk. He inhaled deeply, eyes turning completely gold.

"Fuck," he mumbled. "I've been waiting so long to taste you."

Pushing one finger inside of me, he continued to lap at my

clit. I gripped the edge of the desk, trying to still my trembling body. My pussy clenched around him, and I bit my lip to muffle my moans.

He stared at me, golden eyes like the sun. Daring me to push him away.

I shoved a hand through his hair, pulling him even closer. There was no pushing him away. I needed him, was aching to feel him inside of me, right here on his desk. For his wolf to be over-come with so much fucking desire that he couldn't hold back from thrusting his hard cock right into my tight little pussy and claiming me as his own.

It was what I wanted. For him to claim me.

"Roman," I said between shaky breaths.

He sucked my clit into his mouth, his tongue still moving in torturous circles, and pounded two fingers deep into me.

Someone knocked on the door, and I pressed my lips together, eyes widening. My core was aching with a rising pressure.

Roman didn't stop. He continued to devour me—his stubble tickling my inner thighs, his hands pinning my legs to the desk, his fucking eyes taking in every inch of my body. I gazed at the door, worried.

They knocked again, and I bit my lip to hold in my moans.

"Roman," I whispered. My legs began to tremble, and I knew I was seconds away from releasing myself onto him. "Roman, please stop."

"Alpha!" Vanessa's nasally voice rang out through the door.

Oh my Moon Goddess.

I gulped, trying to draw my legs together again, but Roman pushed them down.

"Stop," he ordered. "Look at me."

I gazed down at him and then back at the door.

He growled and snatched my chin. "Me," he said, voice full of dominance.

I gnawed on the inside of my cheek. "She's going to come in," I said in a hushed voice.

There was no doubt in my mind that she would stroll right into Roman's office in her little fucking bikini.

He released my chin, thrusting a finger back into my pussy and watching me squirm. "I will finish what's mine. She will not interrupt me."

He flicked his tongue against my clit. One hand wandered up my torso to my breast, and he grasped it in his hand, pinching my nipple between his fingers.

I parted my lips, slapped a hand over my mouth to muffle my moans, and came all over him. Wave after wave of pleasure pulsed out of me, sending me higher than I had ever been. My mind was foggy, my whole body tingling. Yet he didn't stop massaging my clit with his tongue.

Pressure rose in my core again. I curled a hand in his hair, brows furrowing. "Roman"—I threw my head back—"I'm going to…"

He wrapped an arm around my waist and picked me up off of the desk. I dug my fingers into his shoulders as he thrust up into my pussy, hard and fast and so damn rough. His canines grazed against my neck, poking the skin just barely.

"Yes," I said softly into his ear. A rush of heat warmed my core. Hell, I didn't even know what I had said or what he had done or what he would do. All I knew was that it felt too fucking good, and I wanted more. "Please."

"Alpha Roman!" Vanessa said.

He growled loudly, and she quieted down, her footsteps becoming quieter and quieter.

Roman pressed his lips against my ear. "I want to hear you scream, Isabella. So fucking loud that everyone at this fucking party hears you." He brushed his thumb against my swollen clit. "Come for me."

I parted my lips, my toes curling, and moaned his name, unable to hold it back.

"Fuck, baby," he said, fingers slowing down until I totally collapsed in his arms. He set me on his desk and leaned over me, placing his hands on either side of my thighs. He hung his head low, taking deep breaths to try to control his wolf.

After I ran my fingers through his hair, admiring it, he lifted his gaze to meet mine. His eyes were a breathtaking gold.

All I could think about was staring into those eyes for the rest of my life. It scared me because alphas were known to sleep with more than a few girls before they mated, and—it was so fucking wrong—but I wanted to be one of those girls. I'd be one of the lucky ones who got to see him under the moonlight, to draw my fingers across his cheeks when he was sleeping, to feel things like this because of him.

We gazed at each other for a few intimate moments, and then he pulled away. I looked down at my lap, eyes flickering over the contents on his desk.

That look he gave me ... it was so ... so ... different.

The crumpled sketch of me was sitting on his desk, next to his journal and a drawing of a moonflower, his mother's favorite. I brushed my fingers across the drawing, watched him retrieve my bikini from the other side of the room, and quickly hid the paper under the waistband of my skirt.

No, I would never be the woman in the sketch he took from me earlier. But the picture was beautiful, and I wanted to keep it for my own selfish reasons.

Roman walked back over and handed me my bottoms. He leaned against his desk, watching me put it on. "Isabella," he said softly, "thank you."

"For what?"

He paused for a long moment. "For giving the hospital a try." His words were sincere, like he thought I had obeyed him for once in my entire life. "I'm really glad that you like it more than you thought you would."

I stayed quiet for a long time, my heart suddenly hurting. Staring into his eyes that were filled with so much passion and at his smile that shattered my heart into a million pieces, I hated myself for going behind his back, for going to meet Ryker tonight, for giving up on this.

Whatever we were.

CHAPTER 18

ROMAN

*S*he stared at me with the most beautiful eyes that I had ever seen; they glimmered under the moonlight that flooded in through my office windows. And that smile. Moon Goddess, her smile got me every time.

But instead of one of her overly joyous or flirty smiles I had come to know and love, her smile was filled with sadness, and I didn't know why. Maybe she didn't like the hospital as much as I'd thought she did. Sure, I didn't expect her to love it. But this morning, when I'd visited her, she had seemed to get along with everyone quite well.

The way she'd walked around the hospital reminded me of Mom, so caring, so nurturing. She'd make a perfect luna someday. Yes, I'd hated going back to the last place I had seen Mom, but Isabella had made it so much easier.

She parted her plump lips and pushed past me. "I have to go."

I wanted to pull her back, to keep her here with me, to show her all of my drawings of her. She might not have liked the first one, but maybe she was just hurt. If she saw the other ones, if she saw every one that I had drawn each night, she would love them. She looked so strong in them, just as she was.

Instead of pulling her back, I watched her leave and sighed through my nose. I couldn't wait until she turned eighteen. Every day was pure torture now that I didn't see her. And every night was pure torture, killing rogues in the woods near her house and knowing that she would be safer with me in my pack house.

"Rogue spotted at the border," a guard said through my mind link.

I clenched my jaw, inhaling her lingering scent. *"Kill him,"* I ordered.

There would be more tonight, like every night. I just needed them to stay away long enough for Isabella and her family to get home safely.

After clearing my head, I walked out of my office.

Vanessa was waiting in the kitchen for me. "What're you up to?" she asked, brow raised.

"That's none of your business."

"You were with Isabella."

I arched a brow at her. "Like I said, that's none of your business."

She placed a hand on her hip. "Why were you with her?"

I growled. *Did she not hear a word that I just said?*

She had no place to ask about my Isabella. She was in no place to ask questions.

"What's your obsession with her?"

Vanessa crossed her arms over her chest, jaw clenched, huffed, and walked out of the house.

That woman was crazy. Absolutely crazy.

I grabbed a spare shirt from my bedroom, tossed it over my shoulder, listened to my guards speak through the mind link about the growing number of rogues outside the borders, and walked out of the house.

"Five spotted to the north," another guard said through the link. There were so fucking many of them.

"Three to the west."

"Two more to the west."

I frowned at Isabella through the window. This was more proof. Proof that I'd made the right decision, keeping Isabella as a nurse. No matter how much it hurt me. Dad couldn't protect Mom, but I would protect Isabella.

Isabella looked toward the house, her gaze catching mine.

"Guard the forest," I said through the link. *"No rogues get within fifty feet of the property until everyone gets home."*

After my parents had died, I'd hunted down all the rogues I could find and killed them. Now, after seven years, they were back. And I would not chance losing Isabella to them too. They'd targeted my family before; I wouldn't put it past them to do it again.

CHAPTER 19

ISABELLA

*a*fter listening to Roman praise me for lying to him, I walked right out of the room without speaking a word. I couldn't listen to him. I couldn't look at that smile of his and that softness in his eyes.

My stomach turned. I hated every second of it. When he found out that this was all a lie, he would be so hurt. He wouldn't look at me the same.

I shook my head and made a beeline for Mom and Dad. This wasn't my fault. If he had just accepted me as a warrior, I wouldn't have even considered becoming a Lycan. Sure, becoming a Lycan was always a goal, but I just wanted to protect. Being a warrior would have sufficed because I enjoyed being in Roman's pack, under his command, *with* him.

Mom was curled in Dad's sweatshirt by the fire, staring at him with the flames reflecting off of her eyes. All I wanted was a relationship like theirs, and I hoped the Moon Goddess would give me that soon with a mate. Then, maybe, I wouldn't feel bad about leaving Roman.

"There you are, Izzy," Mom said.

"Your mother and I are leaving," Dad said.

Good, I needed to get out of here. I had to meet Ryker soon.

"You can stay with Derek a little longer if you—"

"No, let's go home."

I watched Roman walk out of the pack house with a soft expression. For the briefest moment, his eyes met mine. But I looked away, the guilt smothering me.

When we finally got back to the house, it was nearly eleven p.m. I retired to my room, shut my door, and breathed in the refreshing scent of moonflowers. They twinkled on my windowsill, brightening up my room like Christmas lights. I brushed my finger against Luna Raya's keychain and smiled.

I was doing the right thing. I was doing the right thing. I was doing the right thing.

My wolf might've wanted to stay, but I wanted to go. This was my dream.

At eleven fifty p.m., Dad started snoring. I waited anxiously by my bedroom door, grasping the keychain in my hand. If anything could give me strength to fulfill my destiny, it would be Luna Raya.

After another two minutes, I took a deep breath and peeked my head out of the door. Mom and Dad's door was closed, and I could hear Mom cursing the Moon Goddess for having a mate who snored louder than her father.

I doused myself in a foul-smelling perfume to hide my scent from the guards, tiptoed down the stairs, skipping the floorboards that creaked, and then slipped out the door. The moon glowed so brightly in the sky, its light flooding through the tree leaves and hitting the forest floor. Wolves growled viciously in the distance—in the direction of the pack house.

To the west, guards were doubled ... so I decided to sneak out to the east. I hurried through the woods, being sure not to leave much of my perfume's scent on any trees or bushes.

There was an eerie sense of danger in the air. I gazed around, making sure every step was in the right direction—away from the danger and not toward it.

Another wolf growled, and I ducked behind a tree. This one was closer, and it sounded different from any growl I had heard. Rogues maybe? Ryker had been looking for new recruits for a reason.

Either way, I had to be more careful. If *anyone* saw me, I would be screwed. They'd tell Alpha Roman that someone was sneaking outside of the borders. Roman would track my perfume's scent and drag me back to my room, if not lock me in the pack prison for leaving without permission for the second time.

When I thought nobody was around, I walked carefully and quietly through the woods toward the borders. Three guards walked tensely around, gazing everywhere, as if they were looking for something. Or someone.

Nothing could ever go easily for me.

The numbers *11:58* glowed on my phone. I tapped my fingers on the screen, waiting anxiously for the guards to be relieved of their positions at twelve a.m. There would be more of them, but they usually weren't as on guard at that time. I had tried and tested this multiple times, sneaking out and going to The Night Raider's Café with Derek in high school. I just had to be quiet.

That was when I'd take my chance and sprint off of the property. I didn't want to keep Ryker waiting. Tonight was the only time to prove myself.

After crouching down behind another tree, I pressed my lips together. *11:59 p.m.*

I gazed through the woods, trying to find a hidden passageway, when I locked eyes with Ryker. Standing about two hundred yards off of our property, he was looking directly at me. Waiting for me to make a react. Assessing my actions.

Though Ryker stood close enough for his scent to be noticed, Lycans were known to have an abundance of abilities to hide themselves, like scent-cloaking. He didn't move, just leaned against a tree with a smirk on that gorgeous face, and I knew that this was my first test. I would either escape without being noticed or get caught by Roman.

At twelve a.m., the guards didn't leave but continued to walk alongside the borders, watching. Ryker gazed down at his wrist and tapped it, as if to say, *It's time.*

Fuck it. I needed to get out of here. Now.

I stepped out from behind the tree, heard Roman's voice, and scurried back into hiding. *Damn it, Roman.* What was he doing here out of all places?

He should be at the pack house or by my window. Not here. On the other side of his property. This wasn't even along his running trail.

He stood in the clearing and talked to a guard; his muscles were swollen from running, sweat coated the back of his neck, and blood dripped from his lips.

Was he hurt? Had someone attacked him?

My wolf growled inside of me.

"Any more rogues?" Roman asked the guard.

The guard shook his head. "No."

Roman slowly scanned the woods, like he knew someone was out here, and paused when he looked in my direction. After lifting his nose to the air and inhaling deeply, he pressed his lips together.

I froze. He paused for a few moments and then finally turned back to the man. The guard walked off, and Cayden walked up behind Roman. His hands were soaked in blood, almost more blood than Roman's.

"Is everyone okay?" Cayden asked Roman.

Roman nodded.

"Everyone?" Cayden asked.

Roman sighed loudly and ran a hand through his thick brown hair. "Yes, Isabella is at home, safe." His jaw twitched, and I could tell he wanted to say more.

Cayden arched a brow. "And you're upset about that?"

The moonlight bounced off Roman's eyes. "No. She just seemed ... different when she left. Didn't even say bye to me." Roman walked a few steps toward the pack house, fist clenched by his side. "She likes the hospital."

Thanks for making me feel worse about this.

"Isn't that what you wanted?" Cayden asked.

Roman took a deep breath. "Yes, that's what I wanted, but ..."

"But?"

Roman growled. "But she's fine with it!" he snapped, canines emerging from under his lips and nails lengthening into claws. "It doesn't even faze her anymore. She's not putting up a fight."

I narrowed my eyes at him. *Did he want me to put up a fight with him? Is that why he assigned me as a stupid nurse?*

Cayden shook his head and walked toward the pack house. "Why do you always get pissed at her?" He turned around and walked backward, his arms outstretched. "You get mad that she hates the hospital. You get mad that she likes the hospital. Next, you'll be mad that she's hot. It's like you find reasons to confront her."

Roman growled and bared his teeth at his beta, but Cayden didn't back down.

"You wanted her at the hospital. She's at the hospital. Maybe you should leave her alone."

Thank you, Cayden.

Someone was actually talking some sense into him for once. Maybe he would listen. Maybe he would leave me alone.

No. We don't want that.

Roman clenched his jaw and stormed toward him. "I did what I had to do."

Cayden snorted. "You had to assign our best warrior to the hospital." He nodded. "Makes sense."

Roman snatched him by the collar and shoved him against a tree. After quietly whispering something to him in that threatening alpha tone, he stormed away. I clutched my keychain to my chest. Something wasn't right, but I didn't have time to deal with it right now.

When they departed from the forest and the other warrior wolves were taking their posts, I took a deep breath and bolted toward Ryker, staying quiet and out of sight.

CHAPTER 20

ISABELLA

*A*fter almost an hour of running, Ryker and I approached Lycan territory. The trees were bent in every direction, not one of them standing straight, roots crawled along the forest floor, and eerie fog lay heavy around us.

Ryker shifted into his human and handed me some clothes that had been hidden inside a tree stump. I pulled the shirt over my head and followed him through the fog, listening to the hoots and howls coming from deeper in the woods.

When the trees cleared and the fog suddenly dissipated, I gaped at the hundreds, if not thousands, of houses built into the mountainside. We stood atop a mountain with the community of Lycans below us. Though it was one a.m., every cabin had a light on. At the very bottom was a plateau, where Lycans were training in an open field that stretched on for miles.

Near the bottom of the hill was the grandest home—white brick, towering windows, and firewood stacked along its side. The view was more amazing than anything I had ever seen.

A bonfire was lit in front of the cabin, and some warriors sat around it. Each one had scars, moonflower tattoos, and a look in their eyes that promised me death if I got on their bad side.

My heart pounded against my chest as I just took in everything. Though any other wolf would've been terrified by the Lycans, I was excited. So damn excited.

Ryker led me to the fire. As we passed the Lycans, they gazed at me—some looking like they wanted to kill, others giving me that oh-so seductive stare that Roman always gave me.

It felt weird to have that attention from them instead of Roman. Sure, they were hot and were infamous for their feral manners in bed, for both fucking and loving with so much passion because they didn't know if they'd survive the next day with all the rogues and terror they faced. But it wasn't Roman.

I sat down on a log near the fire, letting it warm my face, and Ryker sat next to me. Though I didn't mind those seductive looks and though I wanted to love with as much passion as the next Lycan, my mind kept wandering back to Roman.

His stupid lopsided grin. That stupid glow in his eyes. The stupid way I felt when I was with him. I didn't want to think about how I'd lied to him so easily or how this wasn't some white lie. This was *the* lie. The lie that would destroy any type of relationship that I had with him. The lie that would pluck me right out of my dreaded hospital life. The lie that would make me a damn force to be reckoned with.

Ryker placed his forearms on his knees and leaned closer to me. "These are my warriors. We usually hunt at night, which is when rogues are most active. As you can see, we like to train in the type of environment that we fight in." He smiled at me and placed a hand on my knee. "Follow me. We will watch practice."

We walked toward the open field where warriors were stretching. When they saw Ryker, they bowed their heads, as if he was their alpha. We stood at the edge of the field. My gaze shifted as I analyzed the Lycans while they fought against each other. Muscle against muscle. Brain against brain. Heart against heart.

"Raj," he said to a man, arms crossed. "You're not finishing your throw."

Raj gazed at me, pushing a hand through his black hair, and winked. "I always finish," he said, a slight accent in his voice.

"Finish the throw," Ryker said, a familiar aura of authority to him.

I looked at him to see his jaw clenched just slightly. He reminded me of Roman.

"I bet Isabella would finish the throw on you."

"Me?" I said with wide eyes.

His eyes glowed like the moon. "If you don't want to fight tonight, I can—"

"No!" I jogged over to Raj. "I want to fight." *I was born to fight.*

Raj gestured down to his body. "I don't know if you want a piece of—"

I grabbed his wrist in one hand, turned on my heel, and tossed him over my shoulder, completing one of the hundreds of judo throws I had memorized over the last thirteen years.

He landed on the dirt with a hard thud and then hopped up. "Okay then, she's good."

Ryker smirked, fingers brushing against his stubble. "I know."

Raj shook out his arms and leaned down into a fighting stance. "Well, get ready, killer. You haven't seen anything yet."

Punches, kicks, takedowns, and throws—he tried them all on me. Landing about half of his moves, he came at me for almost an hour, giving me everything that he had.

Training with Cayden had made me aware of my weaknesses and prepared me for this moment. Every night after tryouts, I'd analyzed the positions I had gotten myself into and understood how to get out of them. I was ready for anything Raj could throw at me.

For the rest of the night, Ryker watched me and nodded in

approval when I took Raj to the ground. It felt good to have someone believe in me and to think I was as good as these Lycans.

Every time I caught him staring, I pushed myself harder. This was my only chance to impress him, and I wasn't going to give it up.

After practice, I sat on the ground, leaning back onto my hands and breathing deeply. Sweat dripped down my forehead, rolled down my neck, drenched my shirt. Everyone walked back to their homes up the mountain.

Ryker gazed down at me and took off his shirt, his muscles flexing. Scars were etched into his taut chest, and tattoos covered his forearms. The light from the bonfire bounced off of his body so damn perfectly. "You ready?"

"Ready for what?" I asked, standing.

He cocked a smirk. "For me." He lowered into a fighting stance. "Did you hope that you were done?"

I smiled at him, butterflies in my stomach. "Never," I said, standing up and imitating his stance.

Roman never fought against me, wouldn't even think about it. He never gave me a chance, but Ryker was.

Unlike with Raj, I couldn't keep up with Ryker. He would fake me out with one move and then switch to another one. Fake a takedown, finish an ankle-pick. Fake a jab-cross combination, land a kick to the side.

Adrenaline pumped through my system. Pure excitement. Pure exhilaration. Pure power.

Ryker shot in for a takedown but grabbed my wrist instead and threw me over his hip. I landed on the ground—hard—and he landed on top of me. His body on mine, his chest against my breasts, his lips near my neck. I took a deep breath.

After a couple long moments, he hopped up and pulled me off of the ground. "Let's get you cleaned up before the run back to your pack." He tossed his shirt over his shoulder, leading me toward the pack house. "You did good today."

"Just good?" I asked, brows furrowing together.

"Yes," he said, "just good." He opened the door to the pack house for me. "You shouldn't expect me to compliment you or go easy on you when you begin with us."

I smiled, stomach filling with excitement. "When I begin with you?"

"Isabella," he said, giving me a breathtaking smile, "you're going to be a Lycan."

CHAPTER 21

ISABELLA

I walked through the hospital, clipboard in one hand and Mr. Beck's blood samples in another. My thoughts hadn't stopped racing since this morning.

After Ryker had told me I was going to be a Lycan, I'd wrapped my arms around his neck and pulled him into a tight hug. I couldn't fucking believe that any of this was happening. All of my life, I'd trained for this moment, and I'd thought Roman had taken this opportunity away from me. But now, I was going to be one of the most respected warriors ever. A goddamn Lycan!

After placing the blood samples in a cart to be examined by Dr. Jakkobs, I skipped back to Mr. Beck's room with a big smile on my face. Instead of sitting in his room, where I'd left him, he had rolled all the way to the end of the hallway. He sat in his wheelchair, swaying back and forth and staring at the cardinals outside the window.

"You should break me out of here," he said. "I need to get those whippersnappers in shape."

I raised a brow at him. "Whippersnappers?"

"Those warriors. I see them run past here every morning. Back in my day, we'd run for hours, not just one time around the property."

Oh Moon Goddess. Here we go with another one of his stories.

He turned to me. "I bet Roman's training you real good." He elbowed me and gave me a grin. "You know what I mean."

"I told you, I'm not a warrior," I said. If I were, I wouldn't be here with him.

He slapped the armrest on his wheelchair and burst out in chuckles. "I ain't talking about fightin'. I'm talking in the bedroom."

I blinked a few times. *Did he just ... did he just really say ...*

"Mr. Beck, we're not—"

Suddenly, he stopped laughing and looked at me with a serious expression. "Isabella."

My brows furrowed together, and I took his hand in mine. "What's wrong? Does anything hurt? Are you okay?"

"He's here."

"Who's here?"

"Isabella," Roman said, walking through the door of the hospital with a to-die-for smile on his face.

Mr. Beck burst out in laughter again, and I silently cursed at him for nearly giving me a heart attack.

Roman walked all the way toward me, eyes landing on my chin. "What happened to you?"

"What?"

"You look ... tired, hurt? What happened?" His soft eyes searched mine.

I pulled away from Roman, Mr. Beck's laughter still sharp in my ear, and gazed down at the clipboard, pretending to be busy. "Nothing happened. I slept fine last night without you barging in, like usual."

He growled and grabbed my face in his hand, tilting it to the side. "Why is there a bruise on your jaw?"

Almost immediately, I placed a hand over the bruise, wanting to cover it, if there was one. It ached slightly but not enough for me to have noticed it this morning. And I'd gotten back so late that I didn't even bother looking in the mirror before I had to rush out this morning. Ryker must've given it to me.

I pulled myself away from him and leaned close. "I don't know. Maybe you gave it to me at the party," I whisper-yelled, so Mr. Beck wouldn't hear.

He was hard of hearing ... hopefully.

"It's not a hickey," Roman said, black specks appearing in his golden eyes. "What did you do?"

"I didn't do anything."

He stepped closer to me, eyes intensifying. "What did you do, Isabella?"

I pressed my lips together. "Why don't you ever believe me?"

He stepped even closer, and I pulled the papers to my chest and stepped back, afraid that he would see right through me.

"What happened?"

"Nothing."

"Did you go out last night and kill a rogue?"

"Alpha Roman let a rogue on his property?" I asked, faking surprise.

He shoved me against the wall, clenching my jaw in his hand. "Don't play stupid." His lips brushed against my ear. "I smelled you out in those woods this morning when I was training with the warriors." His fingers dug into my skin. "Now, what were you doing?"

I clenched my jaw. He wasn't going to let this go.

"Like I said before ... nothing."

When his eyes turned gold, he growled. "All I want is to keep people in this pack safe, but you are set on putting yourself in danger."

I snarled in return, pushing him off of me and stepping forward. "I can take care of myself. I'm strong. I'm smart. And"—I crossed my arms—"I think you're intimidated by me."

It all made sense. If I was ranking close to Beta Cayden, that could mean that I might outrank Roman ... someday. All the pieces were fitting together. Well, sorta. Roman had placed me in the hospital, so I wouldn't get better, so I wouldn't threaten his innate dominance and rule. He wanted to shut me down instead of let me rise.

"I'm trying to keep you safe, Isabella! Safe!" He snatched my chin in his hand again and shoved me against the wall with more force. "That is my job, and I don't care if you get angry with me for it. I will be placing a guard at your house at all times. You are not to leave your room at night until I say otherwise."

"And if I do?"

"You won't."

"I will."

"You won't." His voice was hard. "And if you do ... I'll have to lock you up in the pack house with me, so I can keep an eye on you."

I brushed a finger up his forearm, watching him tense. "I bet you would like that, huh?"

He gulped, eyes flickering to my lips. "No, I wouldn't," he said. *Oh Moon Goddess, he totally would.*

"I would rather my pack members follow my orders."

"You know I don't follow orders, *Alpha*." I gazed up into his golden eyes, my heart racing. "Guess you'll have to tie me to your bed to make sure I don't go anywhere."

He growled lowly, and I felt him harden against my stomach. I didn't know why I was still entertaining the idea of him after I'd visited the Lycans. I would have to leave this pack soon and get over this fling ... but right now ... all I wanted was him.

CHAPTER 22

ISABELLA

*H*is minty scent drifted into my nostrils, and I inhaled like he was a drug. I wouldn't mind him waiting outside for me, dragging me to his packhouse and into his room, and finishing what he had started. Staring at me from the foot of his bed, his muscles swollen, the pure dominance dripping off of every inch of him. My wolf purred.

"Fine," Roman said through clenched teeth, his golden eyes fading to green. "No guards."

My brows furrowed together. "What?"

He stepped away from me. "Go out if you want."

Go out? He was just going to let me go out without consequences? Without guards? Without protecting me from rogues?

I arched a brow at him. He would never do that.

"What're you doing?" I asked.

"Nothing." He shrugged his shoulders and stuffed his hands into his pockets. "Do whatever you want to do."

I crossed my arms over my chest. This was not how he

worked. He wasn't supposed to let me do whatever I wanted. He was supposed to fight with me. He was supposed to try to control me, try to dominate me.

"Later, Isabella." He turned and walked all the way down the hallway toward the exit doors.

No way was I going to let him just walk away from me. I stepped forward. "You might not have a guard out there, Roman," I said, "but you'll be out there, waiting for me."

With one hand grasping the doorknob, he gazed back with those dangerous eyes of his. "That's where you're wrong."

Then, he walked right out of the building, leaving me dumbfounded.

I shook my head and growled under my breath. If he wanted me to go out tonight, then I would go out to get myself into trouble. Bratty? Yes. But he liked bratty. He was giving me a chance to do what I wanted. Whether he came out to get me or not, he would be watching.

Mr. Beck chuckled from his wheelchair. "You two are something else."

"We aren't anything."

"I've been around for too long." He gazed back out at the cardinals and grasped his mate's necklace he had around his neck. "I know it when I see it."

"You know what?" I asked, snatching his wheelchair and wheeling him to his room. "That he's an asshole about ninety-nine percent of the time?"

He swayed back and forth. "That you like him."

I scoffed. "I do not like him."

His cock maybe but not him. Not someone who didn't respect me. Not someone who had placed me in the hospital when I was the best warrior he ever had. Not someone who got on every one of my nerves.

"You do, and that's why you'll go out tonight. You'll disobey him to get his attention."

I clenched my jaw. Here I was, standing in the hospital, listening to an old man tell me exactly how I was feeling and why I was feeling it. And the craziest part of this whole thing was that it was all true. Mr. Beck was right.

My wolf and I wanted Roman's attention.

I didn't know why. Maybe we had a connection ... maybe he was my—

No. He couldn't be.

A wolf wouldn't disrespect his mate. Mates lifted each other up; they didn't tear each other down.

After pushing Mr. Beck into his room and turning on the TV for him, I sighed. "Okay, well ... I'll be off."

Before I could leave, he grasped my hand. "Isabella"—he pointed a finger at me—"I'll be expecting those details tomorrow." He elbowed me. "If he doesn't lock you in his bedroom first." Then, he burst into another fit of laughter, his new dentures nearly falling out of his mouth.

I tapped my fingers on the coffee table at The Night Raider's Café, a large tree-shaded café perched between five different packs that doubled as a club during the wee hours of the morning. Men and women from all the nearest packs bustled around it. I gazed down at the two extra-fudge brownies with cute little moonflower-shaped sprinkles that sat in front of me and then the door. Where was he?

While trying to keep my eyes open until Derek got here, I rested my head on the window. It felt like forever since I'd hung out with him even though it was just yesterday. All I wanted was to gush about my time with the Lycans last night, but Derek would blab to Roman about it. He was one of those suck-ups. Not a brat like me.

"Your mate wear you out last night?" Vanessa sat down

directly across from me, her screechy voice ringing in my ears. "Derek is *such* a cutie," she said, annoyance laced in every word.

What was her problem? One moment, she was angry that Roman was flirting with me, and the next, she was angry that Derek was my *mate*. She was so damn confusing, and I didn't even want to deal with her. But ... I had to keep up that lie, so she didn't find out about Roman and me.

When she found out about us, everyone would know. Even though I would leave this pack soon to become a Lycan, I didn't want any rumors like that to spread.

And, plus, there was no harm in having a bit of fun.

"I know." I smiled at her.

She placed an elbow on the table and leaned toward me. "Is he good in bed?" she asked with a blank face and curious yet angry eyes. "Tell me." Her voice sounded almost desperate.

I grabbed her hands, hoping that she would stop. Stop this. Stop prying. Stop being so annoying. "He's amazing!"

Her eyes widened. "No way."

"And ... his fingers ..." I slapped a hand over my heart. "They do wonders when he's giving it to me from behind."

She made an O with her lips, eyes softening. Then, she smiled. "Isabella, I'm so happy for you!" Her voice sounded anything but happy. It sounded jealous.

I bet she was just trying to get with any man who talked to me. Next, she'd be all over Ryker when everyone found out I had been recruited by the Lycans.

The bell on the café door rang, and Derek walked into the room.

When he approached us, she stood. "Well, I'll leave you two *lovebirds* alone for now."

Derek gazed at her for a long moment and then at me. "What was that all about?" he asked.

I chuckled and slid a brownie in his direction. "Nothing." *Absolutely nothing.*

CHAPTER 23

ISABELLA

*L*et's just say that word had gotten around fast.

Vanessa had blabbed to everyone in our entire pack that Derek and I were *mates* and that he was *soooo* good in bed. When we walked back onto pack property, everyone gazed over at us and whispered. Some elder wolves congratulated the newest couple, but most young she-wolves stared lovingly at Derek like he was a sex god who could please them just by looking in their direction.

I walked up the porch stairs to home, smelling the faint scent of meatloaf in the garbage from the other night.

Stupid me for thinking rumors spread about Derek and me were better than rumors about Roman and me. My wolf retired inside of my mind, refusing to speak to me after I'd lied to everyone—claiming Derek was my mate and that Roman and I had done nothing together.

Even though my wolf didn't want it, maybe this was exactly

what I needed. A perfect distraction as I flirted with Roman and began my recruitment to the Lycans.

My phone buzzed in my pocket.

Rachel: Did you find your mate?!?! Mr. Beck is saying you did!

I took a deep breath through my nose and reached for the door, but someone pulled it open before I could.

Mom grinned at me, clapping her hands together. "Izzy!" She pulled me into a hug. "Derek is your mate?! You've been keeping it a secret for, what, five, six months since he turned eighteen?! Why didn't you tell us?"

"Mom ... he's not my mate." I awkwardly patted her back and looked at Dad. "It's just something Vanessa made up."

Dad wrapped his arms around her shoulders, trying to pull her away. "I told you. She won't know for sure until it's her birthday. And besides, sweetheart, if they were mates, Derek and she would've been all over each other when he turned eighteen a few months ago."

Mom playfully slapped his chest, her mate's necklace shifting on her chest. "He might be! You never know!"

Since we had been in diapers, Mom had wanted us to end up together. So, I decided not to argue with her. Derek was the "perfect boy" for me, she had said. But for me, he was too—how do I say this lightly?—submissive. Roman could order him to do anything, and he would do it at the snap of his finger. I wanted someone who was just as hardheaded as I was.

A vicious warrior. A strong wolf. Roman.

Moonlight flooded in through the window. I inched toward the stairs, hoping that Mom and Dad would let me get out of another dinner cooked by Dad himself. I loved Dad, but his cooking was ... for the rogues.

"I'm going out with Derek tonight," I shouted once I successfully snuck up the stairs.

I tossed my white doctor-in-training jacket onto my bed and looked out the window. Expecting Roman to be waiting for me.

Expecting to see his golden eyes. Becoming disappointed each minute he wasn't there.

The woods were empty and quiet. The only light came from the moonflowers on my windowsill and not his glowing eyes. *Damn it.* I hadn't expected him to actually stay home. I'd expected him here.

I tugged on some shorts and a T-shirt, walking back downstairs and right out the door. "Love you," I said to my parents before leaving. "Sorry about lying," I said to *myself* and shut the door behind me.

Like Roman had promised, no guards were perched at my front door. And I felt ... weird. I didn't want him to just let me do whatever. I wanted him to push me back, to scold me. It was exciting to see him standing above me, tugging off his belt, pushing his cock against my lips.

I shredded my clothes, shifted into my wolf, and ran through the woods.

Everything was silent. No wolves. No guards. No Roman.

After blowing out a deep breath and saying, "Fuck it," I ran to the pack house to find him.

Though the pack house was unusually quiet, a single light flickered off on the second floor, and I stood outside his house, my tail wagging back and forth like a dog's. He was here.

Roman appeared downstairs in the kitchen, a black sweater hugging his muscles, his hair tousled to the side. He opened the fridge, took out a bowl of grapes, and walked back up the stairs. The light turned on again.

I growled lowly, glaring up at his window. *Damn him.* What was wrong? Why wasn't he outside, trying to find me? I slammed my paw into the dirt like the immature little brat I was and furrowed my brows together.

All I wanted was a damn good night, running away from him through the woods, letting him chase me. We didn't even have to have sex; we could go to the cave and spend hours there. My wolf was just craving him.

After another minute, I sighed. Well, if he didn't want that, then I was going back home. Settling on Dad's meatloaf, lying in my bed, staring at the moonflowers. Perfect fucking night.

I turned around, growling under my breath again, and stopped suddenly when I saw Roman. Staring at me with those dark eyes, he slowly approached me and kept his head low.

My eyes widened, and I stepped back. Ready to run. My heart was racing inside my chest. He bared his teeth at me. And in a moment, he clamped them into the scruff of my neck and began dragging me to the back door of the pack house.

I whimpered and squirmed in his grip.

When he reached the door, he shifted, and I followed. With his hand harshly wrapped around the back of my neck, he pushed me into the garage—grabbing a thick piece of black rope on the way—and then shoved me toward the stairs.

"Let me go," I said, struggling in his grip, my whole body naked and exposed.

"No."

After pushing me into his bedroom and onto his bed, he snatched my wrists, bound them together tightly, and tied the other end of the rope to his headboard.

I pulled against it, my breasts bouncing. "Let me out."

"This is what you wanted. I'm finally giving you what you want. Be fucking happy."

"This isn't what I want."

His lips curled angrily at me, a golden fire raging in his eyes. "Well, what would please my dear Isabella? Do you want me to get Derek for you? Maybe you want him to fuck you from behind? Would you like that?"

Fuck.

Vanessa the Bitch was at it again.

CHAPTER 24

ISABELLA

*M*y heart thrashed against my rib cage. Oddly, this was exactly what I had wanted. Him to drag me up into his room. Him to slam the door and lock it. Him to take me any way that he wanted me. But I never expected this rage.

Ravenous eyes, razor-sharp canines and claws that could tear me piece by piece, he stood on the other side of the room and stared at me. I had seen angry Roman, but I had never seen furious Roman.

I scurried to the headboard, my tied hands now at my side. "We didn't do anything," I said, struggling with the rope.

His jaw twitched, golden eyes fixed on mine, hands balled into tight fists. He parted his lips, showing me his viciously long canines that I wanted to just sink right into me. "Don't give me that," he growled. "Don't lie to me."

After debating on my options, I decided to be a good girl for once and to tell him the *truth*. A part of me screamed at myself to just obey him, just do what he wanted, but that part of me obviously couldn't see how fucking sexy my alpha looked right now. Dominance dripping off of his every word, his every fucking move.

"Fine."

His nostrils flared. "Fine?"

"I would very much like you to call Derek over. Unlike *you*, he actually fucks me when he tells me he will. He takes me from behind and thrusts his cock deep inside of me until I'm thoroughly fuck—"

By my ankle, he yanked me as close to the edge of the bed as I would go. Then, he flipped me over and pulled my ass into the air. The rope dug into my wrists, becoming tighter and tighter, and I whimpered.

"I'm not going to fuck you, Isabella." He grabbed my chin and forced me to look at his darkening eyes. "Not until you learn." After placing one knee on the bed between my legs, he pressed his hardness against my bare pussy, grabbed a fistful of my hair, and drew me closer to him. "But I guarantee you that when I'm done with you, you *will* have learned a lesson."

My lips curled into a smirk. "But I have work tomorrow."

"Oh, Isabella." He gently caressed the side of my cheek, his lips moving against my ear. "It won't take that long."

"You sure about th—"

He plunged a finger into me, his thumb rubbing small circles against my clit. I tried to suppress a moan as it moved around inside of me. His minty scent drifted into my nostrils, and my wolf purred.

Oh Moon Goddess, this was an amazing way to teach me a lesson.

He groped my breast in one of his large, callous hands and massaged it. Then, he pinched my nipple between his fingers and roughly tugged on it, making me scream out in pleasure. After shoving another finger inside of me, he continued to thrust them in and out while pulling on my nipple, moving in a rhythmic fashion.

I clenched around his fingers, the tension growing inside of me. He growled lowly in my ear, fingers stilling. My mind buzzed with thoughts of his canines inside of my neck, of the pure pleasure that would rush through me like adrenaline. When I thought the pressure in my core had subsided, he curled his two fingers and hit my G-spot. My legs shook, and I collapsed and moaned into the mattress, desperately pushing my hips back and forth on his fingers.

Once I rode out my orgasm, he grabbed my hair, forced me back onto my knees, and rubbed his fingers on my bottom lip, making me taste myself.

"Count for me," he said.

I sucked his fingers into my mouth, my whole body still tingling.

He tugged harder on my hair, holding me close, and seethed in my ear. "Count, Isabella, or I'll make you."

I shook my head. He wrapped his hand around my throat, holding me so still that I couldn't squirm away, and squeezed my nipple hard. I bit my lip and furrowed my brows together.

No. No, I would not count for him. I would not count for him.

Heat pooled between my legs.

He pinched the bud harder and harder and harder, the pain almost unbearable. My toes curled, and I whimpered.

"One," I yelled. "One ..."

Almost immediately, he released my nipple and gently groped my breast, rewarding me. "Good girl." He smirked against my neck, drawing his nose up my jaw. "Someone's learning."

I growled lowly to tell him not to push it, but he just plunged his fingers back inside of me.

"Who do you belong to?" he asked.

"Nobody."

He tugged on my sore nipple again. "Who do you belong to?"

I clenched my jaw, trying to displace the pain. "Nobody."

His growl ripped through the room, and I clenched.

He pushed my face against the mattress, making it hard for me to breathe. "Whose are you, Isabella?" He tugged on my nipple harder until it was bright red and stinging.

My legs trembled as I screamed into the bed, "Yours, Roman." Pleasure pumped out of my pussy. "I'm yours."

He groaned quietly behind me, as if the words brought him delight. Then, he massaged my breast like he wasn't just torturing it.

"What do you say?" he asked.

I breathed heavily against the bed. "Roman, please."

I could barely even think straight. He grazed his fingers against my nipple again, and I flinched, my body shaking with immense pleasure for the second time. My breasts were so sore already.

"Two," I said breathlessly.

"Good," he said, stepping off of the bed. "Now, don't move."

With my ass in the air, my chest pressed against the black bedsheets, and my pussy dripping wet, I pushed my legs together and took a deep breath. I wanted to move, but for the first time, I didn't want to be punished. Roman would hurt me so fucking good, but I didn't think I could handle it.

He grabbed my ass in his hands, shaking it gently. "You're so sexy, Isabella." He placed a light kiss on the back of my hip. "So fucking sexy," he said.

I closed my eyes, trying to calm my racing heart. I had never felt so good and had definitely never been so obedient. A part of me liked the way he ordered me around, that pure strength and dominance oozing from him.

He slapped my ass, making it bounce, and swore under his breath. I gazed back at him, watching him stare at me with those golden eyes and a smirk that told me that my ass was *his*.

All I wanted was for him to thrust his cock into my pussy, to fill me up with his cum, to make me tremble and scream out his name and submit to him.

"Derek would've fucked me by now," I said.

He growled, trying to stay in control of his wolf. My pussy tightened as I just watched his wolf get so jealous at the mere mention of Derek's name.

"Well, Derek obviously doesn't know how to please you."

I scoffed and leaned onto my forearms, "You think this pleases me?"

Barely able to wrap his whole hand around his cock, he stroked it slowly for me and smirked. I gulped, my nipples hardening against the bedsheets.

"I *know* it pleases you, Isabella," he said. "The longer I make you wait, the better it will be." He rubbed it against my pussy, making it glisten with my juices.

"Fuck, Roman." I clenched. "Please … please give it to me." I arched my back. My body was aching for it. My mind was aching for it. I was aching for it. "I need it."

He chuckled lowly. "I don't think you need it that bad."

I pushed my hips against the head of his cock, hoping that he would lose control and just plunge himself into me.

"You won't make me lose control, Isabella." He teased my entrance with his cock, pressing it harder against me. "You're just making yourself hornier, giving me permission to play with this little pussy all night."

"Please, Roman." I breathed heavily. A wave of pleasure coursing through me. "It's yours, Roman. It's all yours."

"What's mine?"

"I'm yours." I pushed my hips back further. "Please."

He laughed again. "You're sexy when you beg for my cock." He stepped back off of the bed again and walked around it until he stood by the headboard. "Come here, Isabella."

I crawled to him, watching him stare at my hips swaying from side to side, feeling my nipples brush against the mattress, smelling the sweet scent of mint waiting for me by the head-board. When I reached him, he flipped me onto my back, making me hang my head off the edge of the bed. The rope dug into my wrists.

He lightly wrapped his hands around my neck and positioned his cock on my lips. "Show me how bad my dear Isabella wants my big dick."

I drew my legs closer together, my core pulsing. "Please, Roman." I wanted to push a hand between my legs and touch myself. "Please, I need it so fucking bad."

He pushed his cock into my mouth and all the way down my throat until I couldn't breathe. Then, with his fingers, he traced the outline of his cock in my throat.

Without warning, he thrust quickly and roughly into me. My hands balled into fists, and spit dripped down my cheeks. I gagged on his big cock and struggled against the rope.

"I love when that pretty little throat of yours talks to me," he said. He reached between my legs and rubbed my clit in small, rough circles, making my legs tremble.

Harder. I wanted it harder.

Each time I neared an orgasm, he pulled his fingers away from me. He rested his forearms on the sides of my hips, spread my legs, and pressed his tongue against my clit. I gagged again on his cock, desperate to breathe.

"Don't come unless I tell you to," he said.

I nodded my head, and he continued to eat my pussy, his facial hair tickling my inner thighs. I clenched, knowing that an orgasm was close.

He inserted a finger into me, making a come-hither motion and hitting my G-spot. I pressed my lips around his cock, sucking him harder.

Fuck, it felt so good.

When he flicked my clit with his tongue, my legs instinctively jerked off the bed. He slapped my pussy harshly.

"Stop it," he growled against me.

I whimpered out, not being able to hold it together much longer.

After thrusting his cock a few more times down my throat, he groaned and stilled inside of me, his cum dripping down the back of my throat. "Fuck, you suck my cock so fucking good."

He pulled himself out of me, and I gasped for air. Spit dripped down my cheeks, into my hair, onto the floor, absolutely ruining me. He placed a finger on my chin, lifting it until my lips were pressed together. And in a daze, I swallowed his cum.

"Good girl," he said, brushing his thumb over my bottom lip.

My pussy clenched.

"Now, do you want to come?"

I nodded my head.

"Use your words."

"Yes, Roman," I moaned. "Please."

He softly rubbed my clit. "Come for me, Isabella."

My legs shook around him, my breasts bouncing slightly as I released myself. I screamed out, unable to form any coherent words, and then relaxed into the bed.

My body tingled, and I felt like I was walking on clouds again. When I finished, I took a shaky breath. "Th-three."

He pulled me back up the bed, so my head rested on the pillow next to him. Then, he brushed his finger against my swollen clit *again*. I struggled against the ropes, trying to pull my legs together.

"Roman, I-I can't." I shook my head. "I can't."

Every part of me was too sensitive.

"You can't?" He pushed his finger inside of me and chuckled against my ear. "But your pussy is already tightening around me again."

I squeezed my eyes closed. This was going to be a long night.

CHAPTER 25

ISABELLA

I had fallen asleep somewhere between orgasm twenty-four and twenty-five. My eyes fluttered open, and I pulled the blankets further up my naked body. All I remember was the constant shift between pleasure and pain.

My clit was swollen. My nipples were stinging. My pussy was raw. And my throat was beyond sore from screaming his name all night long.

After rolling onto my side and curling into a ball, I rubbed the rope burn on my wrists, hoping that the pain would vanish. His minty scent lingered on his pillow, and I inhaled deeply and sighed, my mind numb. It was so damn comforting, but I couldn't understand how it could comfort me after that torture last night.

I took a deep breath and frowned. In a few short days, I would be leaving his pack for good. I wouldn't be able to wake up with his scent lingering in my room or my scent lingering in his. I wouldn't be able to get on his nerves every day. I hadn't met anyone in the Lycans who smelled like him, and I didn't know if I ever would.

Maybe I would change my attitude when I became a Lycan. No more brat Isabella, especially to Ryker. He was someone who admired my strength, not pushed me away because of it. I didn't have to fight him to respect me.

The clock on the wall read twelve thirty-five. My eyes widened. Shit, I was late. Roman would punish me again for it. And my whole body was too sore from last night to survive another punishment.

I shot up from the bed and noticed Roman sitting on a chair across the room, lips curled into a small smile, gaze lingering on me.

"Relax," he said, standing and placing two journals on the dresser.

"I'm late for work," I said.

"Well, it's good that you're not going in today."

I leaned against the headboard, pulling the blankets up my chest. "You're giving me the day off?"

"Seeing as you slept through half the day already … yes."

"That's not my fault."

"Actually, Isabella, it is." He walked over to me and stopped just where the sunlight flooded in through the window and hit his eyes, making them a golden sea. "But I'll let it slide for today."

I crossed my arms over my chest and frowned at him. His eyes were soft, unlike the hard ones he had given me last night. I gazed at the chair, the glass of water, and the journals on his dresser.

"Have you been watching me?" I asked.

For the briefest moment, he peered at his journal and nervously licked his bottom lip. His muscles flexed against his baby-blue V-neck. "Do you want breakfast?"

After arching a brow, I grabbed his shirt from the side of the bed and tugged it over my head. "Why're you being nice to me?"

"I can't be nice to you?"

"You're never nice to me." And I was never nice to him.

We got on each other's nerves, made each other furious, even hated each other at times. That was how we worked, and this sudden niceness was making me uncomfortable.

"Do you like eggs?"

I wrinkled my nose. "Eggs are boring."

"Moon Goddess, you sound like my sister." He groaned and rubbed a hand over his face. "What would you like then?"

"Anything," I said, waving him off and glancing around his bedroom.

Notebooks were stacked on the dresser, clothes were folded neatly inside his laundry basket, and pictures of him and his family hung on the wall. I frowned at Luna Raya and Alpha Guss and twelve-year-old Roman and an even younger Jane. They all looked so happy.

He looked so happy.

After gazing at the picture with me, Roman held out his hand. "Come with me."

"No," I said and crawled off of the bed. "There are people downstairs."

I could smell the dozens of scents that had been here and had gone this morning. So many people, I didn't know who was here now. It could be Jane and Vanessa, waiting to just ruin my whole life. If Vanessa found out and I ended up being the talk of the pack, I'd be that girl who cheated on her mate, Derek, with the alpha. A typical cliché.

"So?" He grabbed the door handle.

My eyes widened. "So?! I don't want people to think I'm another one of your whores."

He stopped, spun toward me, and growled. "One of my whores?" he asked. His words sounded so sour. "I don't sleep around."

I turned my head toward the window. "All wolves who aren't mated do it."

He howled louder this time, canines emerging from under his lips, and stepped toward me. Jaw clenched, almost visibly shaking, he asked, "Is that what you're planning to do when you turn eighteen?"

No, I planned on doing something that would make me feel a lot shittier at first but would hopefully play out well in the end. But he didn't need to know that.

"Maybe ..." I said, my wolf whimpering inside of me.

He roughly grabbed my chin in his hand. "Maybe? What the fuck does that mean?"

I shoved my hands into his taut chest. "It means that maybe I'll get tired of this little game that we're playing and want someone to actually fuck me right." *And to actually love me.* I looked toward the window, soaking in the rays. "And besides, does it even matter?"

"Yes, it matters," he said through clenched teeth. He moved back into my line of vision, golden eyes shimmering.

"Stop getting butt hurt over it." I shook my head. "Do you expect this little thing between us to go on forever?"

"Yes."

"And what happens when you find your mate? Or when I find mine?"

He parted his lips and then immediately closed them. "Isabella." His voice was suddenly softer.

He swayed slightly, and our fingers grazed against each other's. I swallowed hard, tingles shooting up my arm, and pulled my hand away.

We'd been physically intimate before, but that was ...

"I don't expect this thing to go on forever," he said, stepping away from me.

We gazed at each other for a few moments; his eyes shifted slowly between gold and green. My wolf stirred inside of me, wanting to run, wanting to do something. I just couldn't understand what that something was.

My breathing hitched when Roman closed his eyes, his minty scent becoming incredibly intoxicating. He moved away again, and I felt hurt.

"I expect you to be with your mate when you find him. Stay with him, mark him, lie with him, *love* him." Then, he turned and walked right out of the room.

His words had sounded so ... sad. And for some stupid reason, a part of me felt sad for us. This thing was purely physical, but I didn't want to leave. Every single day, he made it harder and harder for me to choose the Lycans.

Roman was aggravating, but I liked aggravating. Roman was infuriating, but I sort of liked infuriating now. Roman was everything I wanted in a man, but he wasn't mine.

Sure, I might've been able to get away with things with him, but he was the alpha, four whole years older than I was and of age to find his mate. He would've told me if I was ... his. Alphas were always so possessive; they would take their mate as soon as they could. The tingles were just because *I* liked him. Not my wolf.

Playing with me, teasing me, dominating me ... it was just his way to pass the time until he found his mate. Just like all alphas did. He would never be mine. He was another girl's alpha. He was another girl's mate.

My wolf growled lowly inside of me, and I shushed her. Now wasn't the time to be growling over Roman. I sat on his bed, digging my claws into the blankets and inhaling his scent.

This was so stupid. I didn't even like him. I never had.

Lie.

He was a good alpha, a good leader, a good guy, and damn good in bed. But that was it. That was all that he could be. He couldn't be my mate. He couldn't. Mates didn't hurt each other. Mates supported each other.

No matter how hard I tried to imagine a life without Roman, I couldn't. Every time I closed my eyes, I saw him.

In my past. In my present. In my future.

Running through the forest with each other. Playfully fighting each other in the snow. Laughing deep into the night under *our* blankets in *our* bed.

I shook away my fantasies and walked aimlessly through the room, fingers brushing against the bedsheets. No, I couldn't think of him that way. I didn't even know who he was. Since his parents had died, he had closed himself off to almost everyone ... but that didn't mean that I couldn't figure out who he really was.

My fingers brushed against the knob to his closet, and it *accidentally* opened. I peeked my head into it. Khakis that made his ass look great. Gray sweatpants that definitely made his ass look even better. T-shirts. V-necks. *Boring. Boring. Boring.*

After searching through the pants he had worn last night for some secret love note and finding nothing and after looking under his bed and finding just one small dust bunny, I sat up and sighed through my nose.

Jeez, Roman wasn't interesting at all.

Two leather notebooks sat on his dresser—a maroon one on the bottom and a navy one on top. Though I was hoping to find his deepest, darkest secrets in them, I bet it was just some boring-ass notes about the pack, scribbled in his messy handwriting.

I opened the top journal. Every page was dated and had some information about the day written on it. The journal dated back to five years ago. Notes about the pack were neatly written on the pages. Some were extremely detailed and serious; others were just mere thoughts. I turned to the last pages, the most recent entries, wanting to find something about me.

5/5/2019

Vanessa is so fucking annoying.

. . .

I laughed.

5/6/2019
Ryker visits the pack. He is interested in recruiting Isabella.

The words were written much darker than all the other pages. At one point, it looked like he'd broken through the page with his pen.

5/10/2019
Isabella's placement is for the best. I don't get to see her often since she is ignoring me now, but she is safe.

He'd wanted to keep me safe, so he'd decided to throw me into the hospital. Got it.

5/12/2019
A rogue found dead on our property. Isabella's scent was in the woods the same night. Something is going on with her.

The last note was dated this morning.

5/14/2019
Two rogues found dead. Isabella was lying next to me in bed while it happened.

. . .

The scent of pancakes drifted into the room, and I closed the notebook and continued my search before Roman came back. The other notebook was probably even more boring. I could just imagine all his little notes about every pack member.

I peeked inside one drawer in his dresser and frowned. Empty. The next one was empty too. In fact, they were all empty. It looked like he had either cleaned it out recently and thrown everything away or he was waiting for someone to move in all of their clothes.

My wolf growled lowly inside of me at that thought.

After slamming the drawers harder than I'd intended, I pressed my lips together. Was he seeing someone else while he was seeing me? Was I a side piece? Was it Vanessa? It probably was. That was who—

A cute light-blue pendant necklace lay on the other side of the dresser next to his watch. I furrowed my brows. What was this? A piece of women's jewelry on his dresser? I picked it up, knowing that I shouldn't, but it was so beautiful, and I was so full of spite.

It was shaped like a moon and looked identical to a mate's necklace.

I clenched my jaw harder.

The door opened, and Roman walked into the room. I sucked in a breath and placed the necklace onto the dresser. He put a plate of pancakes next to it, tensing and glancing at his journals.

"Were you looking through my stuff?"

"No," I said, glancing at the necklace. "Whose is this?"

He stepped closer to me, his minty scent comforting me again. "You seem jealous, Isabella."

"I'm not," I said quicker than I should've. "I just want to know where they got it. The *detail* is beautiful."

His lips softened into a boyish grin. "You like it?"

"It's cute." *Really cute.* "So, whose is it?"

"It was Mom's when she was alive. She didn't want to be buried with it. She wanted me to pass it on to my ... mate." The last word was so faint that it was almost inaudible.

Oh ... it was just Luna Raya's.

He moved ever closer, gaze shifting down my body. I inhaled sharply. The tension between us was back, and it was so damn stronger than it had been. After placing his hands on my hips, he drew me closer.

"You look awfully sexy in my shirt," he mumbled against my ear.

He toyed with the end of the shirt, but I pushed his hand away.

"No, I can't do this again," I said.

He chuckled, pulled me closer, and rested his forehead against mine.

I knew that it was a bad idea to play with him, but I couldn't help myself. I rested my arms on his shoulders and tugged on the ends of his hair. The pull between us came so naturally. Whether it was pure fury, pure jealousy, pure adoration, it didn't matter. It felt so natural that I thought we could be mates.

Could.

Then, suddenly, someone opened the door. I quickly pulled away from him, but he pulled me back, his fingers curling into my hips like they belonged there.

Jane stood in the doorway with wide eyes. She looked between us and then solely at me, her gaze falling on my—Roman's—shirt. "Isabella. What are you doing here?"

"I, um ..."

"That's none of your business, Jane," Roman said.

She smirked at him and shook her head. "Another one, Roman? That makes, what, three in the last week?"

CHAPTER 26

ISABELLA

*T*hree girls … three girls in the past fucking week, and I was one of them.

Why had I stupidly thought this was exclusive between us? Hell, I'd had a chance to flirt with Ryker—kind of, not really. But if I had known that Roman was with other girls, I could've tried not to feel this stupid fucking way for him.

"Three women?" I stepped back from him, feeling disgusted. "Jesus Christ, Roman. I probably have some sort of disease now."

Roman growled. "Jane," he scolded.

Jane laughed, wrapped an arm around my shoulders, and leaned the side of her head against mine. "Ooh, I like you already. Why didn't we hang out more in high school?"

I clenched my jaw tighter, staring at Roman. I couldn't believe it. Three women. Three. I bet it was Bitch One and Bitch Two, and here I was, Bitch Three.

My wolf whimpered inside of me. *Three? Three? Three?*

Jane pulled away from me, still laughing, but I didn't see anything funny.

"I'm just kidding," she said, nudging my shoulder with hers. "It was about damn time that he brought you to the pack house. I'm so tired of listening to him grumble around the house every night. He needed someone to take care of his ass. I just didn't think it'd be you."

I took a deep breath, gazing at her and then back at him. What was her problem? She was exactly like Vanessa, trying to make my life hell.

She grabbed my hand, intertwining our fingers. "So, you're the reason his nightly runs take forever, huh?"

Roman clenched his jaw. "Jane," he said through his teeth. "Leave."

She giggled again, like this was so damn funny, and honestly, I would've probably been laughing, too, if it wasn't me in this situation. But ... she was frustrating.

In a single moment, her smile turned into a frown. "Wait, I thought you were mates with Derek though."

"I am," I answered at the same time he said, "She's not."

I narrowed my eyes at Roman, who had his jaw clenched. His green eyes had golden streaks in them.

Jane raised a brow. "Ooh, tense."

Roman growled at her.

She held up her arms in surrender. "Fine, I'll leave, jeez. You could've asked nicely."

She walked out of the room and closed the door behind her. I crossed my arms and stared at Roman, needing a reason to get out of here. This tension between us was driving me crazy. If I didn't leave soon, I'd end up looking like a damn fool and telling him I didn't want him to sleep with other girls because *I* wanted to be his one and only.

"So," I said, "two other girls, huh?"

No, I didn't believe Jane. But Roman *was* acting weird. Having cleaned out his entire dresser. Having a woman's necklace in his room. It didn't add up.

"I haven't been with anyone else."

His minty scent smelled so damn good. I needed to leave. Now.

"Well, I don't believe you." I walked to the door, being the dramatic bitch that I was, and humphed at him. "I'll be going."

He rolled his eyes and then smirked down at my shirt. "You're going to walk home in my shirt? What will everyone think?"

I narrowed my eyes. "I'll just ask Jane for clothes. Jane!"

As if she was waiting outside the door, begging for drama, she popped her head into the room. "I'd love to get you some clothes." She grabbed my hand. "Come with me."

"Don't tell her lies about me," Roman said.

"No promises," she called down the hall.

She pulled me down the stairs to her room on the opposite side of the house. After searching through some clothes, she handed me a pair of cutoff jeans and a pink crop top. As I tugged on her clothes, she sat on the bed, kicking her legs back and forth.

"So, you and Roman ..."

"What about us?" I adjusted the crop top in the mirror and frowned.

"Are you dating?"

I laughed. "No." *Nowhere close to dating.*

"Why not?"

"Because I don't like him like that."

Lie.

She arched a brow. "Yes, you do. You wouldn't have gotten angry about him being with other girls if you didn't like him like that."

I took off the pink top, deciding that it was too much, and put on Roman's shirt, tucking the shirt into the waistband of my jeans. "The only reason that I reacted the way I did was because I didn't want to get any diseases from Va—" I stopped, knowing that her and Vanessa were friends, and pressed my lips together.

She crossed her arms over her chest and stood. "You're lying. You like my brother."

This was the second time in the past two days someone had accused me of liking Roman. And while a small piece of me did, I didn't want Roman to think I was head over heels about him. It was purely physical between us, and I didn't want to ruin that. Whatever kind of thing we had would have to suffice because I'd lost him after his parents died and I didn't want to lose him again.

"I'm not lying," I said. "He's just ... *hot*."

CHAPTER 27

ROMAN

*W*hile Isabella changed into clothes, I sat in my bedroom. If I didn't control my wolf, he would take her for all that she was when she got back. And she would be back. She had her breakfast here, and she'd had a night that she would never forget.

Hell, I would never forget it. Having her sleep in my arms for the first night. Waking up with her scent all over me. Giving her a real taste of me and my wolf. Getting her closer to submitting.

Her sweet scent still lingered in the room, and I tried my hardest to come up with something to say to keep her here. I needed to keep her here. It was all I wanted. Another minute. Another hour. Another night.

I listened to her and Jane's faint voices and rubbed my palms on my sweatpants. Moon Goddess, I was so nervous, and I knew why. From her almost looking in my journals to her looking at Mom's mate necklace ... to her almost finding out my secret.

That I was in love with her.

Her and only her.

My wolf wanted her to sleep with us tonight. He had been waiting for her for years. And just one taste wasn't enough. He wanted *more. More. More. More. More.*

The door opened, and I stood up, heart racing. "Isabell—"

Jane walked into the room with a smirk on her face. She hopped on my bed, kicked her feet back and forth, and twirled a finger around her hair. "Isabella? Oh, she's long gone."

I growled under my breath. "What the fuck is your problem? You lied right to her face about me and scared her off."

Her smirk widened on that damn irritating face of hers. "I don't have a problem," she said. "You do." She stood up and walked around me. "You like Isabella."

I clenched my jaw. "Jane," I said, my voice hard. Warning her not to push it.

"You're obsessed with her." She opened my maroon journal, gazing at the pictures of Isabella that I had drawn. "You think she saw these when you went down to make breakfast for her? You think that's why she hurried out of the house, why she left you here? Or maybe it was because she was going to meet her mate, Derek."

My wolf took control, a snarl rumbling from deep within my throat. "Derek isn't her fucking mate, Jane."

She grinned at me. "Someone's a little possessive, isn't he?"

I snatched the journal away from her and tossed it onto the bed. "I'm not possessive."

She snorted. "Not possessive? Moon Goddess, Roman. Everyone can see it. You're acting just like Dad did."

"I am not."

"Okay," she said, walking to my door. "Believe what you want to believe. But just to let you know, Isabella likes you too." She gave me Mom's smile. "And not just in this way," she said, looking at the messy bed. "Like, really likes you."

CHAPTER 28

ISABELLA

*A*fter changing into Jane's clothes, I escaped through the back door, avoiding Roman and his intoxicating mint scent, and walked to The Night Raider's Café for breakfast. A part of me had wanted to stay to have pancakes with Roman, sitting on his bed, sharing a plate, smiling at each other like the damn stupid wolves we were.

It terrified me because I had never felt so close to someone who blatantly disrespected me. It terrified me because I was losing control around him. It terrified me because I was falling for a man who would be difficult to let go and leave.

I opened the door, and the scent of baked bread hit me. I stood behind a woman in line and bounced up and down on my toes. Too many people knew about Roman and me. Derek. Rachel. Mr. Beck. Jane. If word continued to spread, I wouldn't be remembered as the strong Lycan warrior from the Silverclaw Pack. I'd be *that* girl who slept with her alpha.

The scent of forest mixed with hazelnut drifted into my nose.

"Someone's a little jumpy today." Ryker stood behind me, arms crossed against his chest, making his biceps bulge. Dark eyes, tousled brown hair, and that sexy sleeve of moonflower tattoos.

I nearly choked on my own breath.

I nudged his arm and smiled. "A little."

He stuffed his hands in his pockets and smiled down at me with his pearly whites. "Few more days until you can officially become one of us. How're you feeling about everything?"

The woman before me stepped out of line, and the cashier called for me to order.

"I'm good," I said after stepping forward and asking for a coffee and a chocolate chip muffin.

From behind her thick frames, the cashier gazed between us. "Are you two paying together?"

"No."

"Yes," Ryker said, handing the woman a debit card.

I wanted to protest, but Ryker gave me a *don't you dare* look, and I pressed my lips together, taking it as a kind gesture from my soon-to-be leader.

We grabbed our coffees and sat at a table in the corner of the café, near the windows. Young pups were chasing each other around the trees outside. Small groups of people were walking up and down the path toward the café. And I hoped that nobody from my pack showed up. That would be hard to explain to Roman.

"Any hesitations?" Ryker asked, sipping his coffee.

I shook my head.

"Well, if you ever have any questions, I'm always available for a coffee date with you." He leaned back in his seat, eyes flickering black. "So, how's Roman doing?"

"He's good," I said quicker than I should've.

"Just good?" He arched a sharp brow. "Rumor has it that you

two are a *thing*."

"Where'd you hear that?"

"I have people." He took another sip, analyzing me. "Rumor also has it that you have a *thing* with your friend Derek."

I took a deep breath. *Great.* If Ryker knew, other people had probably heard about us. Wolves in my pack. Warriors in the Lycans. I didn't want that—at least, not while I was transitioning into a Lycan.

Some people gazed over at us, hushing their voices. These wolves just loved their gossip, didn't they?

I leaned across the table. "In a few hours, rumor will probably also have it that I'm dating you too." I pushed my hand across my face, noticing a couple people from my pack walk into the café, and groaned. "Wow, I sound like such a ho."

He chuckled and placed his cup down, stirring it a bit. "Don't worry about it. Lycans are notoriously known to have more than a few lovers."

"Well, that makes me feel so much better about myself," I said sarcastically.

"You're going to be something else," he said, a smile tugging on his lips. His eyes suddenly became hazy and distant, as if he was talking through his mind link. Then, he clenched his jaw and stood. "I need to go. Rogues are at it again."

The door jingled behind him, and we both looked over to see Derek and Rachel walking in together. Rachel surveyed the shop, saw me, and sighed in relief. I swallowed hard, smoothing out my T-shirt.

"I will see you soon, Isabella." Ryker tossed his cup into the trash. "And remember, if you have any questions before your birthday, come and find me. On the night before, I will be in the forest where I was last time to escort you to the Lycans."

I cracked a smile. "You know you don't need to do that. I can find my way there."

"I don't have to, but I will," he said. Then, he walked away, leaving his woodsy scent all over me.

I inhaled, smiling and watching him walk right past Derek and Rachel. They gazed back at him, brows furrowed, and then walked to me.

"Was that a Lycan?"

"Yep," I said, hoping that my one-worded answer would cut it.

I wasn't sure if I wanted to tell Derek about me becoming a Lycan. It was a shitty friend move, keeping this from him, but he would tell Roman. Roman already knew that something was up with me, and I didn't need to give him any more clues, especially since everyone had seen Ryker and me together.

Word would get around—whether I wanted it to or not—and Roman would ask Derek about it and fuck this all up for me.

"What did he want?" Derek asked, sitting in his seat. He stared at me with those big, boyish eyes, like he had done so many times since we were kids while Mr. Beck screamed at us.

"Nothing." I shrugged my shoulders, a heap of guilt settling into me, becoming a part of me. "He was just asking about Roman."

Derek eyed me, knowing that was a lie. I gnawed on the inside of my cheek.

"Where were you today?" Rachel said before Derek could pry. "Everyone was so worried about you."

My cheeks flushed. "I just … needed a day off."

"A phone call or something would've been nice," Derek said, raising a brow at me and tapping his fingers on the table.

Well, Derek boy, a phone call wasn't an option, as I was tied to Roman's headboard and getting face-fucked by him until the early hours of the morning.

Rachel smirked. "Mr. Beck said you were with Roman, but I wasn't sure if I should believe him or not." She leaned across the table and lowered her voice. "So, were you?"

I gazed between her and Derek and smirked. "Maybe."

She grabbed my hands and squeezed lightly. "You were! Oh gosh!" She fanned herself. "Sorry, I haven't been this excited for anything in a while. My life is so boring. I need some good, juicy drama."

"Oh, don't worry about it." I had all the good, juicy drama she could ever need.

Derek leaned across the table. "Did you guys finally fuck?" he asked, forgetting about my little white lie I had just told him.

"No. He told me I needed to *learn a lesson*." I pressed my lips together and rolled my eyes. "He makes me so frustrated." Frustrated that I *wanted* him.

It was so sad that I'd rather people knew that I'd fucked him than knew that I was falling for my alpha despite his harsh words and his blatant disrespect.

"Maybe he isn't"—Rachel's cheeks flushed—"well-endowed and is embarrassed."

My eyes widened. "Oh, no, he is definitely well-endowed." My fingers grazed against my throat as I remembered how big he'd felt when he was thrusting it down my throat, when all I'd wanted was more and more and more.

"Maybe he's waiting until you turn eighteen," Derek said, drawing his fingers over the calluses on his hand. "He might think it's weird that you're still underage."

I furrowed my brows. "He sure didn't think it was weird when he was shoving himself down my throat."

Rachel's cheeks flushed a darker shade of red. "Oh Moon Goddess, you've gone pretty far." She grabbed my hands again. "Wait, you're not eighteen yet? When's your birthday?"

"In a few days."

Her eyes widened. "We need to have a party! How are you celebrating?"

A party? I just planned on spending some time with Derek and my parents. I had never had a big birthday party before. I didn't even know who I'd invite.

They started talking excitedly to each other. And I smiled sadly at them. Joining another pack for my birthday would be harder than I'd thought—and not just because of Roman. I would have to make new friends and try to stay in touch with the friends I had now.

My frown deepened when I gazed at Derek. I hoped that I could find some time to hang out with him.

Derek beamed at her and then at me. "I'm throwing her a party at my place."

"Are you inviting Roman?" Rachel nudged me. "Maybe he'll finally make his move." She turned to Derek, bouncing up and down in her seat. "Wait, do you think her mate is in this pack?"

"Maybe her mate is that Lycan she was talking to."

"Mr. Beck would say differently."

I shook my head. "Mr. Beck doesn't know anything about my mate," I said.

He was always thinking the craziest things.

Later that night, I lay in my bed. Trying to convince myself that this was the right choice. Trying to convince myself that leaving Mom, Dad, Derek, Rachel, Dr. Jakkobs, and … Roman was the right choice. Leave them to achieve my dreams and goals.

Could I do it? Could I leave for at least an entire year?

Surely, I wouldn't see anyone that often once I left. Ryker had told me that Lycans were busy all the time. With training at night, sleeping during the day, and hunting the rogues in our spare time, I didn't know if or when I'd find a moment to visit them. My heart sank in my chest.

I opened my curtains and sat on the windowsill next to my moonflowers, gazing out into the night. Roman sat, in his wolf form, in the forest and was watching me. I leaned against the window, my fingers grazing against the keychain from Luna Raya.

She'd thought I could be more, and I would be more. I had to let Roman go, no matter how hard it would be, to become everything that I was meant to be.

CHAPTER 29

ISABELLA

"*T*omorrow's your big day!" Mom said, hopping onto my bed that night with a big grin on her face and pulling me into a hug.

Her mate's necklace felt warm against my skin, and I hoped that this was the right choice.

"Fingers crossed that Derek's your mate!"

I smiled and gazed at the moonflowers on the windowsill, twinkling brighter than they had ever twinkled.

"I remember when you were just a little pup," she said. "Now, look at you, about to be a woman, about to find your mate, and about to settle down." She wiped a tear from her eye. "I can't wait when you meet him. When you lay your eyes on him for the first time, when you see his smile, when you smell his scent ... you'll never forget that moment. It'll be the best moment of your life, Izzy. How are you feeling about it?"

My wolf suddenly felt terrible. I wrapped my arms around

myself, took a deep breath, and hoped that I wouldn't cry. How could I leave this? Leave this support? Leave this love?

"I'm okay, Mom," I said.

But I didn't know if I really was.

She crawled off of my bed, placed a kiss on my forehead, and left the room.

About twenty minutes later, Dad's snores drifted through my closed door. I tiptoed out of my room and gazed into theirs. They were smiling as they slept, Mom cuddled into Dad's chest. I couldn't wait to be that way with my mate soon. Smiling. Happy. *Loved*.

A tear slipped down my cheek. Though that guilt continued to build and build until I was nearly drowning in it, becoming a Lycan was my goal. They had always supported my goals before. If I left, I was sure they would support that decision too.

I walked out of the house and through the woods, hoping that I wouldn't attract the attention of any guards. The forest was quieter than the other night when I left pack property. No midnight howling. No wolves running. No Roman.

The pack house came into my view, and I walked toward it like I was drawn to it. I lingered outside his bedroom window. Every moment that I had been here, every moment that I had been with him, seen him, crushed on him in high school flashed through my mind.

But one moment stayed the longest.

It was Roman's eighteenth birthday. Fifteen-year-old me had lingered in these woods, in this exact spot, watching him lead practice, like he had done for four years. Sweat dripped down his forehead, his brown hair tousled on his head, his muscles swollen under the early morning sun.

In the middle of a practice match against Cayden's dad—our beta at the time—he gazed at me and stopped. His green eyes shimmered with golden streaks, and I swore that I could hear his heart racing. He walked right away from his match and toward me, scolding me for being there when I should've been in school.

Though tense, when he grabbed my arm and shoved me through the woods to the school, he relaxed. He didn't let me go, even when he brought me to the principal's office. He had remained close to me, and I wished that we could still be that close.

This decision would tear us apart. But he had torn us apart when he told me I wasn't good enough to be a warrior.

Before I had second thoughts, I ran off the property and found Ryker waiting for me about a hundred yards to the west.

My life was about to change for the better. My life was about to change for the better. My life was about to change for the better.

During the hour run, I tried to convince myself.

Every one of the Lycans waited for me by the bonfire.

"There are two traditions we have for every new member," Ryker said, standing in front of the group and in front of me.

The fire glowed off of his eyes, and I smiled.

"They hunt to prove their abilities, and then they get the Lycan symbol tattooed on their body as a commitment to us."

I bounced up and down on my toes. I'd never thought I would be here. I'd never thought this opportunity would come to me so easily. Not after Roman.

"Are you ready?" Ryker asked me, his woodsy scent overwhelmingly strong.

After I nodded my head, Ryker told me to run to the east, where the rogues had been torturing some alphas by taking the pups in their packs. I had a goal. Kill one of them.

I placed my nose to the ground, picking up and tracking the scent of a rogue to a nearby pack. The Lycans followed me, their paws hitting the ground like a thunderous roar, purposefully making it more difficult for me.

At the edge of the property, a rogue stood and watched a couple guards who were oblivious to his scent. Then, he leaped into the air, right under the moonlight, about to kill one. I sprinted forward and sank my teeth right into the rogue's neck before he could kill anyone.

We tumbled to the ground, somersaulting over and over until I landed on top of him. The rogue struggled under me, but I sank my teeth deeper into his neck and ripped out his throat, letting the blood rain down on his hollow face and earning the respect of the Lycans behind me.

After we walked back to the Lycans' property, Ryker gave me some spare clothes. I changed into them without showering, and I walked with him and the rest of the Lycans to their tattoo parlor.

My final task: to tattoo the Lycan symbol on my body. A permanent mark of my allegiance to them.

I sat down in the chair, trying to still my trembling hands. I wasn't nervous for the needle, but my wolf was whimpering, begging me to stop, forcing me to think about everyone's reactions to this act of betrayal.

Ryker sat next to me as others chatted with each other. He smiled at me, drank, and had a good time celebrating. He placed a hand on my hand, steadying it. "Are you sure about this? You can back out now. Nobody would judge you for it."

No. Not now. I couldn't back out.

"This is what I've wanted for ages, Ryker." I shook my head. "There is no going back now." I gazed around the room, taking in the hundreds of pictures of previous Lycans who had been tattooed here and the rogue canines hanging from the ceiling as trophies from previous Lycan additions.

"Once you have the tattoo, it is final. You will have to train with us for at least a year," Ryker said. Giving me every single opportunity to decline.

"This is what I want. I'll be valued here. I will get to protect everyone that I care about, and I will achieve my goals." There was no better option. Luna Raya would have been so proud of me. "Let's do this."

He paused for a moment and then nodded. "You may get the tattoo anywhere you'd like." He pulled up his sleeve, letting me see the wolf tattoo on the back of his hand and the hundreds of moonflowers crawling up the side of it. "And for each rogue you eliminate, you're allowed to tattoo a moonflower next to your wolf."

I smiled down at his arm, getting butterflies in my stomach. I brushed my finger against his skin and shivered. He had killed so many rogues and eliminated their evils from this earth.

"How many do you have?"

"Moonflowers?" he asked, watching me and smiling. "Two hundred forty."

My eyes widened. "Jeez."

He chuckled lowly, and my heart raced. "You'll be there soon, *Bella*. I know you will."

"I want mine on my back," I said, removing my shirt and my sports bra and leaning forward in the chair to cover my breasts.

The tattoo artist placed a stencil on my upper back and drew the wolf.

When he started the tattoo gun, I grabbed Ryker's hand. Not because it would hurt, but because I was still trying to convince myself. But as soon as the needle touched my skin, I sighed in relief. A wave of pride rolled through me, and I knew that this was the right choice.

The tattoo took almost an hour, and Ryker stayed by my side the whole time. He stared at me, not saying a word, and drew a finger down my forearm to soothe me. My wolf howled inside of me, not wanting him to touch us. It was after twelve a.m., officially my eighteenth birthday, and she recognized that he wasn't our mate. Nobody here was.

When the wolf tattoo was complete, the artist started on my first moonflower. I watched him tattoo me in the mirror and smiled. This was everything I had been waiting for and more. Why had Roman overlooked me so easily?

This was the best birthday I'd ever had, and I hoped it would just get better, but I knew that it probably wouldn't. I would have to tell everyone that I was leaving. Mom, Dad, Derek, Roman.

Once the artist wiped the blood off my back, Ryker smiled at me. "Welcome to the pack, Bella. Your tattoo will heal within the next few hours, thanks to your wolf's quick restorative abilities. I will let you spend your eighteenth birthday with your friends, family, and pack. But I expect you back tomorrow." He handed me my shirt. "And don't forget that you will need to tell Roman that you are leaving his pack to join the Lycans."

I nodded my head and swallowed hard, not sure how I felt at that moment.

This was real. There was no going back.

CHAPTER 30

ISABELLA

*M*usic blared through Derek's parents' windows for my birthday party. Mom and Dad stood behind me with a plate of meatloaf that smelled good for once.

Dad ruffled my hair. "You ready to meet your mate?"

I rolled my eyes. "Mom has actually convinced you that Derek's my mate?"

He gazed at her and then leaned toward me, smiling. "No, but we'll keep that between you and me."

Rachel opened the door, wearing a blue party hat. "Izzy! Happy birthday!" She pulled me into the room of sweaty bodies.

Nearly everyone in the pack was here, even Vanessa and Jane. Rachel swore that Derek hadn't invited either of them, and I was sure they had just shown up without an invite anyway. That was kind of their thing.

Derek saw me from across the room, dancing his way around everyone. He handed me a drink and placed a big, fat kiss on my cheek. "Eighteen never looked so good."

Rachel hopped up in front of me. "Oh, I almost forgot! I have a surprise for you!" She disappeared into another room. "A special someone wanted to see you today!"

Roman.

A few moments later, she wheeled Mr. Beck into the room.

Oh.

"Hey, hey, hey! Happy birthday!" he yelled. He grabbed my hand, leaning in close, and nudged me. "I want to hear those details from the other night that you promised me."

"I never promised you any details."

"So, there are details!" He burst into a fit of laughter, his dentures nearly falling out again, and smacked his knee. "I knew you wouldn't be able to stay away from him."

After giving him a tense smile, I wandered throughout the house. Throughout the night, I waited in the corner of the room with my parents and with Derek for Roman to walk through the front door. I didn't know what I would say or do when I saw him. But I needed to tell him tonight that I had joined the Lycans, so I hoped that he would show up.

I'd promised myself that I wouldn't tell anyone until the end of the night. I didn't want to ruin everyone's day. It was a shitty thing to keep this to myself until the very last moment, but a part of me couldn't admit it out loud. This day was supposed to be happy, especially for my family.

At nine p.m., Jane and Vanessa walked up to me.

"Have you mated yet?" Vanessa asked, voice tense over the music.

"We're not mates, Vanessa," I said.

Jane grabbed my hand, intertwining my fingers like she had the other day. "My brother said that he couldn't make it tonight. Something came up."

"Oh."

My heart sank. *Roman wasn't coming? He wasn't going to wish me a happy birthday?* I'd thought maybe he'd come for one or two moments. Hell, out of everyone who Derek had invited, I'd wanted Roman to come the most. I'd wanted to see him on my special day to make sure we weren't mates.

After Jane broke the news to me, I walked out onto Derek's porch and sat on a stair, gazing up at the stars. People left the party, wishing me a happy birthday on the way out. I smiled as widely as I could, saying good-bye to them for the last time.

At midnight, Derek peeked his head out of the house, asking me if I wanted him to bring me home. I tugged him into a hug, and a tear slipped from my eye, but I pushed it away before he could see it.

"No, thanks, Derek."

I needed time to think to myself.

When he pulled away and I saw the abundance of love in his eyes, I wanted to blurt out everything that had been happening. But it wouldn't come out. I tried really hard to tell him, but I couldn't admit to it.

Vanessa pulled him back into the room, and I smiled at the closed door. I walked down the porch stairs, starting for my house and just simmering in a heap of sadness when I smelled it.

Mint.

So strong.

So good.

So intoxicating.

My wolf howled and pulled me in the opposite direction. I gazed around the woods, my heart racing as I tried to find the source of the smell. My mate was here.

The woods were so dark, and the only light was coming from the full moon above it. I walked around the corner of the house, closing my eyes and breathing in my mate. A branch cracked in the forest, and I stopped.

Roman emerged from the woods, his chest bare and sweaty. And as soon as I saw him, my heart stopped.

Mate!

He smiled when he saw me, his golden eyes devouring mine. "Mine," he said, walking toward me. "Finally mine."

CHAPTER 31

ISABELLA

*M*y wolf did flips in my stomach. *Mate. Mate. Mate. Mate.*

I gazed at him, taking in every inch of his body. The way his abdomen flexed. The way his lips curled. The way his eyes glowed under the moon.

This wasn't real. He wasn't real.

This was the best moment of my entire life, better than the way Mom had described meeting Dad. This was so fucking exhilarating.

Staring at me like I was the only thing that ever mattered, he walked to me, snatched my chin in his hand, and smirked. This *was* real. His fingers ran gently down my neck, making me shiver. "Mine."

"Yours?"

"Mine."

Despite my wolf wanting me to never let him go, I pushed him away from me and grinned. "Prove it."

In one moment, he turned me around and pushed me against the nearest tree. He grabbed a fistful of my hair and brushed his canines up the side of my neck, lingering in the spot where he would mark me. "I could fuck you right here."

"Could?" I mocked, pushing my hips back and feeling his hardness against my ass. "That doesn't sound too promising."

He growled in my ear, and I immediately clenched. Forget being a brat. Forget trying to tease him. I couldn't handle this anymore. He was what I wanted, and he was my mate.

"Take what you want, Roman. Take me," I whispered.

We both knew we had waited way too long for this.

He grabbed my ass through my dress, squeezing it. "You're tempting, Isabella, so fucking tempting." He placed a kiss just below my ear. "I'm going to take you home and finally do everything I've been craving to do to you since the moment I laid eyes on you."

I turned toward him, pulling him closer. "I can't wait that long."

"If I could wait four fucking years for you, you can wait five minutes."

My smile widened. "Make it three, and I'll try not to yawn while you fuck me."

He picked me up, his hands under my ass, and walked me toward the pack house, his eyes darkening. Through the walk, my body buzzed with pure excitement. Roman's minty scent drifted into my nostrils, and I sighed in delight. I couldn't think about anything, except him.

How I wanted to love him. How I wanted him to devour me tonight. How I had been waiting for this moment forever.

When he kicked his bedroom door closed, he let me down, unzipped my dress, pulled down the straps, and pushed me back onto his bed. My hands traveled all over his body, sliding over his shoulders, down his back, up his abs. Everything about him felt like it had the other night, but suddenly, it felt so much more invigorating.

I tugged on the ends of his hair, pulling him to me, and then pressed my lips to his. Like he had wanted to for years, he kissed me back, matching my intensity. We had never kissed, not once. And these butterflies were everything that I had ever wanted.

His fingers danced down my body and slipped into my underwear, rubbing me gently and making me wet with pleasure. I wanted him to be rough with me, but I also wanted to just enjoy this moment with him.

Our first time together.

Maybe our last time together.

He thrust two fingers inside of me, moving them slowly, and groaned.

I smiled and clenched on his fingers. The feeling sent pleasure through me. "So, this is what you were waiting for."

He smirked against my lips, resting his forehead against mine. "You have no idea," he mumbled, fingers moving faster.

I unbuttoned his belt and pulled it off of him, and then I wrapped my legs around his body to pull him toward me. "Well, I don't want to wait any longer." I pushed his pants down and took his cock in my hand, stroking his hardness. It was mine. "I want you inside of me, Roman."

He pressed his lips to mine before leaving soft kisses down my body. He latched on to one of my nipples with his teeth, biting down. I winced, remembering the last time he had done that, and he sucked on it more gently. I brushed my fingers across his forehead, admiring my mate.

His lips moved down my stomach until he reached my core. He hooked two fingers under the hem of my panties, peeled them off of me, and pressed his hot mouth on me.

So slowly, so softly, so sinisterly.

I arched my back, loving every moment of us together, and pulled him back up to me, unable to hold off much longer. With my legs wrapped around his waist, I tugged him down, making him pushed his hardness against my wetness.

"Please, Roman."

He smiled and kissed me. "I love you," he said, golden eyes glowing.

Then, he thrust himself into me until his hips were against mine. My eyes widened as I tried to adjust to his size. Everything about him and about this moment was more than I could have asked for. I was more than glad he had made me wait.

Knowing he was my mate made my first time a thousand times better.

When I adjusted to his size, I tightened myself around him. He slowly pulled out, and I tightened again.

"Fuck," he swore under his breath.

He pushed himself back into me, and I moaned.

"More, Roman."

His fingers brushed against my cheek. "You're so sexy when you moan my name." He pulled himself out and then pushed himself back in, this time quicker.

I dug my nails into his back. His cock filled my tight pussy, and I moaned again. He fucked me harder and faster and rougher, leaving me begging for him to continue. I never wanted him to stop. Not when his fingers brushed against my swollen clit. Not when he latched on to my nipple with his teeth again.

My legs shook uncontrollably. I grabbed on to him, hoping he wouldn't stop and he didn't.

"Come for me, Isabella," he whispered in my ear.

When I screamed his name, he thrust into me once more and then came on my stomach. He looked down at me with so much love, and I stared back up at him with so much guilt.

He was my mate, but I had a terrible secret I needed to spill to him.

CHAPTER 32

ISABELLA

$\mathcal{H}$is fingers danced across my collarbone so softly. They were soothing, and I didn't want him to stop. He snaked them into my hair and pulled me closer, his canines brushing against the nape of my neck.

A chill ran through my body, yet everything inside of me seemed to warm. My wolf and I loved this.

"I want to mark you, my dear Isabella," he whispered against me. "I want to show everyone how wonderful their new luna is. I want to finally show everyone that you're *mine* and only mine."

I stiffened at his words. I should've seen this coming. I shouldn't have let my thoughts get in the way and stupidly believed that he wasn't my mate. Maybe I hadn't blindly thought that; I just didn't want to admit to myself that my mate had denied me a position as a warrior. He knew that I deserved to be on the battlefield next to him, but he refused to grant something so precious to me. That was betrayal. That had always been betrayal, whether we were mates or not.

A stray tear rolled down my cheek as I stared into those golden eyes. They were so comforting. So fucking comforting.

He brushed the tear away with his finger, taking my face in his hands. His brows furrowed together. "What's wrong, Isabella?" he asked, rigidly. "Do you not want me to mark you?"

His wolf was clawing to mark me already. He wanted nothing more to claim me as his, to make sure nobody else would try to take me away from him. But it was too late for that.

My lips trembled. "Roman," I whispered, squeezing my eyes closed, "I have something I need to tell you."

He sat up, eyes full of concern. "What?"

For a few minutes, I tried forming words, but I couldn't. How could I tell my mate that I was going to leave him—willingly? My lips trembled again, another tear slipping down my cheek.

"I have to leave," I said so quietly that I barely heard myself, but he heard me.

He tensed. "What do you mean?"

I parted my lips. No words. I tried forcing them out again. Nothing. "I … I …" I grasped his face in my hand, his stubble tickling my palm. "I have to leave for a year."

Roman didn't move, but his hold on my fingers tightened. "Isabella, tell me."

"Don't hate me, Roman, please. I made the decision before I knew you were my mate, and I can't take it back now." My heart was breaking into a million tiny pieces that I wouldn't be able to put back together. Not now. Not ever.

"Now, Isabella. What're you talking about?"

I frowned at the man above me and did the only thing I could. I turned my bare back to him, so he could see the mark of a Lycan, and I curled my fingers into the pillow, digging them in and waiting for something. Anything.

But it never came. No scolding. No yelling. Nothing.

"I'm sorry," I whispered. "I really am."

After five minutes of pure silence, I turned my head. He had his lips pressed in a tight line. His eyes were gold but not that fiery gold that I had seen almost every night. They were a sad, swelling gold.

"You're leaving me."

"Roman ..." I sat up, pulling the blankets over my naked and exposed body.

"You went behind my back. You're leaving me to be a Lycan." His voice was louder this time, more hurtful.

"We're still mates. We—"

"Mates who don't live together, mates who will never see each other, mates who lie to each other. Those aren't mates, Isabella." He clenched his jaw and stared out of the window, the moonlight glimmering off his perfect fucking face. "The whole reason for mates is to build a life with one another, and you're leaving me!"

I pursed my lips together, suddenly angry with him. "This isn't my fault."

"This isn't your fault? You could've told me about it. You could've told me that fucking asshole was talking to you behind my back. What did he say to you? What did he promise you? Happiness with him? Is that what you wanted? Did you want someone to fuck you because I wanted to wait until you knew we were mates?" He ran his hands through his hair and abruptly stood off of the bed. His minty scent was making this oh-so goddamn hard.

I stood, too, and poked a finger right into his chest. "You cannot blame me for this. If you had welcomed me as a warrior, then we wouldn't be in this position. I accepted a job from Ryker because he'd believed in me from the beginning, unlike you."

"You think I didn't believe in you?" He shook his head and grabbed my hand tightly in his. "That's fucking ridiculous. I had full intentions of placing you on the team until he showed up at practice. I had full intentions of making you the best fucking warrior I had ever known. Tortured myself for days for assigning you as a nurse. But not placing you on the team kept you safe from any danger."

I knit my brows together. "That doesn't make shit any better, Roman."

"Tell me this, Isabella: would you have taken the position as a Lycan if you were a warrior?"

"Tell me this, Roman: why did you tell me I was terrible at fighting? Did you want me to feel bad about myself? You chose Vanessa over me. You know how embarrassing that was. I'd trained my whole life to be a warrior." I shook my head. "You know, maybe if you'd accepted me from the beginning and told me you were my mate, I would've made another choice."

He dropped my hand and stepped back in disbelief. "Maybe?" He held back his wolf. "Maybe?" His voice was louder this time. "You wouldn't have given me a sure chance?"

"You didn't give me a chance."

"That's different."

"No, it's not, Roman. It's not different." I shook my head and pressed my lips together. If we were going to fight about this, we might as well put everything on the table. "Why didn't you ever tell me that you were my mate? Why keep it a secret for the four years you've known?"

Silence.

"Is it because you wanted to fuck whoever you fucking wanted to and didn't have to take responsibility for it?"

He grabbed my jaw. "Stop."

I glared at him. "Is that the reason?" My heart pounded in my chest.

Had he wanted to be with other people when he knew for sure I was his mate? Nobody hid their mate from the world. Nobody could spend a single moment without them.

Something tightened in my chest, and my wolf whimpered. *Did he not want us—both of us?*

Tears rolled down my cheeks. All the hurt, all the betrayal, all the lying the last few weeks—it was finally coming out, and I didn't stop it.

"Don't be stupid, Isabella." His voice was quieter but still tense. "Since I've known that you were my mate, I haven't been with anyone."

I crossed my arms over my chest and pushed him away. I wasn't sure what to believe.

"You don't believe me, do you?"

He shook his head, snatched his journal from off of the dresser, and flipped through it. My eyes widened, seeing the hundred sketches he had drawn of me.

Every one was of me. Me running. Me smiling. Me training in the backyard with Derek.

"I've spent every fucking day since I turned eighteen wishing that I could be with you and only you. You know how long I've waited for this moment? To finally make you mine?"

His eyes were pure rage. I grabbed the notebook from him, my shaky hands flipping through the pages upon pages upon pages. I couldn't believe it. He had drawn that picture of me. He had given it to me to show how much he cared even though he couldn't really show it. I just didn't understand why he hadn't told me.

"Then, why?" I asked, my heart racing with so many emotions that I couldn't tell which was which anymore.

He tightened his jaw and sighed, walking over to his dresser and trailing his finger across the chain of Luna Raya's mate necklace he had in his room. "I wanted you to feel the same way I felt when I found out you were my mate. I wanted it to be real for you, as real as it was for me. I didn't want you to feel like you had to love me just because I was your alpha and said that I was your mate. I hate those people who do that."

He shook his hand and clenched his fist with the chain in it. "I wanted you to feel everything for me naturally instead of it being forced. I wanted to wait to have sex with you until you turned eighteen because I wanted it to be special for both of us, but you made that damn hard each night." His jaw twitched. "You know how many fucking nights I just wanted to tell you, so I could finally have you as my own?" He became quiet. "And now, you know we're mates, and you're leaving me."

When he turned around, I saw the tears in his eyes. Unfallen but still prominent.

I stepped toward him, not knowing what to say or what to do at the moment, but he moved back. And I felt rejected.

"You're leaving me," he said quietly, like he fully understood it now, his lips trembling.

"Roman," I said, my voice cracking.

He held out his hand and gave me the necklace, not bothering to put it on me like mates always did with each other. Mom had gushed so many times about when Dad put her necklace around her neck, how she would never forget that night.

But I wouldn't get my special moment.

My special moment had been ruined the minute Roman assigned me as a nurse.

"Put it on me," I said. Desperate. So fucking desperate.

He paused, the moonlight bouncing off of his skin. His eyes flashed back and forth between gold and green. Then, he finally took a deep breath and said, "I can't."

After another second, he turned around and placed his hands on the dresser, taking a deep breath, the muscles in his back tensing. "You should leave, Isabella."

No. No, I couldn't leave. Not without him marking me. Not without him putting on my necklace. Not without my mate.

"You want me to leave?" I whispered.

Everything hurt. My body. My heart. My wolf.

I pressed my lips together so hard to muffle a sob. This wasn't how it was supposed to be. This wasn't how I'd wanted my eighteenth birthday to end. This wasn't how I'd pictured meeting my mate.

This wasn't a fairy tale; this was a nightmare.

"Yes," he said. His response was short and quick, like he didn't need to think about it.

I clutched the necklace in my hand, holding on to it for dear life. Besides the sketch, it was the only thing I had from Roman.

I gathered my belongings—my dress, my bra, my single ounce of dignity—and walked to the door. Yet he still didn't make eye contact with me. It was like I was an ugly monster to him.

After grabbing the doorknob, I turned to face him. There was one question that I needed answered before I left. The question that my wolf had been begging me to ask since we found out he was our mate. I gazed down at Luna Raya's necklace, rubbing the pendant between my thumb and index finger.

I already knew the answer, but I needed to hear it from him.

"Will you mark me, Roman?"

Moon Goddess, I wanted him to say yes. I needed him to mark me to prove that he still loved me despite my decision, that he wouldn't be with someone else just because he was angry with me, that I was his and he was mine.

The mating process required it. Sex without a mark or a mark without sex—if one happened and not the other, the she-wolf usually went into heat within the next month. And I didn't want to go into heat without him next to me.

Every single emotion faded from his face, and he stared at me like he stared at the rogues who had killed his parents. "No."

CHAPTER 33

ROMAN

*F*uck.

I grabbed my journal and hurled it across my office at the wall, anger pulsing through my veins. It hit with a thud and then landed on the ground. Everything about this situation was fucked up. I grasped the notebook and tore out each sketch of her. One by one. Until my floor was littered with pictures of my mate.

Fuck.

Why had she gone behind my back? Why did she trust Ryker? Why hadn't she told me? She'd lied to my face. She hated the hospital and used it as a fucking excuse to leave me and my wolf. To be with whom? A fucking asshole who she didn't even know.

My hands curled into fists, and I resisted the urge to punch the wall until my knuckles were bleeding. What was wrong with me? Was I too overbearing for her? Had I not given her enough space? Would she really have joined the Lycans if I'd made her a warrior? Could I have even stopped this?

I leaned over my windowsill, my chest rising and falling. She'd left mere minutes ago, and I already felt like utter shit. She was really going to go be a Lycan, and I could do nothing about it.

Being a Lycan wasn't just a job; it was a job done for the Moon Goddess herself. Breaking one's commitment to their team was against divine law, which restricted me from even getting involved.

Someone knocked on my office door at three in the fucking morning, but I let them knock. I didn't have the energy to tell them to leave. Hell, I barely had the energy to hold myself up and not be a fucking wimp about this whole thing.

"Are you okay?" Jane asked from my office door. I listened to her walk into the room and come toward me. "Roman ... say something. Anything."

She placed a hand on my back, and I lost it.

My body caved in on itself, and Jane pulled me into a hug.

"Roman, what's wrong? I haven't seen you like this since Mom died."

I didn't cry. I refused to cry.

Alphas didn't cry.

But, boy, did I want to.

Jane rubbed my back softly, like Mom used to do, and tears filled my eyes. Everything felt so much more intense than it had yesterday. Every single emotion.

I felt like I was suffocating, drowning, dying.

"It's okay, Roman. Whatever it is ... it's okay."

No, it wasn't. My mate was leaving for a whole fucking year. She would be away from me. I would never see her, never get to hold her, never get to smell her sweet scent of vanilla.

I'd waited four fucking years to have her, only to watch her leave me. If I'd marked her now, it would have only hurt us both in the months to come. I would have to wait another fucking year and hope—pray—that she would choose me next time and not him.

CHAPTER 34

ISABELLA

I walked to Derek's house in tears. My own mate hadn't wanted to mark me because he was angry with my decision to follow my dreams. Mates were never supposed to hurt each other.

But all I felt was hurt. All I felt was rejection.

A part of me thought he was being childish. This whole thing was childish. Him not accepting me as a part of the warriors because he hadn't wanted me to join the Lycans. Him keeping that I was his mate a secret. Him not marking me before I left for an entire year.

Fog lay heavily inside the forest, but I continued to walk, knowing these woods like the back of my hand. I had run through them so many times, yet I couldn't get myself to run. My whole body felt too weak.

The pain—his pain, my pain, our pain—was terrorizing me. I didn't want Roman to go behind my back and sleep with anyone else. It wasn't like I would do it.

Though he hadn't officially rejected me and broken our bond, his refusal to mark me still felt like a rejection.

Only more pain would fester inside of me. I'd go through heat within the next month if he didn't mark me. All she-wolves who didn't complete the marking ritual within a month of meeting their mate went through heat. From the rumors, it was pure, agonizing torture, and instinctively, all unmated male wolves would want to put that she-wolf out of her pain.

Didn't Roman know that? Had my acceptance into the Lycans hurt him so badly that he refused to grant me something so sacred, so essential for my peace of mind?

I banged on the door, unable to stop myself from hyperventilating. Tears began streaming from my eyes again and stained my cheeks. I hated feeling hopeless.

A few moments later, Derek's mother answered the door in a plush pink robe, her brown hair set in wild curls. When she saw me, she furrowed her brows, pulled me inside, and yelled upstairs for Derek.

Derek walked down the stairs, wiping his tired eyes. "Ma, it's, like, three a.m.," he said. When his gaze landed on me, he jogged over and wrapped his arms around me. "Isabella, what's wrong?" he asked, his hand gently caressing my hair. "Why're you crying?"

I grasped on to him, nails digging into his back, like I would lose him too. "Derek, he-he doesn't want me. This is all my fault."

"Who doesn't want you?"

"Roman."

He pulled away but kept me at arm's length. "Roman's your mate?" he asked.

I nodded and wiped my tears with the back of my hand, hiccuping.

"Why doesn't he want you?"

My lips trembled. This would hurt him too. Why had I been so stupid? Why hadn't I just told everyone sooner? What was wrong with me?

"Because ... because I have to leave him." I clutched my stomach, trying to stop the hiccups. "I have to leave you too. I have to leave everyone."

Derek's mother rubbed my back, trying to calm me down. It reminded me of the way Luna Raya had calmed me down after Roman and I were play-fighting when I was five and he accidentally took me down a bit too hard. It was right before he shifted for the first time. All of his energy and power and testosterone had built up into one hard takedown.

I savored that moment. I would savor all those moments now that Roman and I were broken. We hadn't been that close for a long time—since his father had begun pushing him to take on responsibilities as an alpha, since he'd started hanging around that one girl from a nearby pack when he turned thirteen, since he'd hurt me.

Derek furrowed his thick brows. "What do you mean?"

"I got accepted as a Lycan," I said, flinching away and waiting for him to scold me too.

"A Lycan?" he said softly, the words lingering on his lips. After gazing between his mom and me, he grinned, lifted me into the air, and spun me around. "That's amazing!"

My loose curls whipped around us, and I twisted my fingers into his hair. Holding on to him for a moment longer. When he placed me down, I shook my head, wiping away more tears.

"No, it's not. I leave tomorrow."

He became quiet, realization hitting him. "For a whole year?"

My lips trembled. "I'm sorry for not telling you."

He paused for a long moment, brushing a hand over his twists, and turned his back to me, his muscles tense. "What if ... what if you came back to visit sometimes? We can meet at The Night Raider's Café?" He turned back to me with a hopeful smile on his face.

"I don't know if I'll be able to. Ryker told me that the rogues are only getting stronger. They go out almost every night for a hunt. Between hunting and training, I'm not sure that I'll have time."

His frown deepened, and he pulled me into a hug. "It's okay, Izzy. I still love you."

We stayed quiet, and then I knotted my brows together. I couldn't believe that this was happening.

"When I told Roman, he refused to mark me."

"He will come around," Derek's mom said.

But I didn't think Roman ever would. We were both hurt, and it would only get worse. When I went through heat, I might—unintentionally—try to get with another wolf to stop the pain. It would hurt him more; it would hurt *us* more.

I gazed down at the ground and pulled Derek into the last hug that I would probably ever give him for the next year. I didn't know when I'd have time to come back—or if I would.

After brushing a strand of hair from his face, I said, "Do me a favor and just watch after him."

"You don't trust him?"

My lips trembled. "I do ... but I don't trust Vanessa, and he isn't in a good place right now. Just let me know if he asks about me or acts weird or anything. Please."

It was my only hope of hearing about him.

When I got home that night, I peeked into my parents' room. I was so selfish for waiting this long, but I hadn't wanted anyone to hate me. I'd wanted them to be happy until I told them I was leaving.

After nudging Mom awake and after she saw the tears streaming down my cheeks, she sat up and pulled me into her arms. "Izzy, what's wrong?"

"Please don't hate me," I said.

She furrowed her brows. "We'd never hate you. Where is this coming from?"

"I'm sorry that I didn't tell you sooner," I said, staring at Dad, who was blinking his eyes open. I collapsed onto the bed and told them I would have to leave tomorrow morning because I was a Lycan.

And neither of them took it as badly as Roman had.

~

I woke up early the next morning with the sweet scent of French toast drifting through the bedroom and a dreadful ache in my heart. After tossing and turning and searching for another minute of sleep so I wouldn't be in so much pain, I walked into my room from my parents' and brushed a tear from my cheek.

My suitcase was lying on my bed, open and empty. I packed my clothes neatly inside, trying to fit everything that I could. And once my closet was bare, I gazed down at the windowsill, where I had placed my mate's necklace next to Luna Raya's keychain and my favorite moonflowers.

The necklace felt so cold between my fingers, so chilling, so fucking distant. I wanted to put it on, but putting it on myself felt so wrong. Mates were supposed to put it on each other to show their love and support and pure connection between them.

But my mate didn't want me because I'd chosen my dreams over him.

After a few moments, I clipped it around my neck anyway. I needed to do it. Even though Roman didn't accept me, he had given me this—which meant something, right? It was his mother's after all. I would keep it on until ... he rejected me.

My heart sank as I just thought about rejection. Though he had given me the necklace, he could still reject me. I knew that it was such a strong possibility; he had probably toyed with the idea all night.

I lugged my suitcase downstairs and set it next to the door. Sunlight flooded in through the windows, and the forest was oddly quiet for the early morning. It reminded me of the days when I had been young—when Luna Raya would invite me over to play with Roman in the forest, when we would hide out in the cave and tell stupid jokes to each other for hours upon hours until the sunlight faded and the forest was this quiet. Everything had been so much simpler back then.

Mom handed me a plate of French toast and ushered me outside to the porch, where Dad was staring at his garden of moonflowers and drinking his black coffee. We ate breakfast in silence because I wasn't sure if I could say anything without crying.

Instead, I listened to the faint pounding of paws against the forest floor and the howls of the warriors when they started practice. I should've been there with them right now. I should've been a warrior. I should've been marked and mated to Roman. But the Moon Goddess hadn't planned that for us.

I brushed my hand against my neck in the place where Roman had wanted to mark me last night. Without a mark, I couldn't feel how Roman felt today. Was he leading practice like every other day? Was he hurting? Did he care? Would he walk through the forest and see me before I left?

No. He would never come see me.

When we finished, Dad put my suitcase in the car. I took our plates and walked to the kitchen with Mom.

She leaned against the counter and frowned at me. "So, Derek isn't your mate?"

I blew a breath out of my nose. "No."

"Is it Roman?"

I gazed up at her. "How did you know?"

She gave me a *you didn't think I was that stupid, did you* look, her right brow arched hard. "We could smell him in the house, and Dad saw him lingering outside a couple of nights. And ... you know ... Mr. Beck has the latest gossip at the hospital, so everyone there already knew."

Oh, Mr. Beck. I hated him, but I was going to miss the hell out of him. "Tell him I said good-bye."

"Roman?"

"No, Mr. Beck."

She smiled, but the smile didn't meet her eyes. "Roman knows, doesn't he?" Her voice was soft, unlike her usual upbeat and lively tone.

I squeezed my eyes closed and pressed my lips together, trying to hold it all in, but a tear slipped down my cheek.

Mom pulled me into a hug and rubbed her hand against my temple. "It's okay, sweetheart. Everything will be okay."

"No, it won't." I sobbed. "He hates me. He refused to mark me, and he refused to put the necklace on me. Everything's ruined. Everything."

She rocked us back and forth. "He will get over it. Mates always do." Her words were kind, but I couldn't find any comfort in them.

Dad walked into the kitchen and clapped his hands together, a big grin on his face. "You ready, kiddo?" he asked. When he saw me, his eyes widened, and he slowly backed out of the room.

Mom rolled her eyes at him and laughed, pulling away just enough to gaze at me. "You know, when I first met your father, I wasn't a virgin."

I scrunched up my nose and choked out a laugh through my sobs. "Mom, I didn't need to know that."

She shushed me. "That's not the whole story, Izzy. When he found out, he refused to talk to me for weeks. I was devastated; I thought he would never talk to me again … but as you can see …"

Dad peeked through the window from the outside, just enough to only see from his eyes up.

"We're in a much better place." She smiled at him with so much love and grasped her mate's necklace. "Roman will get over it. Maybe not now, but soon."

Dad peeked his head behind the front door as I wiped my tears away. "You ready?"

I nodded my head and said good-bye to the house I'd lived in for years. Then, reluctantly, I hopped into Dad's car. Being the sappy guy that he was, Dad decided that it would be a good idea to take a slow drive through the pack to see everything one last time. My high school. The park. Derek's house.

And of course, the pack house.

Roman stood outside, talking to Cayden, with his back turned. When he heard Dad's car, he gazed over, not even bothering to turn his whole body, and tensed when his eyes met mine through my window. I swore that Dad hit the brakes to drive about five miles per hour because everything slowed down.

I so desperately wanted him to run over, to hug me, to apologize. But he didn't.

He gazed at me until I couldn't see him anymore. And that was when I knew that nothing would ever be the same.

CHAPTER 35

ISABELLA

"Ｎew pack, new you, huh?" Ryker asked from the doorway to my room in the Lycans' pack house. He stared at my freshly cut and highlighted hair that sat in loose curls at my shoulders.

A smile twitched on my lips—the first smile in nearly two weeks since I'd left—and I glanced at him through the mirror. Moonflowers twinkled in the corner of my room, near the window. "You can complain about it all you want, Ryker, but I like it."

I wanted him to respond with a sly comment, something that Roman would say, something to remind me of him.

But instead, he walked over to me, tugged on one of my curls, and said, "I like it."

"You like it?" I asked, my finger brushing against my mate's necklace. The metal was cool, cold even.

He gazed down at the pendant, and then he looked back at me and nodded his head. "It fits you, Bella."

I playfully pushed past him and walked into the living room. Though I had barely smiled these past two weeks, I liked this new me. I liked being able to train and to protect others. I liked being able to do what I loved, and I liked having a pack that supported me. I liked everyone here.

But I missed *him*.

It had been an agonizing two weeks without relaxing into his scent or in his arms or even at the thought of him. Mom had been wrong about Roman. He wasn't going to come around anytime soon.

"We're going to be late for practice," I said.

"Practice doesn't start for another half hour." He followed me into the living room and sat across from me on the couch, resting his forearms on his thighs, his biceps rippling. "Now, do you have anything you want to tell me?"

"No."

He raised a single sharp brow. "Not even about the mate's necklace around your neck?"

I fingered the necklace again, heart racing. He had seen it plenty of times since I had been here, and he'd let it slide. I had known he would ask about it sooner or later.

"Is it someone in the Lycans?"

"No."

He raised his brows, amused. "You and Raj seem to get along quite nicely."

I scrunched up my nose. "Raj's attractive, but he's not my type."

"Then, who is it?"

"Why do you want to know?"

He paused for a moment, his lips pursed together. "Because you have a necklace but aren't marked."

Of course. I must've been the only werewolf ever who had a mate's necklace but wasn't marked. One without the other was the first sign of rejection. I sighed, rested my head against the couch, and closed my eyes.

A part of me still didn't blame Roman for not marking me, and I hated it. My wolf wanted him more than anything she had ever wanted. These past two weeks, she'd refused to push herself hard in training. She was hurt that Roman didn't want us for who we truly were—warriors.

I gripped the edge of the couch, trying to hold back the tears. She felt rejected. *I* felt abandoned. And now, I wasn't only adjusting to a new life with a new pack, but I was also adjusting to a life without him.

The threat of rogues *and* the threat of going into heat weighed heavily on my shoulders. It was so stupid of me to cry in front of Ryker, my leader. But I gazed right at him with tears in my eyes. "Roman is my mate."

"Roman?" he asked, almost in disbelief.

Before I could shed a tear, I wiped the corner of my eye with my finger. "Yes."

He ran a hand through his hair and then rubbed his face with his hands. "Let me guess … he was too angry to mark you."

"No, he wasn't." I pressed my lips together. "He was too disappointed in me." I stood up and shook my head. "Too disappointed in my decision to do what I loved. He always seemed disappointed in me, even when I was in his pack. It didn't matter what I did. I never seemed like enough."

"Bella, I—" Ryker started.

"I don't want to hear it, Ryker. Don't apologize for him. Don't defend him. I don't care. I can get through this without him. I have to. This was my decision, and I wouldn't have made a different one if I had known we were mates prior to joining the Lycans. This has been my dream, and nothing will take my dream away."

His lips curled into a small smile. "Independent woman." He stood next to me and stared down at me with his lovely dark eyes. "You surprise me more every day, but I would never make any excuses for him. If he can't see how strong you are, then that's his fault. Not yours. Now, I assume that you and Roman have had sex already? And if you have, we need to talk about you going through your heat."

"I know," I whispered, suddenly feeling rejected.

"You'll be going through your heat in a couple of weeks," he said. "We need to be prepared. Some—most—warriors, especially in this pack, are driven by innate instinct. When the time comes and they feel that you're in heat, they'll try to put you out of it as soon as possible."

"I'll fight them off."

"You won't be able to," he said, a sudden sadness in his voice. "Have you ever seen a she-wolf in heat before?" he asked.

I shook my head.

"You won't be able to fight anyone off. I don't care how strong you are." He brushed his fingers against the scar on his neck. "You won't."

We sat in silence for a few moments, the air thick with tension, and then I nodded and grabbed his hand, squeezing it with mine. "Then, we will create a plan for when I do."

CHAPTER 36

ISABELLA

"*L*ike the hair, killer." Raj rocked back and forth on his heels, sending me one of his signature smirks—the one he said got all the ladies, but I hadn't seen any ladies that he'd ever been with.

I removed my mate's necklace for training and placed it in my bag, where it'd be safe. "Stop calling me that."

"But it suits you." He tugged his shirt over his head and tossed it onto the ground next to me. Up the left side of his brown abdomen, he had a string of moonflower tattoos.

"I've killed two rogues so far." I held up two fingers for emphasis, and then I removed my shirt and pointed to the tattoos on my back to make sure he fully understood that I was no rogue killer—yet.

He rubbed a hand against his scruff, his dark eyes taking in my tattoos. "Exactly, a *killer*."

I narrowed my eyes at him and jogged to catch up with the rest of the Lycans who were warming up. We lunged from one side of the training area to the other, and Raj lunged next to me.

"Are you making fun of me?" I asked, giving him a side-eye.

"Only if you want me to."

I cut my eyes to him. "Yeah, I would love if you made fun of me," I said sarcastically. "It's always been my dream. My only dream."

"I knew it."

Ryker cleared his throat, and we looked over to see everyone had finished with their warm-up and was staring at us. "If you two are done flirting, we'd like to start training," Ryker said with a tense smile on his face.

Raj pointed at me and then to an open corner of the field. We wrestled for about a half hour, taking turns throwing and pinning each other to the ground. Though he was stronger than me, I kept up with him easily. Unlike the first night I'd practiced with the Lycans, I had quickly figured out his movement patterns and could even spot when he was about to try a takedown on me.

With the right practice and the right people, I'd made improvements that I couldn't have ever achieved in Roman's pack.

Ryker didn't practice with us, just watched the way Raj and I pushed each other after every takedown, after every flirty comment, after every pin.

At one point, Raj caught me off guard and flipped me onto my stomach, pressing the side of my head into the ground. Dirt rubbed into my cheek, and I inhaled a whiff. I spit it out, escaped his hold, and turned him over onto his back, holding him to the ground for one, two, three seconds.

Raj curled one arm under my leg, another around the back of my head, and tossed me above him. I did a somersault out of his grip and stood back up to face my enemy. Covered in dirt and bruises that hurt oh-so good, we stalked around each other. My chest heaved up and down, my heart racing.

Ryker nodded in our direction and shouted, "Practice is over for tonight. Bella, stay back," he said. "I need to talk to you."

Raj playfully pushed his shoulder into mine. "Ooh, talking to the big man." He shook his head. "Someone's in trouble."

"You too, Raj," Ryker said.

I gave him a sly smirk and mocked him for mocking me.

Once I clipped my mate's necklace back onto me and he tugged his shirt back over his head, Ryker handed us a manila folder. "I'm putting you both on a mission."

"Just us?" I asked.

Only the best of the best went on missions without the rest of the team.

He nodded his head. "You two work very well together. You have chemistry."

Raj nudged me again. "You hear that, killer? We have chemistry."

I scrunched up my nose. "What does that have to do with anything?"

Ryker paused for a moment, like he was contemplating something, and then nodded. "This is a different mission. Unlike the typical stray rogue who wanders onto pack properties, there is a group of rogues working together. I want you to find out where their hideout is. There will be no killing on this mission. We need information, so we can raid their hideout and stop them once and for all."

Raj took the file from me, read it for a moment, and looked up. "They're going to be at The Night Raider's Café? A bunch of rogues?"

"The café is having a party during the full moon this Friday. All the packs in the area are invited, which means there will be many alphas there. Since this particular group is targeting alphas, I expect there to be some rogues in attendance."

"What do you mean, they're targeting alphas?" I asked, voice wavering.

Though Roman didn't want me, I still wanted to keep him safe. Luna Raya had died in a rogue attack, and I didn't want Roman to have the same fate. If he was in danger, I would do anything to stop it.

"They're killing alphas and taking their land and people."

Raj furrowed his brows. "How many have they killed already?"

Ryker sucked in a breath. "Three."

I nearly choked on the fucking air. "Three?" I shook my head. "How?"

Ryker sighed, looking much tenser than usual. "I don't know, but I need you to figure out where they're hiding out. I don't care how you do it—flirt with them if you have to—but they can't die. We need them to lead you to their lair."

After showering, Raj and I ran to the café to scope it out before Friday, so we could create our best plan of action. So far, our only plan was to flirt with the rogues and hope they'd bring us back to their hideout. But I wasn't sure if I'd be able to flirt with someone who wasn't my mate or my friend.

Flirting with Raj was easy because he was naturally good at it. With rogues who were here to find an alpha, to kill an alpha, to take an alpha's land and his people, it would be difficult to convince one to take me home. I would have to cover my Lycan tattoo and ... take off my necklace.

Raj stepped into the buzzing early morning crowd at the café, seductively shook his hips back and forth, and looked back at me. "Such a tight space for a club, but they don't call it dirty dancing for nothing. A packed room filled with sweaty bodies that you have to grind against just to move." He chuckled. "Seems like my kind of party."

Wait for it.

"Especially if you're my date."

There it was.

I picked my hazelnut coffee up from the counter, yawning. "Why do you insist on flirting with me?"

"I flirt with everyone. It's my job."

"Your job is to kill rogues."

"Killer, you're still so new. You don't know that there are subgroups in the Lycans. Some groups are pure warriors and kill; some flirt and get important information." He smirked and placed an arm around my shoulders. "I happen to do both."

"What about Ryker? What is he?"

He nudged me. "Why, you have a crush on him?"

"No, I just haven't seen him kill many rogues, and he gets awfully flirty," I said, cheeks flushing as I remembered earlier before practice.

"He goes out on a lot of solo missions to kill rogues, but he is highly skilled in flirting." He wiggled his brows at me.

"Well—"

"Long time no see, stranger," Vanessa said in that high-pitched, screechy-ass voice.

I clenched my jaw and gazed over at her.

She walked further into the café, swinging her purse in her hand, wearing an oversize T-shirt and a pair of heels. "I almost didn't recognize you. You look different ... *pretty*." She curled a finger around my hair and watched it bounce.

Her eyes drifted from me to Raj—who suddenly dropped his flirty-boy attitude—to his arm around my shoulders. I shrugged him off.

"Wow, thanks, Vanessa," I said, sarcasm dripping from every word.

Her hair was ruffled slightly, like she had just rolled out of bed. I inhaled and tensed when I realized how good she smelled.

"Two cappuccinos for Vanessa," the barista said.

Vanessa grabbed the coffees and smiled at us. "Well, I should get going. Don't want to keep Roman waiting. I'll tell him you and your *boyfriend* said hello."

My heart dropped.

Roman … that was what her shirt smelled like. Fucking Roman.

I stared at her from behind. Why the fuck did she have his shirt on, and why was she getting him coffee? Was she fucking Roman now? Decided to make her fucking move after I left?

I stepped forward, ready to follow her, when Raj grabbed my arm and tugged me back. "Lycans don't make rash decisions," he said.

I clenched my jaw and watched her drive off in her stupid Mercedes.

My hand tightened into a fist, and my coffee spilled all over my stomach. Though it was hot, it didn't sting as much as this, as much as betrayal, as much as rejection. My wolf whimpered inside of me. We were hurting.

"Isabella?" Raj asked, brows furrowed together.

The logical part of me knew that Vanessa always liked to stir up trouble. This was probably an elaborate scheme to fuck with me, even when I was gone. I shouldn't have believed her, but I did. She was wearing his fucking shirt.

"Izzy!" Derek walked into the café, his brown hair tousled.

Derek tugged me into a familiar, big bear hug. Since I'd left, I hadn't seen him. We texted back and forth every day. But hours between texts weren't the same thing as an instant reaction from him like I was used to. There had been too many rogues lately to see him.

"How have you been?" he asked. When I didn't answer, he pulled away and looked between me and Raj. "What's wrong?"

I should've been as happy to see him as he was to see me since I hadn't seen him in over two weeks. But how could I be happy when Vanessa was wearing Roman's shirt?

"Derek," I said quietly, not wanting to seem weak in front of Raj. "I asked you to watch Roman."

Derek's eyes widened, and just for a moment, his gaze drifted to the ground like he was guilty. I grabbed his hand, squeezing so fucking desperately.

"Derek," I whispered, tears threatening to fall. "Please don't tell me he and Vanessa are together." I shook my head. "Please."

He didn't say anything, just tensed.

My lips parted in disbelief, and it felt like my whole world came crashing down. Two weeks. I had been gone for two weeks. That was it. "Oh Moon Goddess. They are."

Derek sucked in a breath and put his hands on my shoulders. "Isabella, I'm not sure what's going on between them. All I know is that they've been spending more time than usual together. Something happened at Vanessa's house, and she claimed that she couldn't live in it, so he offered to let her stay in the pack house with him."

Raj squeezed my shoulder, and I pulled away from Derek.

"Why didn't you tell me?"

He pressed his lips together. "I thought it would only be for a day or two." He shook his head, wiping the tears from my cheeks. "I even offered for her to stay at my house with me, so she would stay away from him. But they both refused."

My heart ached so fucking bad.

"I'm sorry, Isabella," Derek said.

But it didn't make anything better.

It hurt as bad as Roman's rejection would.

CHAPTER 37

ISABELLA

I gazed at the people dancing in the middle of The Night Raider's Café with a frown on my face. All week, I had been thinking about Roman, about Vanessa being in the house with him, about him giving his shirt to Vanessa to wear. And all week, I'd wanted to march right onto his property and tell him to reject me.

This feeling was beyond me. I didn't know what was happening there, and it was eating me alive. Sure, he might just be acting like a nice alpha to Vanessa. But he hadn't even been nice to me before I turned eighteen. Sure, he might be doing his alpha duties.

But didn't Vanessa have her own damn shirts to wear? Why had he let her go out with his shirt?

This pain was too much, and I hadn't even gone through heat yet. In less than a week, I would go through it. I would scratch and claw through all the walls in my bedroom, begging for someone to take away the pain by mating me.

The pain would disappear if I rejected Roman, but I couldn't get myself to even think about those words.

Music thumped through the hazy bar, and I sipped on my tequila sunrise. Nobody from Roman's pack was here—at least, not yet. Not even that fucking bitch.

Alphas walked through the crowd in The Night Raider's Café gone nightclub. People parted their way for them to walk, gazing up at them—some with looks of respect or with looks of lust. I clenched my jaw and grasped the mate's necklace in my pocket. I hadn't worn it, but I'd brought it with me, so I could thrust it in his stupid face and tell him I was done.

Out of all the alphas who couldn't be here, he had to stay at home. Probably with fucking Vanessa in place of me. It should've been me he was loving. Me. *Me*. Not her.

My wolf growled in the back of my mind, but I hushed her. Whether this was all some fabricated lie or whether it was the truth, I had to think clearly for this mission. It was my first solo with Raj, and I couldn't fuck it up.

Raj curled an arm around my waist and leaned down. "You ready, killer?" he asked against my ear. Lights flashed upon his face, bounced off of his eyes, making him look so much more attractive tonight. His soft black hair, the dark, lustful expression in his eyes.

I brushed my fingers against my neck—where my necklace should've been.

Without it on, I didn't feel bound to Roman. And I didn't know how to take that.

Raj's hands glided against my hips as he pulled me onto the dance floor between sweaty bodies. Pressing himself against my backside, he leaned down, so his lips grazed against my ear, making me shiver. "You remember the plan?"

"Yes."

"Well, start acting like it."

I painted a smirk on my face and turned in his embrace, my fingers crawling up his chest. He didn't have to tell me twice. His muscles felt so taut underneath his thin button-up. So rigid. So big. I pulled him down closer to me and wrapped my arms around his shoulders, resting my forehead against his.

He smelled like butterscotch. Such a sweet and inviting scent.

After wrapping his arms around my waist, he pressed his fingers against my lower back. I spun us slightly and looked up from his shoulder to see the group of rogues in the corner of the room, watching us.

One in particular, with glowing green eyes, stared at me. From the scar on his right cheek to his lips curled into a dangerous smirk, everything about him screamed bad boy. And we all knew who loved bad boys. I did—for tonight.

After giving him a flirty smile behind Raj's back, I gazed at Raj and blushed. He pulled me closer, our bodies pressed hard against each other. *Why did he smell so goddamn good?*

I moved my hips with his, not wanting to get too close, but close enough. My wolf purred inside of me, and I thought Roman was here. She had never purred like that for anyone else but him.

But when I looked around, I realized that Roman wasn't here. My eye caught that rogue's again, and this time, I kept my eyes on him as Raj and I danced together. I could only imagine that Raj was doing the same thing with another one of the rogues somewhere in the club.

I whispered something into Raj's ear and took off toward the bar. For a brief moment, I gazed back at the group of rogues and noticed that *he* wasn't there.

"Looking for something?" the rogue said.

He had one arm resting on the bar, the other holding his drink. I smiled at him and fingered his collar. His sleeves were rolled up his forearms, and I tried my hardest to keep calm. But my heart was racing, and my wolf was quiet.

"For *someone*," I said.

He brushed his thumb against my lips and smirked. "What would your boyfriend say?" he asked, gazing at Raj, who had his back turned to us—just like we had decided he would.

I placed a finger against his chin and turned his head, so he was facing me. "Like you really care what he would say. Guys like you just take what they want, don't they?"

He chuckled and stepped closer, and suddenly, my wolf was purring again. Just like she had with Raj, just like she almost had with Ryker earlier today before I had to scold her.

I licked my lips.

"Let's get out of here," he said in my ear.

I pretended to think about it for a second. When he brushed his fingers up my abdomen, I was terrified that he would see me as way too muscular for an average wolf, that he would know that something was up. But he didn't.

So, I wrapped my hand around his neck and pulled him closer, so my lips were grazing against his. "Show me the way."

He took my hand and led me to the exit. I barely had enough time to look back at Raj to make sure he knew I was leaving to find this hideout. A few of the other rogues from the corner of the room watched us leave, and the rogue with me threw his hand up into the air, like I was a fucking victory prize for him.

But something about it was so sexy.

We walked out of the bar, and even before the door of the bar closed, the rogue had me pressed against the side of the building and had his lips on my neck, sucking harshly. My heart was racing, yet for some reason, I couldn't even push him off of me. He moved his lips up my neck, nibbling even more roughly on it and leaving a red mark.

Jane's car pulled into an empty spot in the parking lot thirty feet away, its headlights blazing in our direction. I tugged him closer to me, so she wouldn't see me working. I didn't need any rumors spreading that I'd turned into a whore after I left the pack.

The rogue moved his lips near mine, but I leaned away from him, shielding my face with my hair. This wasn't time to play. This was work. Work that I had to do. Work that Ryker had assigned to me because he believed in me.

My wolf purred as his scruff brushed against the crook of my neck and made it *burn*.

Jane walked to the front of the building with a few of her friends and two warrior wolves—who I assumed Roman had assigned to her for protection. I could smell their pungent scents, but none of them smelled like Vanessa, so I could keep myself calm. Jane paused for the slightest moment, gazing in our direction. And when she did, I turned and pushed the rogue to the side of the building, my hair falling into my face. He grabbed my ass, and for some fucking reason, my wolf didn't pull away. She didn't want to.

But I did.

It felt wrong.

Jane walked into the building.

When she disappeared, I took a deep breath, and he pressed his lips to mine, his tongue in my mouth. He wrapped a hand in my hair and forced me to kiss him. I placed my hands against his chest and tried to push him away, but I wasn't strong enough— even though I had done more than just push someone away in practice.

My neck burned. Blazing. Scorching. Sweltering.

I took a deep breath, gathering enough strength to push him back. I had a fucking mission.

"I thought you wanted to take me home," I said, keeping my gaze steady.

He licked his lips, and I pressed a hand against my neck and hoped that the pain would stop. I stepped away from the rogue, catching sight of Raj lingering at the entrance to The Night Raider's Café.

I swayed my hips back and forth, walking toward the woods. "So, where are we going?"

He followed me into the woods, his scent becoming overwhelming, and grabbed my wrist. "We're not going anywhere." He stepped closer to me. "You're too damn sexy to take all the way back home."

"But—"

He pushed me behind a tree and grabbed my shirt, ripping it open. "I do take what I want, when I want," he said, fingers grazing against my skin and lighting it ablaze.

My chest burned, and suddenly, my whole body felt like it was on fire.

My core was throbbing. My head was aching. My skin felt like it was searing off.

I squeezed my eyes closed and grasped on to him. His eyes turned black—the color of his wolf's—and he brushed his teeth against my neck, where Roman's mark should've been.

Oh Moon Goddess, no. My heat. It was here. Now.

Before the rogue could take my clothes off himself, I ripped them off of my body. It was too hot for this. Too fucking hot. I was sweating. My breathing became ragged, like I was gasping for breath but didn't want to breathe too deeply or I'd get a mouthful of dry air, slowly killing me from the inside out.

So much pressure built in my chest that I couldn't hold myself up any longer. I collapsed to my knees, and he unbuckled his belt, taking his cock out. I shook my head, but my wolf purred, wanting him. My eyes shifted back and forth between hers and mine, and for a moment, I almost lost control.

But I grabbed ahold of myself. I didn't know how long I'd be able to do this, but I'd made a promise to Ryker that my heat wouldn't get in the way of doing my job as a Lycan. I wasn't about to have Roman not marking me make me lose this position.

The rogue grabbed my arms and pulled me to my feet. Just as he was about to plunge himself inside of me, I grabbed his cock in my hand, my claws digging into it. He released me, grasping himself.

"Stop."

My wolf jumped inside of me, wanting to be released. She had never wanted something so crazy. She wanted him. She wanted this rogue. She wanted him to fuck us.

"You fucking whore." He wrapped a hand around my throat, pinning me to the tree.

A tear slipped from my eye, and I whimpered. *This couldn't be happening. This couldn't be happening.* This wasn't how I'd wanted to be mated.

Without thinking, I swiped my claws across his neck and killed him instantly. I collapsed onto the ground, stretching out as much as I could and trying to cool down in the dirt.

"Raj!" I shouted. "Raj!"

I listened to someone run through the woods, and Raj appeared at my feet. His eyes were wide and wolf gold, and he looked down at me with so much fucking lust that I knew that he wanted the same thing that the rogue had wanted. To mark me. To put a woman out of her heat.

That innate need was coded into every single unmated were-wolf. It was so natural to want to help a she-wolf through her heat, to stop her from hurting, to make her his.

Some rogues exited the bar and saw me leaning against the tree—clothes torn off, body dripping with sweat, need radiating off of me in waves. And suddenly, they raced toward me.

Raj slowly approached me, controlled by his wolf and his wolf only. His ears lifted, listening to the rogues.

"Raj," I said, tears streaming down my cheeks.

I could barely move. Everything ached beyond belief. He

grabbed my arm, pulled me up, and wrapped an arm around my waist. His skin on mine was the only cool thing on my body.

It felt so good that I couldn't help but beg for him to touch me more. My wolf took control.

"More, Raj," I begged. "It's too much."

CHAPTER 38

ROMAN

I gazed at the man in the fucking mirror and sighed. I could barely recognize myself after I let my mate leave me without putting up much of a fight. A part of me had hoped that she wouldn't go through with it. A part of me had hoped that this was all some fucked up dream. But she was stubborn, and this was all my fault.

She should be with me. She should've been on the team. Not Vanessa. But I had been so fucking jealous and terrified that Ryker would take her away from me that I couldn't let it happen. Now, it had happened.

My mate was at his pack, living in his house, getting close to that asshole.

Any day, she could go through her heat. Any fucking day. And I had no way of knowing when it would be. Would she be strong enough to resist any other guy who wanted to mate her? There were plenty of wolves who would love the chance. Would she be strong enough to fight off the men to keep herself for me? Not with Ryker living in that house with her. He would take her, and he wouldn't even care.

Why had I let her leave again?

I shook my head and adjusted my tie. She would be at The Night Raider's Café tonight for the full-moon party, and I was going to go to get her back.

I'd drag her back if I had to, I'd place her on the warriors, I'd—

I stopped. I couldn't. She was to be a Lycan for at least a year. A vow to the Lycans was as sacred as divine law, and she couldn't break divine law.

Tonight, I would go to see her even if it was in passing. To smell her vanilla sweetness again, if I had a chance.

I gazed down at my dresser, which was covered with all my late-night drawings of her. It was the dresser I'd emptied for her, the dresser I'd left her mate's necklace on. And when I looked at it, all I saw was the devastated expression she had given me when I told her I wouldn't mark her before she left me.

Vanessa knocked two times on the door and walked into my room—uninvited.

Why the fuck had I even let her stay with me? Did I not respect my mate that much to force her out?

I'd lost all my damn respect for myself when I told her yes and told Derek that I would take care of Vanessa's living arrangements after one of her water pipes burst.

She drew her finger across my dresser, and then she touched me. Yes, she touched me.

Her finger grazed up my neck, and I let her. So fucking stupid. But it felt better than nothing. All I could picture were her fingers as Isabella's. Teasing me like she always did. She never even had to try.

"You look so good," she purred. "So, you decided to be my date for tonight?"

I swallowed hard and took her hand off of me. "Vanessa, what did I tell you about overstepping your boundaries?"

She gazed up at me through her long lashes that she had dressed in over a hundred coats of mascara. "Oh, come on, Roman. Don't act like you haven't ever thought about me." She smirked and hopped onto my bed, breasts bouncing as she did. "I know you have."

She was right. I had.

"Thinking about all the things you would do to me." She grabbed my hand and put the column of her fragile neck. "Wrapping your hand around my throat, fucking me like you used to fuck Isabella."

I grasped her neck, dug my claws into her flesh, and thrust her off the bed and up against the wall. Then, I squeezed.

This was the only thing I had thought about doing to her, but I hadn't been man enough to do it yet.

"I should've never let you live as a warrior. You're beneath me. You're beneath her. You're beneath us," I growled. "You will never have a chance with me. I have a mate."

Her cheeks reddened. "A mate?" she spat. "She's at the café right now with someone else."

My hand tightened around her throat. She was lying.

"Jane sent me pictures of them," she said. "She even said that she was *marked*."

Both my hands slipped around her throat, and I lifted her off the floor. I wished that I could snap her neck right here, right now. She dug her nails into me, her eyes wide.

"Leave, before I kill you," I growled in her ear. It took everything I had to let go of her.

She fell to her knees and gasped for breath as I walked to the other side of the room, trying to calm myself down. A minute went by, then another, and that bitch was still in my room.

"Get out, Vanessa." I gazed out of the window, clenching my jaw. "Don't make me say it again."

She scurried out of the room, and when she was gone, I sat on the bed and dug my claws into the bedsheets. My Isabella was marked. My Isabella was with another man right now.

I had waited three years for her, turned down everyone and anyone for her, and then fucking refused to mark her.

My wolf growled inside of me, ready to kill anyone who dared to touch our mate.

Vanessa had to be lying. She had to. She always did.

I needed to get down there now to see with my own eyes, to see what my mate had done because of my stupid decisions. My mind was too scrambled to believe anyone anymore, even myself.

CHAPTER 39

ISABELLA

*R*aj pushed me into the side of a tree and pressed his lips to my neck. They moved so effortlessly on my skin and felt so cool. I rested my head back against the tree bark and closed my eyes.

His scruff tickled my skin, and I pulled him closer. Everything about him felt so good. His muscles rippling under his shirt, his sweet butterscotch, the way he grabbed me and held me against him.

When his canines brushed against my soft spot, I shook in total pleasure. Just waiting, wanting, craving to be marked. My wolf howled inside of me, not able to resist his touch.

"Please, Raj," I whispered. "It feels so ..." I let out a small moan. "It feels so good."

He gripped my hips, and instinctively, I pushed my body against his. He was so much cooler than I was. And when he licked the crook of my neck, I moaned louder, letting everyone hear me and not caring at all.

The moonlight flooded through the trees and made my mate's necklace glow on the ground, near my clothes. I tensed. *My mate, Roman. What would he think about this? He'd hate me.*

He already hates us, my wolf howled in my mind. *Raj doesn't. Raj wants to help us!*

My breath hitched. I didn't want this. I couldn't want this. No matter how much I hated him, I couldn't betray Roman until he rejected me. It was too wrong.

"Raj," I said, trying my hardest to keep my voice steady. I lifted my gaze from his shoulder and stared at the group of rogues coming our way.

Mate! Anyone will do! So hot. Please.

I pressed my hands to his chest, my palms cooling from the contact, and pushed him back. "Raj, stop."

His teeth grazed against my neck again, and I resisted the urge to moan.

"The rogues."

Immediately, Raj tensed. He pulled away, his eyes flashing back and forth between his wolf and his human, tore his hands off me, and placed them in fists next to me on the tree. He parted his lips. "Isabell—"

"The rogues," I said, pointing behind us.

My wolf jumped up and down inside of me. *More people for mates! More people! Just our type!*

They were all staring at me. They were all coming for me. They could all feel me.

Soon, everyone would be able to feel my need to be satisfied, and it terrified me. All I could see were werewolves tearing each other apart to see who could get to me first. All I could hear were them growling viciously over my body. All I could feel was dread and misery.

"Raj," I said again.

He gazed over his shoulder, sucked in a deep breath, and bared his teeth. I wasn't sure if he had done so because he was about to kill them all or because he wanted to sink his teeth into me and claim me.

Claim us! Claim us!

"Go," he ordered.

I shook my head. "No." Even though I wanted to leave.

There were far too many of them for him to take on alone. I needed to suck it up and fight with him, or he'd die. When I'd joined the Lycans, I had taken an oath to protect my partner. I wasn't about to—

"Go! I'll keep them off of you."

"But—"

He snapped his head in my direction. "If you don't go now, I will sink my teeth into your neck." His eyes flickered to my neck and darkened, and he shook his head. "Go!"

And with that, I ducked under his arm and sprinted through the woods. My wolf was trying to hold me back, begging me to stay, to let someone else mark me, to put us out of this misery. But I fought against our natural instinct and continued to run. I ran and ran and ran.

When Ryker and I had talked about my heat, we had decided that when it came, I should go to the only place where I would be safe—the Lycans' pack house. But with all the unmated wolves in the Lycans, I couldn't go back there.

So, I ran through the woods, never shifting into my wolf, in fear that she would betray me and mate with whoever she wanted. I needed to get away from everyone. I needed to get through this. I needed my mate.

When Roman's pack house came into my view, my heart thumped in my chest. His scent lingered everywhere. On the lawn, on the dirt, on the door. I barged through the back door and sprinted to his bedroom. Vanessa's smell drifted out from one of the spare rooms, and I nearly ripped her door open, but I was too far gone.

Roman. I needed Roman, my mate.

Everything was so hot. So fucking hot. Sweat rolled down my forehead, and I wiped it off with the back of my hand. When I made it up the stairs, I ran to Roman's room and pushed the door open. Ready to be marked and mated.

Roman's scent floated in the air, so strong yet so weak. I walked into the empty room and slammed the door shut. After pushing the short dresser in front of the door and the tall dresser in front of his window, I clenched my fists.

He wasn't here, and that made everything hurt worse. Since I'd stepped onto this property, my body had been burning hotter. I felt like I was standing in a firepit with the sweat lathering down my forehead and the unruly boiling of my blood.

Nobody would find me here, and if I shifted into my wolf, I wouldn't be able to leave. It was perfect enough to make it through the night.

I shuffled through Roman's closet, sticking my nose into his clothes and smelling his scent. It was so calming, yet it just made me hurt more. I wanted him to mark me. Needed him to mark me now. But he was probably out with Vanessa at the damn nightclub, doing things to her that I didn't even want to think about but couldn't stop.

My wolf growled and bared her teeth at the thought. Another rush of heat hit me, making me pant for something—anything —cool.

I flung open the bathroom door, started the cold water, and watched it fill up the bathtub. When the bath was half-full, I jumped in, unable to resist it. It was cold, freezing almost, but it didn't stop that lasting ache.

Why the fuck did this hurt so bad? Why the hell was my life like this?

Roman didn't go through heat. Roman didn't know how fucking hard this was because he'd refused to mark me. Roman didn't know how much pain I was in. He didn't. He wouldn't. Ever.

My heart throbbed, and when the cold water wasn't doing it for me anymore, I turned the faucet back on and rested the crook of my neck right on the rushing water, letting it cool me slightly. The bath filled until the water was sloshing over the edge.

I leaned back and groaned loudly. This was too much. Too fucking much.

In a bath full of cold water, I was sweating. No goose bumps, just pure disgusting sweat. My wolf clawed her way through me. I needed to get out. Out of here. Now.

Mate. I needed to find a mate. My mate. Any mate.

I jumped out of the water, trying to fight my wolf but not being able. I landed on all fours and shifted into my wolf, listening to my bones crack but not feeling anything other than this heat. She sprinted to the door, on her hands and feet like the wild fucking animal she was.

She growled at the dressers in front of the door, shook away the sweat, and clawed at the wood. Small pieces jammed into the pads of her paws, but she didn't care. Over and over and over, her claws dug into it, destroying it and ripping it to pieces.

Stop, I demanded, but my wolf didn't listen.

Mate. Need mate. Need a mate now.

I could barely breathe. All this fur was making me warmer, hotter, and dryer. She continued to claw and claw, and I wished Roman would just break through the door at any moment.

My head hurt. My vision blurred.

After what seemed like hours with no success, I whimpered. I begged my wolf to stop. I couldn't handle it. She was suffocating me.

Wave after wave of heat washed through me. I shifted and lay on the warm ground, tears streaming down my cheeks. I rolled into a ball and then stretched out, unable to find a comfortable position.

I stumbled to my feet and away from the door, so I couldn't move the dressers myself. Honestly, at this point, I didn't even think I had enough strength to do that. I eyed the one by the window, which had been untouched by my wolf. And a part of me wanted to just hurl myself out of the window, smack against the ground, and pass out.

Everything was more intense than it had been—and much hotter. So much hotter.

Bed, my wolf said. *Cool down.*

I held on to whatever I could as my legs shook uncontrollably. I couldn't see anything. I moved around the room, my hands on the walls, searching for the thermostat. When I found it, I turned it down as much as I could. I wanted to freeze.

Then, I collapsed onto the edge of the bed, crawled desperately to the pillows, and lay spread eagle on Roman's bed. Cool. I needed to be cool.

I stared up at the ceiling, but I could see nothing but darkness.

Tears fell from my eyes. Everything hurt so bad.

I needed my mate. I needed him.

Couldn't he feel the pain I was in? Why wasn't he coming to get me? Why wasn't he coming to save me?

CHAPTER 40

ROMAN

*C*ayden pressed a hand against my chest, trying to stop me from storming toward the café. "Calm down, Roman."

I pushed him away from me and snatched his collar. "I'll tell you one last time to get out of my fucking way."

My body shook with rage. Isabella was so close that I could smell her.

"Or what?" he asked, eyes wide. "You'll kill me for your senseless mistakes?"

My wolf growled, and I bared my teeth at my beta.

He shook his head, unafraid of me. "If you go into that club while she's working and approach her like that, everything is going to fall apart."

"She's not working. She's with a fucking guy who fucking marked her, having a good fucking time."

I released him and continued to storm through the woods to

the nightclub. Music thumped through the forest, the scent of alcohol becoming almost unbearable.

Suddenly, someone screamed at the top of their lungs, and the music stopped. I collapsed onto all fours, my nails lengthening into claws and my bones snapping, and lifted my nose to the moon, taking off toward the nightclub as Cayden followed us.

Outside of the café, a group of people was huddled together and whispering. Some people had drinks in their hands, and others were crying. Grasping on to each other in their tight clothes, tears falling from their eyes. Warriors scouted the area, trying to calm everyone down. It was pure chaos.

I shifted into my human, scanning the crowd for Isabella. Jane and Vanessa were holding each other by the doorway.

Jane's cheeks were stained with black streaks. She gazed at me, pressed a hand to her chest, and then ran in my direction. "Thank the Moon Goddess, you're all right!" She threw her arms around me. "I thought I'd lost you too."

My brows furrowed together. "Where's Isabella?"

She wiped a tear from her cheek and nodded to the side of the woods, where a group of alphas was huddled. I pushed Jane away and hurried to them.

Mate. I needed my mate.

Cayden followed me, trying to keep up with my quickening pace.

My heart thumped against my chest when the scent of alcohol faded into the stench of blood. Blood. Blood everywhere. I pushed through the alphas, not caring who I pissed off, when I saw the rogue. Dead and lying in a puddle of his own blood. He smelled like her.

Where was she?

A few yards from the rogue was another. His face was torn apart, completely unrecognizable. And a few yards from him was another with a dislocated limb. Five more dead rogues lay throughout the woods, each a distance from each other.

And the mate's necklace that I had given Isabella was in the center of the madness. Painted with blood—not Isabella's, but the rogues'. I grabbed the necklace and deposited it into my pocket. I needed to find her.

Gore covered a few trees and was splattered all over the ground. This hadn't been planned. If Isabella was here on business with someone, they would've taken out each rogue without a mess.

I sniffed the air for any trace of my mate, needing to make sure she was all right and hadn't mated with anyone else. I followed the only scent I could pick up and came to a small stream. A Lycan was in it, washing blood off of his body. His brows were pulled together in pain, and he clutched the open wound on his abdomen.

"Where is she?" I asked, stepping closer to him.

The Lycan gazed over at me, jaw clenching as he pulled himself out of the water and put more pressure on the open wound, which sat almost perfectly along the line of moonflowers tattooed on his side.

"Who?"

"Isabella. Where is she?"

He stiffened and then scoffed, "So ... you're her mate?"

I stalked over to him and grabbed him by the neck. "Where is she?"

"Take your hands off of me before someone gets hurt."

"I asked you a question."

"And I told you to take your hands off of me."

I growled, baring my teeth at the man who had Isabella's scent all over him. Her scent was so strong—too strong. "Where?"

"I don't know where your mate is. I asked her to leave."

"Don't give me that shit! I know you Lycans have an oath to each other that'd you never leave a mission. Where is she?"

He pushed me away and grabbed his wound again. "I asked

her to leave, so I wouldn't mark her. She's going through heat, you dumbass." He shook his head.

Heat. My mate. She was in heat.

"Don't act so fucking surprised either. If anything, you should be thanking me. If I wasn't here, those rogues would've devoured her."

She was in heat, and I wasn't there to stop it. If she lost control, if someone found her ...

"Where did she run to?" I asked.

He pointed toward the direction of my pack, and I ran faster than I ever had to find my Isabella.

CHAPTER 41

ISABELLA

*M*y whole body ached.

I turned onto my side and groaned softly into my pillow. At least the heat was over—for now. That was something I never, ever wanted to happen again. I'd do anything to avoid the pain of the heat. It was like a million knives jabbing into my stomach and cutting me open, like searing in an inescapable burning house.

But it was over so soon. I'd expected it to last two or three days, not just a single night.

Someone wrapped their arm around me from behind and pulled me closer.

My eyes widened, and I thrust back an elbow to hit whoever it was hard in the chest. "Get away from me!"

I hopped out of the bed, tugging the blankets around me and refusing to look at whoever had lain with me last night.

This wasn't real. I'd ... I'd really ... I'd really slept with someone last night. Had I let him mark me too? Was that why I couldn't feel any more pain?

My vision was blurry still, halfway between my wolf's eyesight and my own, as I stared down at my bare feet. The last thing I remembered was lying in Roman's bed, trying to calm my wolf, and being deathly hot. Then, I'd blacked out.

What if, when I had, she had taken control of me? What if I had mated with someone without knowing about it?

"Oh my gosh. I can't believe I did this … I can't believe …" I doubled over, curling into a ball and covering my face with my hands. "I'm a terrible mate."

My body heaved up and down. *Roman would never forgive me now.*

Someone placed their hands on my waist and picked me up.

"Get off of me!" I screamed.

I pulled myself out of the man's grip and turned around, baring my teeth at him. But when I blinked back the blurriness, my eyes widened.

Roman.

After a few moments of breathing heavily, I gazed around the room. Everything was back to normal. The water had been cleaned up, and the dressers—though nearly ripped to shreds— were back in their original spots.

My hands traveled up to my neck, and I sighed when I didn't feel a mark. Nobody had marked me. Tears welled up in my eyes. Nobody had marked me. I was still me. I was still Isabella. Not anyone's.

Roman watched me from the edge of the bed, and I swallowed hard. I hadn't seen him in almost a month. And now, he was staring right at me with a wild mess of curls on his head, dark circles under his eyes, and thick, tan muscles that seemed to have gotten bigger since I'd last seen him.

I wanted him, and my wolf still wanted him. Despite everything.

But I couldn't imagine what he'd say if I told him that.

If you wanted me, you shouldn't have left. If you wanted me, you would still be here with me. If you wanted me, you wouldn't be sleeping under the same roof with another man.

I parted my lips and then closed them, not knowing what to say. It was probably best not to say anything at this point. Showing up in his house. Tearing up his furniture. Lying naked in his bed. I stood there, staring at him and waiting for him to reject me.

When I had enough of him judging me with his eyes, I tore my gaze from him, suddenly feeling stupid for coming here. It was clear that he wasn't going to reject me or mark me. He would've done either already. He wanted me to suffer more, to suffer longer for leaving him. And so, I would.

"I'm sorry. I shouldn't be here," I said.

Next month, when I went through my heat, I'd just lock myself in my room, tie myself to my bed with a silver chain, and call it a day.

I turned toward the door, dressed in Roman's sheets without a care in the world that someone would see me leave Roman's pack house, naked. Nothing had happened between us. Nothing would ever happen between us at this rate.

Roman grabbed my hand and pulled me back into his chest. Then, he pressed his lips to mine. So hard. So passionately. So desperately. By the second, my body relaxed, and I kissed him back. All the stress, all the anger, it melted away. It was stupid and cliché, but it was true.

I wrapped my arms around his neck and pulled him down to me. I would take all that I could get from him at the moment. I didn't know if I'd get another.

When I was out of breath, I pulled away and rested my forehead against his. A tear slipped down my cheek. My heart hurt. So bad. I'd missed him so much, and I never wanted to leave him again.

We didn't say anything to each other. I just stood there and enjoyed it because I was afraid that even after that kiss, he'd tell me to leave. Without a mark. Without a mate.

After pressing his lips to mine once more, he lifted me off the ground, walked to the bed, and gently rested me on it. He sat across from me and brushed a tear from my cheek with his thumb. "Turn around," he said softly.

My jaw twitched. I was still nervous and afraid. But I turned around and faced the mirror on his dresser. I was a total mess. My hair sat in unruly curls around my face, my makeup was smudged on my cheeks, my eyes were red. And my neck was bare. No necklace.

I sucked in a breath and touched my fingers to my neck. No, it hadn't been on my neck last night … but I'd left it in the woods. Somewhere. Somewhere in the forest, near the café.

"Roman," I whispered, "I-I didn't mean to lose my necklace. I had it on me. I swear, I had it on me."

I hopped up, needing to go get it. He probably hated me even more for losing his mother's necklace. Hell, I was a mess. I wouldn't even blame him for rejecting me now.

"Sit, Isabella," Roman ordered.

And I hesitantly obeyed.

He sat behind me on his knees and pulled my necklace from his pants pocket. My eyes widened, heart thumping loudly. He unhooked it and placed it around my neck.

"You're mine, Isabella." He pressed his lips to my skin, right where he would mark me one day. "Mine."

CHAPTER 42

ISABELLA

I smiled at the glowing necklace on my chest and then at Roman in the mirror. With his dark golden eyes, he stared at it too. He wasn't going to reject me. He didn't want me to hurt anymore. He wanted me to be his. That was all.

He snaked one of his hands around my throat, pulled me closer, and then brushed his lips against my neck. I sucked in a breath, tingles shooting down my arms.

"Mine," he murmured against my ear.

His fingers moved down my forearm, and he rested his large, callous hand on my inner thigh. Inch by inch, he pushed his bedsheet from my legs until I was bare to him.

Grasping my jaw in one hand and fingering my folds with the other, he smirked against my neck, his breath fanning my skin. "Mine."

He slipped two fingers inside of me and began to slowly and softly push them in and out. I clenched, already feeling the wetness pool between my legs.

"Roman," I breathed, eyes fluttering closed.

He growled lowly in my ear, "Look at me, Isabella."

I opened my eyes and gazed at him through the mirror, my pussy tightening again.

"Mine." He gripped my chin tighter and placed his lips just below my jaw. "You're mine. *This*"—his fingers stilled for the shortest moment—"is mine."

Pure pleasure pulsed through me. My pussy tightened around his fingers, and I nodded my head. "It feels so good." My toes curled into his bedsheets. "Please don't stop."

He pulled me closer to him until he pressed his hardness against my backside. I parted my lips, trying to form coherent words. He curled his fingers, hitting my G-spot, and I cried out.

"Say it, Isabella," he said, his thumb gently stroking my jaw.

Golden eyes stared back at me through the mirror, devouring every single inch of my body, and I furrowed my brows.

"Tell me you're mine."

"I'm yours, Roman." I gripped on to his fingers as they moved faster, massaging my G-spot. "Oh Moon Goddess, I am yours."

When he tugged on my nipple, I threw my head back and came. I pulled my trembling legs together as wave after wave of pleasure rolled through me and pumped out of me. My whole body felt like it was on fire—a good kind of fire.

He gazed at me through the mirror and watched his mate come.

When I fully relaxed against his body, I whimpered. Oh Goddess, I hadn't felt that good in almost a month. I turned to face my mate, my wolf needing more and more and more from him. With his hard cock pressing against the front of his gray sweatpants, he rested his hands on the pillows behind him and leaned back, eyeing my bare breasts.

I grasped him through his pants, moving my hand up and down his length and needing him inside of me, and then I leaned down to press my lips against his waistband. He stared at my ass in the mirror, and I arched, knowing that he would love every moment of this.

He pushed a hand through my hair and swore under his breath. "Bend over more," he said, pressing a hand onto the center of my back, making me arch harder for him.

I pulled down his pants and took him in my hand.

"I want to see your pussy drip while you suck my cock."

I clenched as I leaned down further, giving my mate the view that he wanted, and wrapped my lips around the head of his cock. After swirling my tongue around it, I took him down my throat until my lips pressed against his hips, and I gagged. He shuddered with pleasure, grasped harder on my hair, and held my head down on him.

"Fuck, Isabella," he groaned.

I took his balls in my hand and squeezed lightly, flicking my tongue against them.

He leaned back against the bed again and relaxed. "Damn, you do that so fucking well."

After forcing him deeper down my throat to get him as far down as I could, I gazed up at him through teary eyes. My nipples pressed against his thighs, and I groaned as I let them glide against his skin.

He reached under my body, groped one of my breasts, took my nipple between his fingers, and squeezed lightly. "Your tits are so fucking nice," he said.

I pressed my thighs together, clenching, and watched him smirk into the mirror again.

"Look at your pussy." He pinched my nipple harder, and I moaned. "It's dripping for me." He pressed his hand against my head, holding me down on him again. "I bet you can't fucking wait for me to fuck you, can you?"

I whimpered, and he trailed his hand down to my pussy,

brushing his two fingers against my clit. When they pressed against it, my ass jerked up into the air, the pressure from his fingers almost too much to handle.

He growled, picked me up off of him, and set me on my hands and knees. After grasping a fistful of my hair from behind, he spit on his fingers, pressed them against my clit, and made me watch him touch me in the mirror.

My pussy tightened, wanting to be filled, and I pushed my hips back against his to feel his hard cock graze against my wet pussy. "Please, Roman," I begged, curling my fingers into the mattress. "I need you."

He seized my hips and thrust his cock harder against my entrance, making me clench. "Mine," he said, pushing himself inside of me and filling me. He grabbed both of my elbows and pulled me back to him, so his chest was against my back.

This was what I had been craving all night. Just him. Burying his cock deep inside of me. Thrusting against me. Taking me. *Claiming* me.

He pulled out and then slammed himself back into me, making my breasts bounce. He stilled, breathed against my ear, and then finally began to pump in and out. My pussy tightened around him, and he pulled me even closer. I watched his biceps bulge in the mirror each time he thrust into me, each time my breasts bounced, each time my pussy tightened harder and harder around him.

His body glistened with a thin layer of sweat, and a dark piece of his hair bounced against the middle of his forehead. Brows furrowed together, eyes on me and me only, canines emerging from his lips, he grasped my chin and pressed his lips to mine, kissing me hard.

"Fuck," he mumbled on my lips. He pulled out of me, hopped off of the bed, and grabbed me by the ankle. "Come here."

I wrapped my legs around his waist as he picked me up and

thrust me against the wall. He kissed me softly, sliding his cock back into me. I drew him closer to me, as close as I could get him, and kissed him hard. I never wanted to stop this. I never wanted to stop kissing him, to stop loving him.

Roman was mine.

He kissed down my neck, still pumping in and out of me. His lengthened canines brushed against my soft spot, and my core tightened.

"Please, Roman." I needed his mark.

When his teeth brushed against my skin, everything slowed down. Every breath he took warmed my neck, making me hot and needy for him. It was like my heat, but it actually felt *good*. He slowed his thrusts and grasped my ass tighter.

My toes curled as I waited and waited and waited for him to finally sink his teeth into my neck. And yet, he still seemed to resist me.

Instead of biting me, he pressed his lips hard to my skin. And though pleasure was pulsing through my body, I couldn't help feeling bad. Even after everything I had gone through, he still didn't want to mark me. After all the pain and all the heartbreak and all the heat, he'd rather I was not marked by him.

He thrust one last time up into my tight pussy, grasped on to my shoulders, and held me to him. When his cock pulse inside of me, I felt myself release.

"Oh Goddess," I said.

After sighing into my neck, he pulled out of me and rested me onto his bedsheets. He stared at me, his brows drawn together. "Isabella, you're so beautiful."

My chest felt tight, and I didn't know what to say.

He lay next to me, his head on my shoulder, and wrapped an arm around my waist. Though his mint scent always calmed me, my heart was beating rapidly in my chest. I was overwhelmed.

Everything that had happened this past week—these past two

days—was too much for me. From the necklace to not going right to the Lycans' property when I was going through my heat, like Ryker had told me to—after all that, I'd ended up here in my mate's arms.

And that was when the first tear fell.

vled again, and my wolf purred for him.
cting like a child."

or suddenly opened, and Roman's wolf stared down at
g the one spot on my neck where my wolf had been
im to bite me.

CHAPTER 43

ISABELLA

I cried out every single emotion I had felt this past
month.

Hurt. Betrayal. Sorrow. Rage. Passion.

My fingers grazed against my necklace, sending a wave of
heat through my body. It felt different around my neck. It meant
something now.

Roman pulled me to his chest, placed a kiss on my forehead,
and massaged my scalp. "Why are you crying, my dear Isabella?"

I threw my arms around his neck and held on for dear life.
Roman wanted me. He really did. He might've still been angry
with me—I didn't know—but this necklace and lying in his bed
with his strong arms wrapped around me proved that he still
wanted me.

"I thought you were going to reject me," I whispered through
my tears.

"Reject you? What made you think I'd reject you?"

My lips trembled. "Because you refused to mark me, you told

me to leave without even placing the necklace on me, and you let Vanessa into your home. I-I didn't hear from you for almost a whole month."

He tugged me closer to his chest, lips against my ear. "I waited three years for you. I would never reject you, especially since this is all my fault."

When I stopped sobbing, I pulled away from him and stared into his golden eyes. I needed to tell him everything. I didn't care if it hurt him. I didn't care if he didn't tell me what had happened here. I wanted the air to be clear between us.

"I was going to let Raj mark me."

"I know," he said tensely. "I could smell him on you."

I swallowed hard, on the verge of tears again. "And that rogue … I was only doing it for work. I didn't mean to kiss him. I didn't want to kiss him."

"You kissed one of them?"

I pressed my lips together. There was no hiding *anything* now. I wanted to start clean. "Yes, I kissed one of them, and then I killed him even though my mission didn't call for it." I swallowed hard. My mission was supposed to be to get information out of the rogues, not to kiss them, not to kill them, not to run to Roman's house afterward. I'd fucked up my one solo mission by getting my heat and killing the rogue. "I killed him," I whispered.

What would Ryker say about that?

"You *willingly* kissed one of them," Roman repeated, hurt showing in his eyes.

I ran a hand through my hair. I should be back at the Lycans' now, reporting to Ryker that I'd failed the mission … but I wanted to be here with my mate, who was now seething because I'd told him I kissed that rogue.

"Roman, stop," I pleaded. "It was for my job."

He stood abruptly, tugging on his sweatpants. His teeth lengthened into canines, and he eyed my neck. My body shuddered as I just thought about him plunging them into my flesh

and claiming me. But instead, he
and slammed the door.

I grabbed his shirt and follow
"Roman, where are you going? I don
this game. Come on." This was ridicu
to kiss that rogue, but I'd had to for *wor*

The muscles in his back were tense.
Please." He shut and locked his office doo

And just as it did, the bitch herse
bedroom, dressed in only a T-shirt—Rom
one from the day at the café. She curled her
a smirk.

"Isabella?" She furrowed her brows toge
doing here?"

I glared at her. "You need to pack your bags
"Leave?" She grabbed my chin, inhaled dee
"You don't make the rules around here, *Izzy*. R
Roman wants me around."

I snatched her elbow and twisted it, making
I'm not in the mood for you. Two, I'm not going to
anymore like I used to. Three, if you touch me like t
pull your shoulder out of its socket so fast that you
know I did."

I released her elbow, and she pulled it back and the
on Roman's office door.

"Roman!" Her voice was so high-pitched and squeak
thought I was going to lose my mind. "Roman!"

He growled from inside of his office, "Leave, Vanessa."

She pouted her lips. "Please, Roman."

"I'm not going to tell you again."

She marched straight out of the hallway and slammed
door shut. What was the goddamn point of that? To get on
nerves?

I pounded my fist on the office door. "Roman, let me in."

EMILIA
He gro
"Stop a
The d
me, eyein
begging

CHAPTER 44

ROMAN

J'd walked out of the room, so I wouldn't mark her out of anger. Just listening to her tell me she'd willingly kissed one of those rogues made me furious. All I'd wanted was to thrust her against the bed and sink my teeth into her.

But I'd waited three years—three fucking years. I wanted our moment to be special. Not rash.

I wasn't Ryker. I wasn't going to mark a woman out of pure rage—even if she was my woman.

She glared up at me. "You can't be angry with me, Roman. It was work. It wasn't like I willingly let someone that I knew liked me live in the pack house and walk around in my own fucking clothes while my mate was chasing her dreams."

I clenched my jaw, trying to hold back my wolf, who could never relax when he was with her. He was always there, always vying for her attention, always wanting her to submit to him.

In the heat of the moment, I pulled her into my office, slammed the door shut, and pressed her against it. She smelled so fucking sweet; I couldn't help stuffing my face into the crook of her neck and inhaling. My teeth brushed against her soft spot. "I'm not angry with you," I said tensely, fighting with my wolf to stay in control. I pulled away momentarily. "I just want you too fucking bad."

I needed to put space between us, or I would be one more moment away from taking her out of rage and pure, innate need. I stepped back but grasped her hands. "All I want is to mark what is mine." I eyed that lovely little neck of hers again and resisted my wolf. "To show everyone that you are *mine*."

Her cheeks flushed. "What's stopping you?"

She always knew exactly what to say to bring my wolf to the surface. I stepped back, bumping into my desk so I wouldn't jump at her.

"I don't want to mark you out of anger," I said slowly.

She frowned, thinking for a few moments, and then she took my hand and placed it on her fragile neck. When my fingers brushed over her soft spot, she shook with utter bliss, and I growled.

She was mine. Only mine. All mine.

"Isabella," I warned.

"Roman," she whispered. "Don't make me *make you* mark me."

She brushed her hand across the front of my pants, and I hardened at her touch.

"You know I have ways of making you do things."

She had gushed about her parents' *moment* when we were kids, hanging out in my parents' backyard. She always told me how she imagined her moment—finding her mate, kissing him under the moon, inside a garden of moonflowers. I wanted to give her that; she deserved it after what I'd put her through.

But now … it was all about to be ruined.

I growled one last time, and she tilted her head away from me, giving me a clear view of her neck—right where she wanted me to mark her.

"Roman," she whispered again, "imagine your mark right here." She gazed up at me with those big blue eyes and drew my fingers across her neck. "Your teeth sinking into my neck, claiming me." She blushed and sucked in a breath. "How good it would look on me."

I cursed under my breath. She would break me. Right here. Right now.

She slipped her hand into my pants and grasped my hard cock. "Don't you think your mark on me would look sexy, Roman?"

Control, Roman. Control.

She stepped around me, hopped up onto my desk, and pulled me closer to her until I was pressing against her wet … fucking … pussy. "Mark me, Roman."

Mark mate.

I wrapped my hand around her throat and pulled her closer to me, my teeth against her neck. I brushed my thumb against her jaw and growled. She was mine.

"Let me show everyone—Cayden, Raj, Ryker—that I'm yours and yours only."

"Mine," I growled. "*Mine.*"

"Yours," she said breathlessly.

My canines brushed against her skin. She was mine, and I was going to claim her.

CHAPTER 45

ISABELLA

*S*omeone knocked at the door, and Roman pulled away from me but didn't stop staring. The sunlight bounced off his eyes, making them a golden sea. All I wanted was for him to drop this tough-guy act and sink his teeth into my neck. Claiming me.

Roman readjusted himself and opened the door.

Cayden stood outside, running a hand through his thick locks and pacing back and forth. "Where have you been? We have a—"

Ryker appeared down the hall, storming toward Roman's office with a tight jaw and even tighter fists. "Isabella, I need to talk to you. Now," he said.

My eyes widened. *Shit. Shit. Shit.* I had known I should've called him or gone back to the Lycans' or something.

Without giving me a chance to speak, Roman growled and pulled me behind him. Ryker stepped forward, but Roman didn't back down. He growled again, his nails lengthening into claws.

Vanessa opened her door. "What's going on out here?" she

asked. "Ooh, a love triangle." She leaned against the doorframe and looked between us three. "I didn't think you had it in you, Isabella."

Roman and Ryker both growled, causing her to snap her lips closed—thankfully. Because if they hadn't, I would have done it myself.

"Get out of my house," Roman said through his teeth to Ryker.

"I'm not talking to you. I'm talking to Isabella, one of *my* Lycans."

Oh no. This was bad. Bad. Bad. Bad. Bad. Bad.

They stepped closer to each other, and I moved between the two of them, placing my hands on each of their chests before they could kill each other.

What was wrong with these two? Hell, what was wrong with all these big-headed, testosterone-filled men?

Roman pulled my wrist away from Ryker's chest, but I held my arm steady. "Stop it."

"This is your fault, Roman." Ryker seethed, eyes flickering to a vicious black.

"My fault?" Roman growled. "What the fuck is my fault?"

I gnawed on the inside of my cheek and turned to Ryker, placing both of my hands on him. They needed to be as far apart as I could get them. Two leaders—two violent and vicious leaders —facing off in the middle of Roman's hallway with me between them both ... that would end badly. Roman wrapped one arm around my waist, holding me close to him.

Cayden stood behind Ryker, running his hands through his hair. He gazed at me with eyes that pleaded for me to stop them because he sure as hell couldn't. "This isn't the time for—"

Roman pulled me out of the way again and pushed Ryker. "Get off of my property. This is, what, the second or third time you've shown up without my permission?"

"I don't need your permission to talk to one of my Lycans."

"She's not yours," Roman growled.

Cayden cleared his throat, yet neither one of them heard it. So, I stepped around them to Cayden to see what this whole fuss was about.

Vanessa stood next to him, her eyes wide, hanging off of every single word Cayden said. "She's what?" she asked, her voice barely audible. A tear rolled down her cheek.

Cayden frowned at me. "Jane is gone, and so is Raj—that Lycan from your pack—Isabella."

"What do you mean, they're gone?"

"How do you just disappear?" Vanessa cried out, black drops of mascara running down her cheeks.

"They're gone," Cayden said again, nodding to Ryker, who shoved Roman into the wall.

They were seconds away from going at it, but I couldn't care at that moment. The one reason I had become a Lycan was to protect, and now, my partner and my mate's sister had been taken.

"Ryker said that the rogues took them."

"The rogues took them?" I asked in disbelief.

When Cayden nodded his head, I marched right over to the two men and pushed them both back.

"Stop!" I shouted, my jaw clenched. Both of their heads snapped to me, and I gazed at Ryker. "Is it true?"

Roman growled, but I placed a hand on his chest, hoping that it'd calm him enough to get us through this.

"Were they both really taken?" My voice wavered.

"Who was taken?" Roman asked.

Ryker gave him a long look, and then he nodded at me. Despite his overt anger, Ryker seemed calm about the situation, as if something like this had happened before. "Jane and Raj are gone."

I pressed my lips together, a heap of guilt washing over me. This was my fault. "How do you know that rogues took them?"

"Jane? What was my sis—" Roman asked.

"Their scent was all over Raj's last known location."

My heart sank in my chest. I should've been there with him. I should've been there. This was my fault. They were gone because of me, because I had been afraid of being marked by him or some rogues. If I had been there, I could've helped him. Now, he had been ... taken.

Roman tensed behind me, suddenly becoming quiet. Vanessa wiped her tears with the back of her hand, her hiccups louder than before. Cayden awkwardly patted her shoulder, trying to calm her down.

"Maybe they're just mates and decided to sneak away," she cried.

"This is my fault," I said. "If I had just come back to the Lycans' when I started my heat, like we'd decided ... if I had stayed there and not run away like I did ..."

It was written all over Ryker's face that he thought it was my fault, too, but he said, "It's not your fault." He sighed deeply through his nose and gazed back at Roman. "It's his."

The vein in Roman's neck pulsed violently, and his eyes turned darker than I had ever seen them. "It's my fault that my sister got abducted by rogues? Okay. Keep telling your dirty little lies to my mate to get her to like you." He seethed.

Ryker growled, "You tracked his scent. You were the only person at his last known location. You refused to mark your own fucking mate. If you had just done it, we wouldn't be in this situation."

"If you hadn't gone behind my back to take my mate away from me, we wouldn't be in this situation."

"If you weren't so fuck—"

I drown them out. I couldn't bear to listen to their bickering anymore. Not when this was neither of their faults. It was mine.

~

"I can't believe it." Vanessa sobbed. Her cheeks were stained with streaks of black mascara. "Why is this happening? Why would they take her?"

I sat in Roman's chair in his office and rubbed my sweaty palms together. It didn't make sense. These rogues were after alphas, not ordinary wolves. Roman paced around the room, ordering his warriors to guard the perimeters and to track any scents that they could find. Ryker sat on his phone, talking to someone back at the pack house and gazing at me every few seconds.

This was my fault. And he knew it.

Roman growled. "Crying will get us nowhere, Vanessa," he snapped at her, his teeth already lengthened into canines.

Derek ran into the room and sighed in relief when his eyes met mine, but I looked away. He pulled me into a hug, and I barely had enough energy to hug him back. My stomach was twisting with uneasiness.

Why take Jane? She wasn't an alpha. Neither was Raj.

If these rogues were after the alphas ... she shouldn't have been taken.

This was not the rogues' original plan. This might've been done in the heat of the moment after hearing that seven of them had been killed at The Night Raider's full-moon party. They might've left clues or forgotten to hide their tracks.

Ryker gazed up from his phone and nodded to me. "Yeah, she's fine. I'll talk to you later."

When he shut off the phone, I stood up. "Let's go," I said. "We need to find them before something happens." I pursed my lips. "Because of me."

Roman snatched my wrist. "You're not going. You're not leaving this house."

Ryker growled at him, "She's going. This is her job."

I rolled my eyes. Not this again. They were about to waste

another fifteen minutes growling at each other and getting nothing done. I gazed at the warriors in the room.

"Can we have a bit of privacy?" I asked, nodding to Roman.

Ryker eyed us. "Two minutes." He looked back at his phone and tapped on it. "Then, we have to go."

Once everyone left, I shut the door and pressed my hands against Roman's chest, resting my forehead against his. "I have to go, Roman," I whispered.

He grabbed my hands. "No."

"I do."

"They'll take you too," he said, a sudden sadness in his voice. It was like everyone he had ever loved was taken from him, over and over and over, and he could do nothing about it. He squeezed my hands. "They can't take you. I've waited too long."

"Nobody will take me, Roman." I smiled. "I hope you have enough confidence in my abilities to believe that."

"I do." He nodded and leaned back against the oak desk, pulling me into his taut chest. "I'm sorry that I didn't put you on the warriors. I really am. I regret that decision every single day of my life, and now, I'm paying for it."

I pushed a stray piece of hair out of his face and gently caressed his cheek. This man.

"But you can't go."

I clenched my jaw lightly. Why couldn't it be easy? Why couldn't he let me protect him and his family?

"I'm going whether you like it or not," I said.

"They'll take you. They took Jane to get at me. What makes you think they won't take you too?"

"Why do you think they took Jane?" I asked, trying to claw at any piece of information that I could.

He paused for a moment. "To weaken me. Just like they had taken Mom to weaken Dad."

I gnawed on the inside of my cheek and shook my head.

"They haven't done this with anyone else in the past seven years. No other pack. What makes you so special?"

Of course, he was very special to me, but why was he special to these rogues? His parents had died years ago, and if these rogues were a new group, like Ryker had told me, then they shouldn't have any information about his parents' death; They shouldn't even care.

Roman quickly gazed at the closed door, clenched his jaw, and growled lowly, "I don't know."

I gently patted his chest. I didn't know either, but I knew that something wasn't right, and I would find out what that was before things turned from bad to worse.

CHAPTER 46

ISABELLA

I grabbed Roman's collar and pulled him into a long, passionate kiss. "Nothing will happen. I'm going to bring Jane and Raj back. Your sister will be okay," I said.

His breath warmed my neck. And I ached for him to have me now, claim me now, take me as his now, but we had a situation that we couldn't ignore for another second.

He pushed some hair out of my face and drew his thumb down my lip, making me shiver.

"When I get back, I expect you to mark me, Roman. I want the whole thing—a bouquet of moonflowers, a date under the moonlight, your teeth in my neck."

He chuckled. "You want it romantic?"

After curling my fingers around his belt loops, I pulled him closer. "Of course not. I want you to lay out a nice dinner for us and then spread my legs and eat what you really want to eat," I said.

He growled lowly, making me clench. All I wanted to do was

push him against his desk, climb on top of him, and let him have me, but someone knocked on the door, ruining the moment.

"Isabella," Ryker said from outside, "time to go."

I frowned at Roman and walked to the door.

He watched me with those dark eyes. "When you come back to me, my dear Isabella, I'll be waiting to claim every inch of your body."

"Remember that, *Alpha*." I smirked back at him. "I expect no less."

Ryker stood outside the door, tapping his fingers against the doorframe, and raised a brow at me. I brushed past him, trying to hide my happiness that Roman had promised to mark me. It should've been done by now, but his promise that he would made me all giddy inside.

The ride to the pack house was silent, only the stiff sound of Ryker's breathing filling the car. I gazed out the windshield, watching the trees fly by. This wasn't right. Something had gone terribly, terribly wrong.

"What're you thinking about?" Ryker asked, one hand on the steering wheel, the other on the gearstick.

"This is my fault," I said.

He sighed deeply through his nose. "Bella, it's not your fault. At least you didn't let one of those rogues mark you. Do you ... do you have any ideas about who it could've been or why they would've taken Jane and Raj?"

Think, Isabella. Roman should've been taken, not his sister. Why target Roman and his family?

"I think something is going on with Roman." I dug my fingers into my palms, breaking through the skin. "He's acting weird."

Ryker suddenly became quiet. "He's been acting weird. Why wouldn't he mark you, even after your heat?" He pulled onto the Lycans' property.

Lycans ran back and forth in front of our car, trying to organize as quickly as possible to defend the surrounding packs from the rogues.

"Exactly," I said, watching him. "Don't you think it's weird that they didn't take an alpha, but his sister?"

He nodded his head, jaw twitching just a smidgen.

"The only explanation I can think of is that Roman did something that angered them, something that he's not telling me."

Lie.

I kicked my feet back and forth under the seat and gazed out the window. "And he wouldn't mark me, even after everything I've been through, after the heat, after running from rogues. He didn't even seem like he wanted me. He looked at me with so much disgust and pity. Barely would touch me the whole time I was there." Lie. "Only when you came to the house."

Ryker furrowed his brows. "His wolf seemed to want to keep you there, but *he* did seem a bit distant. Do you think he's in on this?"

I shook my head. "I don't know, but I want to find out."

He parked the car in front of the pack house and rested one hand on the steering wheel. "This is your mate that we're talking about, Bella. If you do this, you'll have to go against your innate instincts. And if you find that he is working with the rogues, you know what you'll have to do, right?"

"I'll have to kill him," I said quietly.

He gazed at me, nearly making me squirm. "You know, if it comes to that, there are plenty"—he paused for longer than a moment—"of wolves here who'd step up and be the man that you've always needed."

I took a deep breath, my gaze drifting to his lips for a second. "I know."

He nodded his head. "Why don't you lead this mission then?"

I raised my brow at him. "Me? You want me to lead?"

"Yes." He smiled. "I think it'd be perfect. Redemption for you."

CHAPTER 47

ISABELLA

During this dire time, I delegated duties to the Lycans. Some people were to watch Roman. Others were to meet wolves from my pack at The Night Raider's Café to talk about Jane's disappearance. Ryker was to search the outskirts of Roman's property with me every night.

It went well for the first week. I cut off communication with Roman, and I spied on him.

Nothing was off, and I was just hoping that he would do something—anything—fishy to get Ryker off my back, so I could breathe and complete this mission. I wanted nothing more than for him to trust me again. Jane and Raj were in trouble, and if my suspicions were correct, I *needed* Ryker to trust me.

That was the only way any of this would work.

Ryker appeared at my door, dressed in a tight gray spandex training shirt. "You ready?"

Outside, it was dark, and the moonlight flooded in through

the window. I pushed some papers into my desk drawer. "I need to go over paperwork. I'll meet you there?"

Ryker nodded his head, lips curling into a smirk. "I can do a sweep of his property by myself. Finish your work."

I stood up and placed my hand on his hard chest, curling my fingers into the thick muscle. "No. When I finish, I'll be there." I smiled up at him, my gaze traveling down the scar on his neck. So large, so prominent, so sexy. "I promise."

He paused for a few moments and then nodded his head. I could hear the quickened pace of his heartbeat, and I looked down his body for a moment—a mere moment—*unintentionally.* He tensed, his biceps flexing under his shirt.

My cheeks flushed, and I looked away. I shouldn't be feeling this way. I didn't want to feel this way. "I'll be there," I said.

When he left, I sat in my room. I didn't have work to do, and I didn't have papers to read. I had something else that I needed done, something that required Ryker leaving in order for me to do.

I picked up my phone and called Derek.

After the third ring, he answered. "Izzy, what's up?"

"I need you to do something for me."

"Anything."

"Get me Roman's journal with pack notes. It's on his desk. Meet me at The Night Raider's Café in a half hour."

He scoffed, "You want me to steal Roman's journal?" I could hear the confusion in his voice. "Why? Do you think he has something to do with this?"

"Please, Derek," I said, tapping my fingers on my wooden desk.

After a few moments, he sighed, and I knew that I had him.

"See you there," he said.

~

Derek stood at the entrance of The Night Raider's Café with a notebook stuffed under his shirt. "I can't believe that I stole his fucking notebook for you. You'd better have a reason—"

"Is it the right one?"

He furrowed his brows. "What do you mean?"

I grabbed it and flipped through the pages, sighing when it was his actual journal and not the one with sketches of me. If Derek had brought that one, I'd have been screwed. Though I didn't need the notebook for any particular reason. I needed it to distract Ryker for a bit longer. Maybe it'd even help me get entry into his guarded office.

After pressing my lips to Derek's cheek, I thanked him, shifted back into my wolf, grabbed the notebook in my teeth, and ran through the woods.

"Hey! You know he's going to be looking for that!" Derek shouted after me.

I howled in reply and raced toward Ryker's scent.

When I found him at Roman's borders, I shifted into my human, standing bare and naked in front of him.

He looked at me with furrowed brows. "What's that?"

"Roman's notebook."

His eyes widened. "How'd you get it?"

"Vanessa—that bitch who was living with Roman—gave it to one of the Lycans when they met at The Night Raider's Café earlier this evening. She gave it to me just as I was about to leave."

He took the notebook from me. "What's it say?"

I swallowed hard and shook my head. "Let's read it at home." I gazed at Roman's property, knowing that *he* was in these woods, probably watching us. "If we find anything important, we can confront Roman about it tomorrow."

Ryker nodded his head in agreement. Once we did a thorough sweep of Roman's property, Ryker led me back to the Lycans' and to his office.

For the first time, he unlocked the door for me and let me

walk into the room. Unlike Roman's office, Ryker's was a mess. Papers all over the place, his workout gear slung over a chair, locked cabinets that looked *neat*.

I sat on one of the spare chairs and watched him unlock the top drawer of his desk and put the notebook inside of it. After shutting and locking the drawer, he put the key into his pocket. There were so many locks for someone so open with his Lycans about who he was and what the missions were really about.

"We should go through the notebook tonight," I said. "I won't be able to wait until morning."

He chuckled lowly and walked around the desk, placing his hands on my shoulders from behind and squeezing lightly. "You need rest, Isabella. You've been working for far too long on this. I will go through it by myself, and tomorrow, I'll tell you what I found."

"But—"

His hands traveled down my arms, light enough to make me shiver. He breathed against my neck. "Go, Isabella," he said into my ear.

I swallowed my fear of what would happen next—what I would allow to happen next—and turned around to face him. The room was dimly lit, making his features look more alluring. This was my plan, and I wasn't about to let it slip through my fingers.

"You should get some rest too," I said quietly, suggesting something more sinful than I could ever even imagine. I brushed my fingers against his forearms.

We stared at each other for a few moments, and then his gaze fell to my chest. "Where's your mate's necklace?"

"I took it off."

His eyes darkened. "Why?"

I stepped toward him, so we were inches away from each other. "Why do you think?" I asked quietly, keeping my gaze on him.

Again, he paused and just stared at me, and I was terrified that he'd see right through me. That he'd see that this was all a lie. My heart raced when he stepped closer, pushing me against his desk.

"For this?" he said.

I swallowed hard and drew a finger down his chest, flirting just like Raj had told me. And in a moment, Ryker's lips were hovering over my own, millimeters away from pressing against me. My breath caught in my throat, and I placed my hands on his hips, fingering the waistband of his pants.

"For this," I affirmed.

He pressed his lips to mine, and I tugged him closer by the pants pockets, snuck my hand into his right pocket, and stole the key to his office.

CHAPTER 48

ROMAN

I hadn't slept in the past week.

Every day that Isabella wasn't here and wasn't marked killed me on the inside. She was doing her job, being the Lycan that she was, and trying to find my sister while I tried desperately to find some kind of trail.

For the first time in a long time, I was all alone. No mate. No sister. No family. And it was my worst fear—to have nobody that I loved and cared about with me. All I had ever asked the Moon Goddess for was a family who loved me as much as I loved them, a family I could cherish every day.

It was funny how life turned out.

No, I hadn't wanted Isabella to leave, but I'd needed to let her go. It was the only way that I could get her to see that I really cared about her and that I valued her strength and saw beauty in it.

A sharp, piercing pain shot through my chest. I lay in my bed, staring up at my ceiling, and let my wolf whimper. There was only one time that I had felt this pain before, and it was the night of the full-moon party. Right before I left to find my mate, right when she was off, *working* and kissing one of those foul-mouthed rogues.

I didn't want to think about what she was doing this time because, this time, it was for me. Whatever she was doing was to find Jane and Raj, and I had to trust her. I had to trust her to come home to me when all of this was finished. I had to trust her to choose me. I had to be enough for her.

CHAPTER 49

ISABELLA

From the dark forest, I watched Ryker through his office window. He sat at his desk on the first floor of the Lycans' pack house and pushed a hand through his hair, reading Roman's journal. Exactly three hours ago, I'd had the chance to sneak into the office, to go through every piece of paper in his desk, and to confirm every one of my suspicions.

I'd invited Ryker over at eleven p.m. to *talk* about the information in Roman's journal. Only he thought this *talking* was code for fucking me. He'd had that small, *innocent* smirk on his lips when I asked him, the one he had given me at the stream the day he told me I'd be a good fit for the Lycans.

Though he had only kissed me once last night, he'd pulled me toward him like he had wanted me for far longer than I had thought—for days or even weeks—and told me he was thankful that Roman hadn't marked me. That Roman didn't deserve me.

Ryker flipped to another page, slammed the book closed, and stormed out of the house. He appeared at the back door and took his shirt off. My heart raced at the sight, and I crouched behind a tree. I couldn't believe that I was doing this.

Once he surveyed the woods, he stripped his pants off. My gaze raked down his body. Nothing was physically different about him, but something was off.

Something had always been off about him. Making me go behind Roman's back to become a Lycan. The sudden influx of rogues after he became leader of the Lycans. Telling me to go directly to the pack house instead of to my mate when I was going through my heat. It was like he didn't want me to be with Roman.

He stepped into the moonlight and shifted into his large black wolf. He gazed around once more and then sprinted into the woods. I waited a few moments and ran after him, keeping a good distance. I wanted him to take me wherever he was going.

But he didn't run in any unusual direction, like I'd thought he would. He took his normal route through the pack. The one he took every night, passing my room, passing the pack house, passing our training area. We must've run for an hour.

I didn't know if he knew that I was following him, so I slowed my pace. And finally, he ran off of the property. We trekked through the woods, going deeper and deeper into uncharted territory, known only in myths as Rogue Territory.

There were vines and jagged rocks hidden in the unkept grasslands. The ground was wet, like a dirty swamp. We ran through it, mud matting my fur and hiding my scent.

He continued to run faster, navigating like he had run through here a million times and making it difficult to keep up, but again ... he wasn't about to leave me like that. I was going to uncover the truth.

We ran for another fifteen minutes until a stone wall appeared over the grass. He slowed by it, sticking his nose to the ground and sniffing. I stayed back, hiding behind a tree.

Was this the rogue hideout? Had he known where it was this whole time?

My brows furrowed, and when he gazed in my direction, I ducked my head behind the tree and waited a few moments. He let out a low growl, one that was supposed to frighten whoever was watching him, but he didn't intimidate me. Not anymore.

After a few moments, he shifted, walked to the wall, and pulled out one of its stones. A clean pair of clothes was sitting on the other side. He tugged them on, the material fitting him perfectly.

What the—

He gazed around again and waited another five minutes for a rogue to appear at the gate connected to the stone wall. It opened, and my eyes widened.

It was true. It was all true. Ryker knew the rogues. Hell, he could've been working with them if this was what I thought it was.

When they were safely inside of the hideout, I crept up to the wall and leaned against it, ear pressed onto the cold stone.

"You got what we need?" the rogue asked.

"Release them. People are catching on," he said.

My heart pounded. Me. I was the one catching on. Nobody else because they all trusted him. I'd trusted him at one point, but he had tested that trust time and time again.

The rogue growled, "We had a deal. I supply you with idiot rogues who don't know what the hell they're doing so you can kill them, and I get my money."

"Deal's off," Ryker said.

From somewhere deep within the borders, a whole pack of rogues growled, trying to warn him off. I crouched even lower, my heart racing. There were so many of them. So many who could easily overpower anyone—even Ryker.

But it all made sense—from learning rumors of Ryker's past in Roman's journal to snooping around in Ryker's office, figuring out that it was true. He'd turned out to be the one hiring the rogues, so *he* could reap the rewards, so he could clear his name, so he could make the nasty rumors of him raping a woman and getting her pregnant during her heat go away.

And ... I could've been just like that woman, just like Michelle, if I hadn't been careful.

"If we don't get our money, then I'll have to keep them, kill them even. They've been so fucking annoying anyway with all that lovey-dovey shit."

The rogue was talking about Jane and Raj. Were they mates? Maybe they were acting that way to get out. Maybe Raj had a plan.

A branch snapped, and I turned around to see a rogue standing behind me, about to leap at me. Drool was dripping from his bare teeth.

Before I had the chance to kill him, he stuck his nose to the air and gave the most vicious howl, alerting the others.

My heart pounded. Everyone could hear it. Every single rogue around. Even Ryker.

He would know that I'd followed him.

He would know that I really knew.

He would know that he would have to kill me.

So, I leaped into the air, sank my teeth into the rogue's neck, and pulled out his throat. Then, I sprinted through the woods as fast as I could. Knowing that I needed to run for my life.

CHAPTER 50

ISABELLA

*T*he thunderous echo of hundreds of paws hitting the ground followed me through the forest. All coming for me. All wanting to kill me.

I knew that they would find me and that they would in fact kill me. Ryker was the one leading them. He'd lied to me, lied to everyone about the rogues. He had countless alphas being tracked and hunted like animals, hurting them instead of protecting them.

And I was about to be next.

My heart beat wildly against my chest. Beads of sweat matted my fur. I ran faster and pushed myself harder, letting my wolf take control. She had trained for this moment forever. And although Roman hadn't believed in me, although he'd lied to me to protect me, although I'd made the stupid decision anyway to join the Lycans, this was not how I would go out.

I would not be stopped by a pack of rogues that I had been

trained to kill. I would not be killed by a man who had betrayed us all for whatever selfish reason he had.

The trees stopped any moonlight from hitting the forest floor, but I ran in the dark, focusing on the path in front of me—my self-made path—jumping over branches and running between trees.

The rogues' faint, pungent scent drifted into my nose.

Moon Goddess, help me, please.

All I wanted was to see Roman, the only man I had ever loved, the man I wished I had stayed with weeks ago. This wasn't how I wanted my life to end. I wanted to see him one last time.

A tree branch cut into my fur, and I whimpered, but I didn't stop. I ran for another mile, sprinting right off of Rogue Territory and toward the familiar scent I had always called home. Mint.

When the pounding slowed and became fainter, I paused behind a tree and shifted into my human. Blood spewed out of my side, and I put as much pressure on it as I could. I rested against the tree, muffling my whimpers with my hand.

Then, when the rogues became louder again, I gathered all of my energy and ran—in human form—to Roman's pack house. The next mile was longer and harder than the miles I had run through Rogue Territory. But I trudged on through and let out a cry once I was within fifty feet of Roman's property.

Pain shot up and down my side, making me dizzy, making my vision blurry.

Derek—one of the border guards tonight—caught my arm before I fell to the ground and mind-linked Roman. *"Rogues."*

I stumbled out of his grip toward the pack house.

Roman. I wanted to see Roman. I needed to see Roman. I loved Roman.

After throwing the back door of the pack house open, I sprinted into the room—naked and covered in a mix of blood and mud. I couldn't believe this was happening. *What was all of this for?* Every single day that I'd spent getting to know Ryker was all a lie.

"Roman!" I shouted. "Roman!" My Roman.

A light turned on upstairs, and someone shuffled around. I sprinted up the stairs, taking two at a time. Roman appeared at the end of the hallway, rushing out of his room and wearing nothing but some sweatpants.

When he saw me, he hurried to me and pulled me into his chest. "Isabella? Isabella, what's wrong?"

"Rogues," I breathed out, glancing out the window. "Rogues— they're coming."

My first instinct was to kiss him, so that was what I did. I pressed my lips to his, comforted in the feeling of him, wanting him and wanting us and hoping that this wasn't the last moment that I would be with him.

He pushed me away slightly. "You're covered in mud, Isabella." He gazed down at my body. "And blood. You're hurt. Wh—"

"They're coming to kill me," I said.

I knew that they would try to kill me, that they would try to take his whole pack out with them. And again, this was *my* fault. I should've run to the Lycans ... not put Roman in more danger.

But I wanted him, I needed him, and I didn't know who I could trust anymore besides him.

If Ryker hadn't known who I was before, he knew who I was now that I had run directly to my mate. The man he hated. The man who hated him.

Roman furrowed his brows together. Then, his ears flew back, hearing the howls of the rogues. They were approaching the borders quickly. My stomach tightened. Roman's eyes glazed over as he spoke to his warriors through the mind link.

When he turned to me, his teeth had lengthened into canines, his eyes were pure gold, and his minty scent was stronger than ever. "Why are they here?"

I grabbed his hand and squeezed lightly. "Because I know why they took your sister. I know how they did it too." I brushed my hand against the side of his face. "You were right, Roman. You were always right."

"What do you want me to do?" he asked.

It was such a simple question, and I knew exactly what he was planning to do to that man when they caught him.

I grabbed his chin, pressed my lips to his, and pulled away. "Be the alpha that I've always loved. Lead this pack. Kill them."

"We're not ready to take a whole pack of rogues alone," he said. He pulled me down the stairs to the door. The forest was dark and so damn eerie. "You're going to lead us, Isabella." He clenched his jaw and turned toward the woods. "Now, I'll ask again. What do you need me to do?"

Roman wanted me to lead.

The thought made me feel butterflies, but I couldn't think about them for long. I tapped into the disorderly pack mind link, trying to sort through the million and one things being said in it.

Give me the damn strength to figure this out, Moon Goddess.

After stepping into the forest, I gulped. *"Don't attack them,"* I commanded through the mind link.

Roman and I walked farther into the night to see the whole pack of warriors standing at full attention in front of the pack house.

"They're here for me."

I stepped forward, but Roman grabbed my wrist.

"What are you doing?"

"What I need to do. Trust me." I removed myself from his grasp. "You want orders? I order the whole pack to stand down. Don't attack unless I tell you to attack."

The warriors parted for me to walk through them. Ryker stood at the edge of the forest, watching and waiting for me, with the whole pack of ferocious rogues behind him.

He stepped into the moonlight, but none of the other wolves

moved. They all stood there, staring. And I stepped toward him. He took a defensive stance, not nervously but cautiously.

"I already contacted the Lycans," I said. "They know where the rogues' hideout is."

Nobody spoke a word, and then he stepped forward again. "You're lying."

"You don't intimidate me, Ryker." My nails lengthened into claws. "Is Michelle at that rogues' place?" I asked.

He tensed, his jaw clenched. "How do you know about her?"

My teeth lengthened into canines. "Or did you kill her?"

"Stop." His voice was low, and he was shaking with anger.

"Michelle, the woman who used to be a Lycan before me, the woman who you let stay in your pack house, the woman you marked when she was going through her heat, the woman who gave you a child."

He growled.

"It was all inside of your desk. Everything that I needed to figure it out." I shook my head and actually let out a laugh. "You know, that's not even the funny part. The funny part is that she tried to kill you." My fingers brushed against the side of my neck, mimicking the scar on his neck. "Too bad she didn't succeed."

He shifted and ran at me with full force. The wolves behind me got into their stance, but I didn't move.

Instead, I let him leap in my direction, and then I swiped my claws right on his scar. The weakest part of him. They cut into his skin, shredding it almost instantly. He leaped back. His wound was bleeding profusely, and I held my side tighter to stop *my* blood.

"You always told me not to fight when angry, Ryker. You should've listened to your own advice." I transformed into my wolf and sprinted at him.

The difference between us was that I wasn't angry. I was a protector, born under the Second Wolf Moon to keep people safe, and that was what I would do.

Leaping at him, I latched my teeth into his shoulder and somersaulted over him, taking him with me. Ryker sank his teeth into my arm, and I howled. Roman inched his way closer and closer to me, and when he heard me cry out, he shifted and snatched Ryker by the neck.

Like they had done in the hallway a few days ago, they fought, but this time, claws were scratching, blood was spewing, flesh was flying.

Roman's pack started for the rogues, though I told them to stand down, but the rogues wanted no part in a war that they were bound to lose. They ran through the woods, and Roman's pack followed.

Before I could react, Ryker bit into Roman's thigh and tore a hefty piece of flesh right out of it. Roman shifted back into his human form and cradled his leg. My heart raced, and I growled loudly, sinking my teeth into Ryker's thigh and tearing his muscle out of it too.

A thigh for a thigh.

Ryker shifted into his human, stumbling into a tree.

I bared my teeth at him and jogged to Roman, who struggled to stand. After shifting, I pressed my hand to stop the bleeding. And when I turned back to Ryker, he was gone. Roman shook his head, standing strong and trying to follow him. But I knew that it was too late.

I wasn't leaving Roman like this just to chase Ryker. We would destroy him tonight but not before finding our friends.

CHAPTER 51

ISABELLA

Though the path to Rogue Territory was difficult to find, the trail of my blood made it easier. I led Roman's entire pack through the forest, so we could save Jane and Raj before the rogues killed them.

Hundreds of paws pounded against the forest floor, thunderous, like the sound of the rain. But this time, the paws belonged to Roman's wolves, wolves from my pack, wolves that I trusted.

The closer we got to their territory, the more stray rogues were walking through the forest, rogues so weak that I picked them off one by one and didn't stop until we were near their borders.

About half a mile ahead of us, the stone wall was guarded heavily. I stopped, and everyone behind me followed, even Roman. He wanted me to lead because—I was assuming—it was his way of showing me that he trusted me, that he wanted me back for good. The frightened look in his eyes told me that this was the most difficult thing he'd ever faced, but he didn't complain about it.

We ducked behind some trees to stay out of sight. Just like I had done so many times with Ryker, I commanded that the group surround the borders. There weren't as many of us as I had hoped since we still needed to protect the borders at home, but I had to make it work.

When everyone was in position, I turned to Vanessa. She was not the person I'd wanted for this job, and she would probably fuck it up for me, but Roman had insisted.

"You know what to do, right?" I asked her.

She gulped and gazed over at the wall. She had drawn moon-flowers on her arm with Sharpie before we left, pretending to be a Lycan. "Yes," she said quietly. "Anything for Jane."

I gazed over at Roman, who stood a few trees away. *"You sure she's the right person for this? I can—"*

"She is."

I raised a brow at him. She was the fastest runner in the warriors, according to Roman. I didn't believe it, but I needed to believe it. She was our only hope. I pushed her toward the wolves and watched her walk toward them.

Slowly, she approached the rogues. She was to get their attention, get them to chase her, so I could kill each one of them.

When she was a few trees away from the stone wall, she intentionally broke a branch under her foot. "Oops."

Oops, my ass.

Every rogue at the borders turned in her direction. They paused for a moment. Then, they saw the Lycan tattoos on her arm and immediately raced her way. She'd better be fast and not fuck this up.

All she had to do was run all the way back to our pack and not stop once.

She stood there, waiting, and then just as one was about to snatch her, she turned on her heel and ran through the woods as quickly as she could. She whizzed by me, and I listened to that pounding of paws against dirt.

When they all passed me, I waited a few moments. Then, I hopped out from behind the tree, slapped a hand over the slowest rogue's mouth so he couldn't scream, and cut his throat with my claws. Killing him instantly.

I followed behind the group. Picking them off one by one while the rest of Roman's pack moved into the borders to fight anyone inside of the stone walls. Through the mind link, Roman gave the orders to the pack, the exact ones I had given him earlier, leading like the true alpha he was.

Vanessa ran faster than I'd thought she could without faltering. After fifteen minutes of running through the mud, the rogues began to notice that their friends were missing. One turned around, saw me kill his friend, and howled. The rest of them stopped chasing Vanessa and turned on me.

She looked at me with fear in her eyes.

"Go!" I said to her.

She would get killed this way.

She shook her head and sprinted at one of the men. Then, she jumped into the air and sank her teeth into his neck.

In a moment of pure chaos, the rogues turned and sprinted at both of us. Foam dripped from their mouths, rainwater matted their ratty fur, corruption flared within their dark eyes. I bared my bloodied teeth at them and latched on to one as he leaped toward me. Slamming him into the ground, ripping out his neck, watching—only for a moment—as he cried out to the Moon Goddess and shifted into his human, dead.

While Vanessa took on one rogue by herself, I took on the other two. Throwing back my hind leg, I kicked one straight in the jaw and sank my canines into the one in front of me. They both whimpered, but I wasn't finished. They would not only pay for their sins, but they'd pay for Ryker's too.

My claws dug into one of their undersides, swiping over and

over, creating gash after gash, soaking my paws in his blood. It was what I had trained for since I was four, since Luna Raya believed in me, since old man Beck used to tell me his war stories.

Vanessa spat out a jugular, growled in my direction, and then leaped over me to kill the last rogue. She tore his ear off, smacked her paw into the side of his face, and murdered him in cold blood.

Vanessa stood over one of the dead wolves and looked at me, gaze lingering on my side. Though it was still bleeding profusely, I couldn't feel it anymore. All I felt was the potent urge to protect. Protect myself. Protect Vanessa. Protect my mate. Protect my pack members.

When we shifted into our humans, she clamped down on my wound to stop the bleeding. "How can I help you?" she asked, brows furrowed.

I smiled at her and winced. Despite everything, she was actually improving as a warrior. And a small part—a very small part —of me was happy that she was training. She could protect herself now.

"Find me some pine sap. I'll be by the stream fifty yards ahead, washing the wound out." I grasped my side.

With fresh stream water and pine sap, I washed and sealed the wound as best as I could. At least I'd learned something when I worked at the hospital. Dr. Jakkobs would be proud.

Growls from Rogue Territory echoed through the woods, and my stomach turned. The rogues that Vanessa and I'd killed weren't nearly as many rogues that had chased us earlier. There had to be hundreds of them, hiding out in this darkness, that Roman and his pack were fighting.

"I need you to go back to the pack house and ready Dr. Jakkobs and my mom for our arrival back home. Make sure they're waiting at the borders and that the hospital has as many free beds available."

She widened her eyes and drew her brows together. "You think that there are more rogues?" she asked, grasping my fingers. "Do you think Jane is okay?"

"I don't know, Vanessa. I just need you to go, please."

She gazed toward the rogues' hideout. "Are you sure?"

"Yes."

She pulled me close to her, her strawberry scent comforting for once. "Bring Jane back."

I nodded my head and watched her run toward Roman's property. When she disappeared behind the hundreds of trees in the distance, I shifted into my wolf and ran back to the stone gates.

Outside of the borders, the forest was completely empty. I pushed the cold gate opened to find a sea of dead rogues, soaking in blood and gore. After navigating through the bodies, I followed the sounds of Roman's growls into a two-story stone house. People were yelling, rogues were falling, and pups were running through the house.

My heart raced as I just took in the pure chaos. Roman walked into the foyer with a skin-and-bones woman in his arms. Her arms were around his neck but kept slipping down his bare chest. I had the urge to growl at her, but I stopped myself.

Roman was just doing what I had asked of him. Saving the people here.

"Did you find Jane?" I asked him, brows furrowing together.

The woman looked severely malnourished, her lips blue and her ribs poking out of her abdomen. He nodded his head and gazed back into the room. "Someone is unlocking her cage."

I brushed my lips against his, sighing in relief. He was safe. We were safe. For now.

He smiled at me and gazed down at the woman in his arms. "This is Michelle."

My eyes widened at her. Michelle. This was her. The woman

Ryker had raped. The woman Ryker had marked during her heat. The woman he'd left in a cage to hide.

Her eyes were dull and nearly lifeless.

I curled my fingers into his chest. "Find someone to get her home as soon as possible. She needs food and water and to rest in a bed." I smiled at her and walked into the back room to find the rest of the warriors.

Silver dog cages lined the perimeter of the room. Raj sat in the smallest one in the corner, his naked body crouched awkwardly together. His face was bruised severely, and he had a big gash in his side.

After finding a key on one of the rogues' dead bodies, I pulled him out of the cage and into a hug. "I'm so glad you're safe."

Roman walked back into the room, alone, and tugged Jane into his chest. Tears were streaming down her face.

"I'm so sorry," she cried. "I should've been more careful. I should've—" She gazed over Roman's shoulder and growled lowly at me.

I dropped my hand from Raj's shoulder and tossed him a shirt from off of a rogue. Jane frowned at me and curled into Raj's side. He kissed her forehead, and I smiled.

Mates. They were really mates.

"Sorry for being such a bitch to you, Isabella," Jane said. "I should've thought more of you."

Roman placed a hand on my shoulder and squeezed. "We should get back to the pack and create a plan on how to move forward."

Raj furrowed his brows at me. "A plan? For what? You just killed all of the rogues."

Yes, we'd killed the rogues, but we hadn't killed the man who had caused all of this.

But we would. Together.

CHAPTER 52

ISABELLA

*V*anessa and Cayden waited for us at the borders of Roman's territory with Jakkobs, Mom and Dad, and a few other people.

When Vanessa saw us, she threw her arms around Jane and buried her face into her neck. "Thank the Moon Goddess that you're safe."

As Mom ushered a few warrior wolves to the hospital, Dad winked at me and mouthed, *I'm proud of you, kiddo,* waving a moonflower from his garden in his hand. He tossed it to me and then helped Mom with transporting the wounded.

When Vanessa released her death grip on Jane, she turned to Roman and threw her arms around him next. "Thank you!"

Roman stood there, completely still, not daring to hug her back. I pressed my lips together and cleared my throat.

Vanessa immediately pulled away and tugged *me* into a hug. "Isabella, thank you! Thank you so much. I literally can't thank you enough for finding my best friend."

My brows furrowed together, but I awkwardly patted her back.

"We have to talk," I said to Raj and Roman.

Raj nodded his head and pulled Jane to him, placing a lingering kiss on her lips. She brushed her hair behind her shoulder, and for the first time, I saw the mark on her neck, which must've been from Raj.

My eyes widened at the large scar. They'd known each other for only a few days—in a prison—and Jane was already marked. I gazed at Roman. I'd known Roman all my life, and my neck was still bare.

"Come see me before you leave, babe," Jane said to him.

With a lustful glint in her eyes, she smiled and turned away.

Come see me before you leave really meant *come fuck me before you leave.* And if those six little words didn't describe my entire existence, I didn't know what did.

A part of me was jealous of her and of them. I wished I could've taken Roman up to his bedroom and spent just a moment of peace with him, but Ryker was plaguing my mind and haunting me.

When Vanessa and Jane started toward the hospital, I walked to the pack house.

"What's this plan?" Raj asked. "Contact Ryker and tell him we killed the rogues?"

"Ryker ordered the rogues to take you," I said.

He stifled a laugh. "No, he didn't," he said. I stayed quiet, and he furrowed his brows. "You're being serious?"

"I followed him from the Lycans' last night. He ran right to Rogue Territory and was talking business with the rogues. I think he's been giving them money to kill people."

Raj stiffened. "Why would he do that? He's our leader."

"Maybe he wanted power. A few years back, the Lycans nearly wiped out all rogues, didn't they?" Roman said.

Raj nodded.

"No rogues. No Lycans. No power for him."

His motivations hadn't made sense before, but they were starting to all become clearer.

I clutched Dad's moonflower in my palm. "Maybe he felt powerless after Michelle decided to leave. Maybe he thought his masculinity and his alpha-like qualities were being threatened. He wanted to prove himself."

Raj shook his head and stared at the pack house, where warriors were hurrying in and out of.

"You know, I thought it was too easy for the rogues to find us. When you left The Night Raider's Café, I killed all the rogues there. No one from their hideout would've known anything about me being there unless they had an inside contact. I found out that Jane was my mate right after Roman left and we walked to the lake."

"What happened while you and Jane were locked up?" Roman asked, opening the pack house door for me.

"They treated us like prisoners but didn't torture us." He chuckled lifelessly. "At least, Ryker cared so much as to not hurt us." Raj walked into Roman's office, which was scattered with sketches of me, and crossed his arms. "We need to warn the Lycans. If he's there, he'll tell everyone that this was your fault, Isabella. He'll tell them you're the one who betrayed the pack. And he'll spread lies about me, too, since I know now."

Roman clenched his jaw, his muscles tense. "Let's go."

I shook my head and handed him the moonflower. "No, you're staying here." I brushed my hand against his cheek. "You're hurt, and your pack needs you right now."

Roman paused for a long moment, staring down at me with so much pride and ... happiness. "You're not doing this alone."

Though I wanted to protect him from Ryker, I nodded my head.

We were a team. We needed to start acting like one.

CHAPTER 53

ISABELLA

"*R*yker won't hurt me," Raj said softly to Jane as we waited in the woods for everyone to gather.

But neither he nor I believed that. Ryker had killed hundreds of his own people, and both Raj and I were next on his kill list. Another flower to add to his ever-growing tattoo garden of them.

Raj brushed his knuckles against Jane's jaw and smiled.

Roman grasped my hand, drawing my attention toward him and leading me deeper into the woods for privacy. "You knew about him all along, didn't you?"

I smiled up at him, curling my bloodied fingers into his shirt collar. "When did you figure that one out?"

He chuckled and pushed me against a tree, placing his hands on my hips. "So, tell me, how'd you do it?"

My fingers danced up his abdomen to his neck. "None of it added up."

The midnight moonlight bounced off of Roman's face, and I got butterflies. Even with his hair matted with mud and blood soaking through his shirt and those tired eyes, he was the most handsome man I had met.

"What didn't add up?" he asked.

"Since the moment I met him, he wanted to hide me from you. He always hid things, kept his office door locked, kept his desk locked, kept his bedroom locked." I pulled Roman closer to me, inhaling his scent that I had missed so much. "I didn't go to the Lycans without suspicion. I hope you know that. I was watching him the whole time, but … the pain of your heartbreak blinded me for a bit, to be honest."

"He was trying to take you away from me." He sucked in a breath and closed his eyes, inhaling. "He couldn't resist trying to get someone like you to be his mate and lead the Lycans with him. You're strong and powerful. A perfect woman to lead."

I rested my head on his chin. "He was trying to replace Michelle with me." I squeezed his hands in mine, feeling his calluses against my knuckles. "She looks just like me," I said, remembering Roman carrying her out of the rogues' hideout. "And her stats … he had them hidden away in his desk, but when I saw them, they were nearly identical to mine."

After letting out a low growl, I clenched my jaw. Ryker would regret adding me to the Lycans. He would regret ever marking Michelle during her heat. He would regret lying to every one of the Lycans because I would destroy him. He'd trained me to be strong; he just hadn't known that I was stronger than him.

Thanks to Roman for denying me my dream.

Thanks to Ryker for believing in me.

Thanks to my damn self for not trusting my innate instincts.

"Well, you're mine," Roman said, lifting my chin. "And nobody will take what's mine away from me again." He paused for a moment. "But I have a lot of shit to make up for, Isabella, I know."

I brushed some of his mud-coated hair behind his ear and smiled. "We can sort everything out when Ryker is dead," I said because I couldn't stand to have him lie to the Lycans any longer or to listen to him boast and brag about the number of rogues he'd killed.

He'd ordered the attacks. He'd paid the rogues to kill. He was the root of his own evil.

Just as I was about to pull away, Roman grasped my wrists and held them to his chest. "No." He shook his head. "I'm not making the same mistake for a third time." He gazed down at me, his eyes glowing as golden as the sun.

I pressed my lips together, yet my heart fluttered with so many butterflies when I saw his canines emerging from under his lips. "Roman, we talked about this. I have to leave."

"I'm not letting you go without my mark."

Without his mark.

Without his teeth in my neck.

Without his claim on me.

My heart hammered against my rib cage. Though I was covered in blood and mud and dirt from killing the rogues, this moment couldn't have been more perfect. We were both warriors in the midst of the biggest battle we would probably ever face. Marking me in the time of war was the ultimate proclamation of acceptance.

I rested my hand on his chest, feeling his heart beat as quickly as my own. With his fingers lightly digging into my hips, he pulled me toward him and kissed me. One long, passionate kiss on the mouth.

And I didn't taunt, tease, pester, or defy him that simple pleasure.

This time, I wanted him. I really wanted him. More than I'd wanted those late nights. More than I'd wanted to hurt him the way he hurt me. More than I'd wanted sex. Him. I wanted every part of him. The good. The bad. The worst.

I rested my head back against the tree and closed my eyes. He placed light kisses down my jaw to my neck. I shivered when his stubble tickled my skin, and I moved my head further to the side, so he could claim me.

He drew his nose up the side of my neck and breathed unevenly in my ear, like he was holding back, like he was waiting for me to tell him that it was okay, that I needed him.

"Mark me, Roman," I said breathlessly. "I've been waiting so long."

In one moment, he laced his hand through my hair, pulled my head to the side, and grazed his teeth against my collarbone. My breathing hitched, and I curled my fingers into his chest. My wolf was quiet, awaiting his bite.

"I love the way you react to me, my dear Isabella."

He drew his canines up my neck until he found my soft spot. I moaned, my heart racing. And without waiting a second more, he plunged his teeth into my skin and *finally* claimed me.

My body shook with pleasure. Every emotion that I had ever felt for him hit me like a wall, and my eyes filled with tears. This moment … this was the moment that I would remember forever.

A tear slipped from my eye. I'd never thought I would get my moment.

Mom had been right. This was pure joy.

He sank his teeth deeper inside of me and stilled. After drawing me closer, he inhaled my scent, took me in, and connected with my wolf on a deeper level than alpha and omega. We were alpha and luna. King and queen. Warrior and warrior.

When he pulled his teeth out of me, blood dripped from them. My wound closed almost instantly, but his mark remained. I could feel a part of him whirling around inside of me.

I brushed my fingers against it and grinned. We had lied to each other, kept things from each other, been so damn angry with each other … but we'd ended up here. Together.

"Mine," he whispered against my lips.

"Isabella," Raj called through the woods.

I turned my head in his direction, but Roman turned it back to face him.

"Mine."

"Isabella! We have to go."

Roman held me in place. "Mine."

"Yours, Roman. Only yours."

Raj appeared behind a tree. "Isabella?" he said. "If your plan is going to work, we have to leave now."

After squeezing Roman's hands in mine, I placed a kiss on his lips. "You know what to do?" I asked.

He nodded and pushed a strand of hair behind my ear to see his mark.

"And Derek? Will he be able to—"

Roman took my face in his hands, brushed his thumbs alongside my cheeks, and chuckled. "Yes, he's with Michelle at the hospital. They'll meet us there."

"Good. This will work." I pulled away from him. "It'll be perfect revenge."

Raj started into the empty forest, away from the pack house.

Roman tugged me closer one last time and placed a lingering kiss on my ear. "When this is over, I'm going to—"

"Ravish me?" I asked, smirking.

"No," he said. "Fuck you."

I walked a few steps away, glancing back at him. "You're all talk, Roman ... all talk."

CHAPTER 54

ISABELLA

*T*hough it was the late hours of the night—when the Lycans trained and hunted—the forest was eerily quiet. No guards surrounded the perimeter of Ryker's property. No warriors ran on the trails. Nobody—and I meant, nobody—was outside.

At least, that was what they wanted us to think.

Raj and I led Roman and his warriors toward the pack house, not even glancing at the Lycans perched in the trees and hiding in the bushes. There was no trying to tell our side of the story. Ryker had already corrupted their minds with lies about us. They needed proof, and we would deliver it.

Before we could make it within fifty feet of the pack house, they emerged like vultures, surrounding us and stalking around their *enemy*. Baring their teeth. Narrowing their eyes. Lowering their stances. Getting ready to fight with everything they had to protect the people from rogues. But we weren't here to fight.

"Thought you could just waltz in here after what you've

done?" Ryker asked, walking from behind the trees. "You two are nothing but rogues and traitors to the Lycans."

I stepped forward and pressed my lips together. "I'm not here to talk to you, Ryker. I'm here to show every single Lycan that you've been lying to them," I said.

The Lycans stood their ground, not fazed by the noise from a traitor.

"He has been going behind your back, hiring the rogues to kill alphas, killing them so he could feel powerful after he brutally destroyed Michelle and her name."

A short burst of whispers erupted at the mention of her name before Ryker scoffed, "You're really going to use my ex-mate to try to convince them of your sad sob story? Try harder."

"Michelle was never his mate. Were you, Michelle?" I asked, focusing my gaze on Ryker in case he tried to kill her this time.

Locking her up in a cage so she wouldn't talk had been bad enough.

Michelle had her arm curled around Derek's to hold herself steady, yet she walked forward—through Roman's pack—with so much grace and an expression filled with only hatred. Ryker's eyes widened, and he lunged forward, but Raj pushed him away and held him by his throat.

The Lycans broke into another fit of whispers as they stared at her in surprise.

"She's alive."

"The rogues didn't take her after all."

"Ryker said that the rogues had killed her."

Ryker growled again, the sound echoing through the forest, and tried to push Raj away from him. He lunged in her direction again, so many emotions crossing his face. She walked in front of him, barely lifting her gaze toward the rest of the Lycans. Though she was still weak, I admired her strength to face Ryker.

"They're telling the truth," she said, her voice soft. "Ryker had me locked in a cage for the last five years."

Ryker growled and stared at Michelle. Raj dug his claws into his neck and forced him onto his knees.

"She's lying. They're both crazy fucking liars."

This was the real Ryker. This was the man he had been hiding the whole time. He wasn't a strong Lycan; he was a weak man who used people's weaknesses against them, who spoke lie after lie to make himself look better than he actually was.

Michelle clenched her fists, her claws digging into her own palms and drawing blood. "I'm glad she's smarter than I ever was. Refusing to be with you. Refusing to believe you. It looked like those five fucking years that I was trapped there was not for nothing." She stepped closer to him. "You're going to *hell*."

The Lycans were suddenly quiet, each one taking in this new information that Ryker had been lying to them the whole time. If he was lying about this, he had more he was lying about.

"This is why I kicked you out of the Lycans," he said to her. "You come up with the most outrageous lies, Michelle."

I stepped forward, finished listening to him try to talk her down.

"I don't care if you kick *me* out of the Lycans for this," I said. "I'm going to give the order to kill Ryker, and if anyone wants to fight me about it, then I'll fight."

One moment passed.

Two moments.

Three moments.

Nobody dared to step forward.

So, I smiled at the man who had made Michelle's life absolute hell, brushed my fingers against Michelle's fragile shoulder, and said, "Kill him."

Michelle screamed, tears welling up in her eyes, and slashed her claws right into his neck. She held nothing back. Instead, she clawed at his neck over and over and over until blood was spewing out of it.

She was strong, and strong women weren't intimidated by insignificant men.

With one hand, she grabbed his hair and roughly tugged it back. "Do you remember doing this to me, Ryker? Do you remember me begging you to stop?"

Tears streamed down her face. She eyed his bloody neck, bit right into his flesh, and tore out his throat. His body smacked limply against the ground, and Michelle cried out in pure bliss.

CHAPTER 55

ISABELLA

*R*yker was dead. Michelle was showering in the Lycan pack house bathroom. And I was lying on my bed, staring up at my ceiling and thinking about how different everything suddenly was. Without Ryker breathing down my neck and without the pain of Roman refusing to mark me, I felt free.

So, I did the only logical thing to do after you killed the leader of the Lycans, slaughtered hundreds of rogues, and got marked, all within twenty-four hours. I rested my head against the headboard, spread my legs, and slipped my hand into my underwear.

My eyes fluttered closed as I played with my clit, rubbing my fingers around in small circles. Wetness pooled between my thighs. I needed this. Something to help me relax after tonight.

"You're your own woman, huh?" Roman asked.

I opened my eyes to see Roman standing in the doorway. He stepped into my room and closed the door behind him, crossing his arms over his chest and leaning against the door.

Moonflowers twinkled on my windowsill, just like they had at my parents' house, bouncing off of his golden eyes. I smirked at him as he walked over to me so slowly that it was almost terrorizing.

He stood over the bed, drawing his hand up my thigh and parting them, giving him a better view of my pussy. "You remember what I told you I would do to you, don't you?"

"Ravish me," I teased, still touching myself for him.

His fingertips danced up the inside of my thighs, and I shivered. They hovered over my underwear, teasing me with their heat. I raised my hips, trying to maneuver his hand to touch my core, but he just chuckled lowly and pulled his hand away.

"No," he said, finger under my chin. "I said that I was going to fuck you." He brushed his thumb against my mark, and I moaned. "Now, take off your panties."

I batted my lashes at him and continued to touch myself through my underwear, feeling the heat rush to my core. All I wanted was for his fingers to touch me, to make me feel good.

"Take off your panties," he said again, voice hardening.

"You take them off of—"

He lay on the bed next to me and wrapped one hand around my throat, lightly squeezing. "Be good for once"—he drew his fingers against the hem of my underwear—"and maybe I'll reward you," he mumbled against my lips.

I gulped and drew my legs together, not able to deal with the pressure rising inside of me. He continued to dance his fingers along the hem of my underwear, brushing two of them under the material.

I moaned softly to myself, brows drawn together, and pulled down my panties, aching for him to touch me. He smirked and took them from me, playing with them in his fingers. Then, he tossed them to the side of the bed and lightly pulled one of my thighs over his leg, so they were spread wide for his viewing.

When he trailed his fingers up the inside of my thigh, my pussy clenched. He pressed his hardness against my leg, and I moaned. My fingers hovered over my core as I waited for him to touch me himself.

"Don't stop touching yourself," he mumbled against my lips, his hand still around my throat.

His fingers lightly continued to brush against the inside of my thigh, sending shivers through my body.

"Please, Roman," I said.

"Please what?"

"I want you," I said.

He smirked against my lips. "You want me?" He grabbed my hand that was touching my pussy and wrapped it around his hard cock. "You want this?"

I nodded my head, desperate for him, and stroked him through his pants. Waiting. His knuckles brushed against my clit, and I whined softly.

"Please."

"Whose are you?" he asked, fingers hovering over me.

I pursed my lips together, my heart racing, and lifted my hips off of the bed, trying to get him to touch my clit, but he pulled his hand further away.

He grabbed my chin in his hand. "Are you mine, my dear Isabella?"

I sucked in my bottom lip and gnawed on it, my core tightening.

"Are you mine, Isabella?" he asked, his voice more demanding.

"Yes," I breathed. I stared up into his beautiful golden eyes. "Yes, Roman, I'm yours."

He shoved his fingers into my pussy, pumping them in and out of me, slowly tormenting me. But I didn't just want his fingers anymore. I tried rolling us over, but Roman squeezed his hand around my throat, pinning me to the pillow.

"Stay still, Isabella. Enjoy this."

When he pushed them all the way inside of me, he curled them over and over, making the pressure in my core rise.

Without stopping, he sucked one of my nipples into his mouth and softly bit down on the flesh.

My body jerked up, my back arching, and he smirked against me. Heat rushed to my center. He bit down harder, and I gripped the bedsheets in one hand and his cock in the other. He continued to thrust his fingers into me, harder, faster, rougher.

It felt so fucking good, knowing that I was his, knowing that he only touched me like this. Nobody else. Me.

He released my neck and curled his arm under my torso, lifting me off of the bed and shoving his fingers deep inside of me. I placed my hands on his shoulders to steady myself as he thrust me into the air over and over. My core tightened around him, wave after wave of pleasure coursing through my body.

I cried out and relaxed against him for a moment. When he placed me back down on the bed, I pushed him onto his back, pulled down his pants, and wrapped my lips around his cock. Goddess, I had been waiting for it to be inside of me again for weeks.

When I took all of him down my throat and spit was dribbling out of my mouth, I grabbed his hand and placed it around my neck. Letting him feel how big he was inside of me. I bobbed my head up and down on him until his hips began to spasm slowly. Right when I got him close to the edge, I sat up and crawled over to him.

He grabbed my hips as I hovered over his hard cock. Gripping the base, I pushed his head against my hole and slowly lowered myself onto him.

He growled lowly, "You're so fucking sexy, Isabella."

His fingers glided against my mark, and as they did, he raised his hips, shoving himself all the way inside of me. He continued to thrust up into me, but I pushed his hands off of my hips and placed mine onto his abdomen, moving my hips on his and taking control. Over and over and over. I rode him until my legs were shaking.

He pinched both of my nipples between his fingers, tugged me toward him until my chest was pressed against his, and then gripped my ass in his hands. "Your ass is so fucking nice." He pulled my cheeks apart and thrust into me so hard.

My teeth lengthened into canines, brushing against his neck. When his stubble grazed against my mark, I sank my teeth deep into his neck, tearing right through the muscle. I inhaled his scent, my mind becoming fuzzy.

Marking him was everything I'd imagined it would be.

Pure bliss.

He moaned loudly in my ear, his body trembling with pleasure. I continued to ride him until his cock pulsed. My pussy clenched harder on him, and he pulled out of me. Resting his head on my shoulder, draping one arm over my body, he lay on the bed, his abdomen uncovered, his cock glistening with my juices.

Moonlight flooded in through the window, making his skin glow. I sat up against the headboard, resting my head against the wood, and sighed. In a weird kind of way, we were back to normal.

Someone knocked on the door, and I pulled Roman's shirt over my body and walked over to answer it. Roman sat up in the bed and rested one arm behind his head, his bicep flexing.

I peeked my head out of the door to see Derek standing there with Raj.

He had his arms crossed over his chest and was raising a suspicious brow at me. "Are you done?" he asked.

I narrowed my eyes at him. "Don't *are you done* me, Derek."

"You're needed," Raj said. "The Lycans are holding a meeting."

"We'll be out in a minute." I closed the door and tossed Roman his clothes.

Before we left my room, he gazed in my mirror at his neck and smiled, his fingers trailing alongside it.

I rested my head on his shoulder and smiled. *"Mine."*

"Always yours, Isabella," he said.

He grabbed my hand and tugged me out the door and to the training area, where all the Lycans were talking war with each other. When they saw me, everyone quieted down, and Raj walked forward.

"Isabella," Raj said, "we talked for a while about what will happen to the Lycans since Ryker is gone, and we came to a decision."

Michelle grabbed Raj's arm. "Wait. Can I tell her? As a thank-you?" When he nodded, she gazed at me with a soft smile on her face. "Would you like to lead the Lycans?"

My eyes widened, and I squeezed Roman's hand. I gazed around at all the men and women who I had trained with relentlessly this past month. They had been nothing but good, loyal people. My people. Lycans.

I gazed up at Roman and frowned. But I had found my mate, and we had mated for real. I wasn't about to give that up again. I would never give up my mate again. I knew now that he respected me.

Roman paused for a few moments and then smiled. "I think you should do it, Isabella. You're stronger beyond belief."

"But ... but I won't be able to be with you."

Raj stepped forward again. "Actually, that was a rule that Ryker had put in place. You are free to stay with Roman whenever you'd like as long as you're committed to helping us."

Roman nudged me, and I smiled up at him with so many butterflies. I couldn't believe that this was real life. This was my moment, and my mate was supporting me through it.

I nodded my head. "I'll do it."

To be continued...

Defying the Alpha (Submission Trilogy Book 2)

Are two alphas too many to handle?

Defiant wolf-shifter Isabella loves toying with her mate Roman. But between Isabella leading the Lycans, Roman strengthening their pack, and a darkness slowly overtaking wolves' minds, they have rarely found time for themselves.

And one of the worst problem of them all is that Alpha Kylo Marks—the most powerful alpha in the nation—wants Isabella's and Roman's heads.

When the Moon Goddess brings Kylo and Isabella together to help stop the darkness from overtaking the werewolf species, Kylo finds himself treading on uncharted territory.

Can Roman and Isabella's relationship withstand the bloodthirsty alpha? How will Isabella juggle the two enemies who are vying for her?

Read Defying the Alpha, the second book in the Submission Trilogy, by international bestselling author Emilia Rose!

This book is considered a menage romance which includes one female with two alpha mates.

ALSO BY EMILIA ROSE

The Twins (Submission Trilogy Spin-Off)

Two pairs of hands. Two intense stares. Two men who want Naomi on her knees.

Naomi hasn't been touched by a man since her last boyfriend, Oliver. When the Shadowcrown Pack hires her to help strengthen their weakest links, she meets the notorious twin alphas, Jax and Noah. From the moment they meet, these bad boys are determined to have their way with Naomi.

Come Here, Kitten (God of War Series, Book 1)

Taming an alpha is never easy, even when you're his mate.

Warmonger Alpha Ares promises to kill anyone who has the Malavite Stone—a crystal packed with ungodly powers and healing properties. From slaughtering packs to building himself an empire, he will stop at nothing to find it. That is, until he meets Aurora.

Excite Me (Excite Me Duet, Book 1)

Dating your best friend's dad is never easy.

Find out what happens in this forbidden romance between Mia and Mr. Bryne, Mia's best friend's father.

ABOUT THE AUTHOR

Emilia Rose is an international bestselling author of steamy paranormal romance. With over 3,000 monthly subscribers on Patreon and over 18 million story views online, Emilia loves creating the newest and sexiest paranormal romances for her fans.

⬛ facebook.com/authoremiliarose

⭕ instagram.com/emiliarosewriting

▐⬤ patreon.com/EmiliaRoseWriting

Made in the USA
Coppell, TX
21 March 2021